I0824459

Praise for Faye Snowden and the *Killing* Series

"This brutal and beautiful story about secrets and survival, and the legacies that fathers leave their daughters, haunted me. Snowden's best work!"
Rachel Howzell Hall, *New York Times* and *USA Today* bestselling author, on *A Killing Breath*

"I would recommend *A Killing Fire* to crime fiction and mystery lovers and fans of Ruth Ware and Gillian Flynn."
Black Girls Lit

"Full-bodied and dynamic characters carry this one along a mystery, tying a brutal past with a bloody present that will keep you guessing right up to the finale."
Unnerving Magazine on *A Killing Fire*

"The prologue alone sent chills up my spine, and that was just the beginning. This is a book that grabs you by the throat and doesn't let go until you reach THE END..."
Ann Parker, award-winning author of the *Silver Rush* series on *A Killing Fire*

"A polished gem of a crime novel, replete with deftly crafted characters, unexpected but riveting plot twists, and a memorable finale."
Midwest Book Review on *A Killing Rain*

FAYE SNOWDEN

A KILLING BREATH

Book Three of the *Killing* Series,

Following *A Killing Rain*

This is a **FLAME TREE PRESS** book

FLAME TREE PRESS
6 Melbray Mews, London, SW6 3NS, UK
flametreepress.com

US sales, distribution and warehouse:
Simon & Schuster
simonandschuster.biz

UK distribution and warehouse:
Hachette UK Distribution
hukdcustomerservice@hachette.co.uk

Publisher's Note: This is a work of fiction. Names, characters, places, and incidents are a product of the author's imagination. Locales and public names are sometimes used for atmospheric purposes. Any resemblance to actual people, living or dead, or to businesses, companies, events, institutions, or locales is completely coincidental.

Thanks to the Flame Tree Press team.

Cover art by Nick Wells/Flame Tree Studio from sketches and layered files created using new photos and stock images from Colin D. Young, andreiuc88 and CarlosBarquero (Shutterstock.com) combined and crafted in Photoshop. No AI, AGI or LLM was used in this process.
The font families used are Avenir and Bembo.

Flame Tree Press is an imprint of Flame Tree Publishing Ltd
flametreepublishing.com

A copy of the CIP data for this book is available from the British Library and the Library of Congress.

1 3 5 7 9 8 6 4 2

HB ISBN: 978-1-78758-972-8
ebook ISBN: 978-1-78758-973-5

Printed and bound in the UK by CPI Group (UK) Ltd, Croydon, CR0 4YY

Represented in the EU for product safety and compliance by Authorised Rep Compliance Ltd, Ground Floor, 71 Lower Baggot Street, Dublin, D02 P593, Ireland. Contact at www.arccompliance.com

FAYE SNOWDEN

A KILLING BREATH

Book Three of the *Killing* Series, Following *A Killing Rain*

FLAME TREE PRESS
London & New York

To Eric, my husband, my love, my rock and one of the few people who is willing to put up with all of my shenanigans

Prologue

Ruth Jefferson was no stranger to the blues, but it was jazz that carried her troubles. She'd sit on the porch of her shotgun house in a line of shotgun houses strung along the ten freeway in Byrd's Landing, Louisiana while listening to old Satchmo's trumpet talking about a beautiful world, or Jelly Roll's piano crave, crave, craving. The opposite notes of joy and longing took her mind off all plights and predicaments.

This included the notorious serial killer Floyd Burns, who, on the run, slipped into the third shotgun from the top of the hill with his daughter, Raven Burns, some months ago. Of course, Miss Ruth didn't know about his past. He had taken on the name Floyd Baxter to escape the law. He knew Miss Ruth, but they had gotten off on the wrong foot from the moment they met. Even though she never stood in front of a preacher with a man she intended on marrying, Floyd insisted on calling her Mrs. Jefferson. But she was Miss Ruth to the neighborhood she and her family had been living in since Jesus was a baby. Her house had a magic that captured the entire neighborhood in that long-ago summer, grown-ups and children alike, especially Raven.

Floyd reckoned that the reason was because the woman told stories all the livelong day. Some child would ask a question, or one of the neighbors would carry over a sweet potato pie, and Miss Ruth would start talking about her granddaddy. Pretty soon she'd be going on and on about random things like kitchen gardens, patty rollers, root workers, house parties (*chile, you should've seen us then*), and the uncle who choked to death on his own false teeth. She ended every crazy tale she told with 'true story'.

At first Floyd abided her because she helped him keep an eye on Raven, his Birdie Girl. But soon enough all that jibber-jabbering made him want to slice his own ears off. But that's not where the trouble between him and Mrs. Jefferson got too hot for his liking.

Beyond the crooked strut of shotguns was a hill, and beyond that hill a chain-link fence, and beyond that a fat highway where people drove shiny cars so fast it was as if they were trying to lay all four tires on the wind. And for all the care the drivers had for the poor folk on the other side, that chain-link might as well have been made of cinder blocks.

But not for a notorious and still-free serial killer.

Floyd could see straight through the links to the speeding cars on the other side. That fence served him. It fed him some.

Drivers sometimes lost control, and their cars would twirl in the bright afternoon air like a drugged-up ballerina before plunging onto the shoulder with a thunderous, glorious sound. The most self-assured drivers wouldn't be wearing seat belts and Floyd would be gifted with an entire human body flying like a missile straight for the chain-link. Afterward, it would be like someone tore flesh into rags and set them on the fence to dry in the sun.

While everybody in the neighborhood would go running out of doors to see how they could help, Floyd would stroll over with his hands in his pockets and his white fedora on to take it all in. He'd feast on the blood still warm and pumping with the music of dying heartbeats. Sometimes he'd get close enough to hear the death rattle, the last sound made by a torn body on its way to the charnel house.

On one such day, when crumpled metal lay in balls all along the shoulder and cries and screams rode the wind, Floyd paused near a particularly unlucky traveler. He knelt, bent down so his ear was near the bloody mouth to wait for the death rattle. But instead, he heard a voice. That voice.

"Your daughter is right behind you."

It was Mrs. Jefferson standing there like a big, sturdy mountain, judging him, taking his measure with no fear and finding him wanting.

He slowly lifted his body up. He knew how it looked. Blood on his ear and a primal gleam in his eye while everybody else was doing

CPR, shouting questions back and forth asking who called 911, or sending barefoot children back to the house for blankets or water or anything useful that could soothe the dying. He tried to think of something clever and Floyd-like to say, but the look in that woman's eyes sealed his lips shut. It reminded him of the avenging God he used to preach about from the pulpit, the one who'd turn you away from heaven's door, so you'd have no choice but to go to hell and bunk with the devil.

He turned in the direction Mrs. Jefferson had shown him to see his little Birdie Girl wearing a t-shirt with yellow daisies all over it and a pair of cut-off shorts. Raven eyed him with a fixed, dead face, what Floyd liked to call her thinking face. What ticked Floyd off most was that Raven was barefoot, which she knew as sure as sunshine was against the rules. Other kids in these matchboxes could go around without no shoes on, but not Raven Burns, not his daughter.

But Raven wouldn't listen to him because that's how this stout Black woman ran around, shoeless, her feet untouched by cloth or leather, like she had a pact with the earth, like they was such good friends it would never hurt her.

"Why, Mrs. Jefferson," he finally said. "Raven looks fine to me."

And she was. She had seen worse.

"She ain't fine. She's in shock," Miss Ruth said. Without waiting for him to answer she went on, "Since your ass ain't helping, you can go on and take her back home."

Sirens pierced the silence that followed and screamed closer with the approaching night. Fire trucks and ambulances would be there soon if the highway patrol didn't beat them to the scene. It just wouldn't do for him to be here when the police rode up. Him with an ear smeared with blood and everybody looking at him like a poop stain. Hell, even the now-dead man he had knelt by was staring up at him.

He wiped the blood from his ear before curling his wet fingers into his pocket. As he strolled back through the hole in the chain-link with a hitch in his step and Raven at his side, he thought about all the things he could do to a busybody like Mrs. Jefferson.

Miss Ruth

She shouldn't have opened the door.

It was nearly ten at night, already dark. She had lived on this hillside of leaning houses all her life. Her mother and grandmother had lived in the same house before her. Miss Ruth knew where to place her bare feet to avoid both scrape and scratch while roaming from house to house. During the day she was invincible. She looked out for the children, soothed loneliness where she found it and when she could.

But at night people who needed Miss Ruth were on their own.

Everyone knew this. They would joke about it. "Y'all know Miss Ruth ain't coming to some cookout when it gets dark. If you want her greens, you better do that shit in the daytime."

Night was when people got up to no good no matter if it was as new as a baby wet from afterbirth, or as toothless as an old man eager to die with the dawn. It was in the dead of night, her grandmother told her, when White folk came for her grandfather. For Byrd's Landing, it was mostly in the stinking dead of night when they carried people off and hung them from trees and bridges, leaving them there until the sun rose and the days passed and bleached their bones to birch. Her night phobias had become particularly worse since Floyd and that child settled on The Hill.

On this night she had long ago closed the front door, which signaled that she had stopped accepting visitors. No more stopping by asking for a recipe or bringing news about so-and-so who thought the only way to get the hell out of the poor house and Byrd's Landing was to join the Navy, or wanting to gossip about whose girl was pregnant and what boy was smoking weed and who might or might not be selling dope. She was especially afraid because she was alone. It was the Fourth of July. Fireworks needed the dark. Those who were able had gone to the park for a cookout and to watch light exploding in the night sky. No one should be knocking at her door.

But there it was again, someone on the other side rattling the screen door as steady as a woodpecker.

"Go on from here," Miss Ruth said. "Y'all know I'm done for the night. If you looking for the cookout, they at the park."

The rattling stopped. She felt a twinge of guilt, but she planned to stick to what she knew. Her house was boarded up. The windows were locked. She wasn't about to let anyone inside.

Then she heard the cry of a child. If a child was hurt that door needed opening. There was no way around a child in trouble no matter how afraid of the dark a body might be. She took two deep breaths to steady herself. Then she lifted the two-by-four lying across the door and set it aside. She twisted the deadbolt open, took one more deep breath before turning the lock on the doorknob to the open position. Her final act of opening the door was to undo the chain. She expected to see a child's face covered in tears. But there was no child. The man she knew as Floyd Baxter stood there instead.

Ruth slammed all of her weight against the door, but it was too late. Floyd pushed through it. She grabbed the two-by-four, but Floyd easily snatched it away. He flung it aside like a bag of beans.

"Good evening, Mrs. Jefferson," he said. "I know you don't take night visitors, but you and me need to have a conversation."

It was then that she saw the butcher knife, a long one with a silver blade. He pushed it into her stomach while walking her backward into the house.

Floyd

No sooner than he had driven the knife into Mrs. Jefferson's gut did she start screaming like a banshee. And it was just old Floyd. A man half her size, and her being a good heft of a woman, a sturdy woman. Why, she was even armed. After all, she did have a knife. It may have been sticking out of her gut but it was a weapon she could get to. Floyd wasn't at all surprised when she did just that. He'd seen dying people do plenty of things to try and stay on this earth one more day than the good Lord was willing to give them.

Mrs. Jefferson didn't disappoint.

She yanked the knife out of her belly and even with her bleeding everywhere and her plumbing threatening to fall out, she started slashing away. But she was so disoriented that she got nowhere near to cutting him. He grabbed her by the wrist, took that butcher knife away and stuck it in her again. This time he kept a good hold on both her wrist and the handle. He slit her right up the middle. She screamed so loud that the earth itself would have split in two if it cared enough to listen. She screamed for so long that soon Floyd heard footsteps on the tail end of her last caterwaul.

Lucky for Floyd, the fools who had come running pounded on the door first instead of trying the doorknob. Floyd was so excited about finally giving Mrs. Jefferson her comeuppance that he had forgotten to lock it. He looked at her with regret. Her large brown eyes twinned fear and hope in a way that unsettled even him. He got hold of the knife and ran out of the back door and into the woods behind the houses. One of the people who had discovered the unfortunate woman was chasing him. It sounded like a teenage boy cussing him with such eloquence that Floyd thought he'd make a mighty fine orator one day. What kind of teenager would chase a killer through the dark Louisiana woods? But Floyd knew the answer. A killer, like he himself was. Floyd ran faster.

He lost the kid by running through the woods to the backroads and then doubling back toward the neighborhood. Soon he was at the back door of the shotgun he shared with Raven. Floyd slipped into the house. It was as quiet as a cloud, a welcome break from the noise at Mrs. Jefferson's place. He had told Raven before leaving to draw him a bath, one too hot to sit in. That way he figured it would be warm when he got back. She did as she was told without question. Raven had learned long ago that being hellbent on asking got you answers you didn't want to hear.

The water in the old clawfoot tub was as clear as forever. He stripped off his bloody clothes and set them in a pile near the door. He would burn them later. He sank into the tub and adjusted his thinking about the water as it claimed his hips and softly rippled against his chest. It was not only clear as forever, it was as warm as the womb. Pink clouds floated up all around him. Leaves and dirt from the woods settled atop the water.

He sat for a few moments enjoying the warmth before picking up a full bar of Irish Spring. He rubbed the bar on his wiry blond hair until the suds dribbled down his neck and onto his chest. He used a loofah to clean his torso, and a nail brush to scrub his fingernails and between his perfectly angled toes while murmuring the 'This Little Piggy' nursery rhyme. When he was done with the soap he rinsed and rose. After toweling off, he splashed himself with Stetson cologne and dressed in his best pajamas.

He walked into the middle room, where Raven slept on a twin bed pressed against the window. She was a child who fell asleep quickly. When the dream world required her presence, it snatched her down without delay. Her face in the moonlight shining in the window was troubled. Floyd smoothed her hair back and watched her. Before long her nose twitched. He grinned.

"What is it that you smelling, my Birdie Girl?" He stroked her hair some more. "You smell my soap, my Stetson?"

She frowned when he kissed her.

"Just sleep," he said. "You don't have to give me an answer."

His smile was wide as Raven's frown disappeared. He looked forward to the day when she was all grown up, the day when she could be a proper partner.

Chapter One

After hearing three sharp raps on the screen door of her new house, Raven opened the door to find her ex-partner, Billy Ray Chastain. He stood on the porch in all his handsome six-foot-four glory. The only thing marring his good looks was the keloid that started at the corner of his right eye and disappeared into his hairline. Her fault. Billy Ray got that scar when Lamont Lovelle tried to burn him alive. Lovelle also killed Raven's friend Oral Percival Justice within these walls. Oral left her this old Craftsman-style home in his will.

She and Billy Ray used to be partners in New Orleans. When Raven got the call to come back home to Byrd's Landing she couldn't imagine police work without him. She was in town for only a few months when she asked him to join her. He came.

What a mistake.

Yet he stayed and helped her stay sane by not tolerating her foolishness. That's why she needed to talk to him tonight. She had decided to stay in Oral's house and she wanted his approval. She didn't think it would be a good conversation with him studying her like she was a butterfly on a pin.

"You gone let me in?" he asked. "I thought you wanted me to see the place. It's done, right?"

"Done as it'll ever be." Raven stuffed her hands in the back pockets of her jeans. She didn't make a move to open the screen door.

He checked the Breitling watch he picked up at an estate sale for twenty-five bucks. He told Raven he tried to tell the son of the man who died about how much the watch was worth. The kid didn't care. He just wanted the watch gone, like his father was throughout his childhood. *All the mean ole bastard cared about was money and flashing money*, the son said. *He wanted to be buried with the watch, but I wasn't about to oblige. I'm getting rid of all his shit. He'd probably find a way to haunt me if I kept it.* Billy Ray bought the watch. He didn't like letting anything go to waste. And he didn't believe in ghosts.

"It's late. Are we going to stand on the porch until daylight?" Billy Ray asked.

"It's only late because your highness couldn't meet before zero-dark-thirty," Raven said as she pushed open the screen door.

"I got a business to run," he said. "I work from can-to-can't-see and I have to clean the kitchen after. I can't be at your beck and call, Raven."

"Yet, here you are," she said.

Billy Ray walked in and regarded the spacious but empty living room. She told him that the entire dark wood floor had to be replaced because Oral's blood had seeped between the floorboards. Billy Ray said nothing.

She continued, "Willie Lee told me this story about when he was cleaning up after a crime scene."

"You mean when Byrd's Landing was still letting that freak of nature clean up after crime scenes," Billy Ray said.

Willie Lee. That long, tall, jangly drink of water whose amateur taxidermy and shed of horror made him a murder suspect in the serial killings of young boys. He was eventually cleared but he had a lot to answer for, and for that matter, so did she. They were both now pariahs in the town of Byrd's Landing. After the Sleeping Boy case, he needed money and she needed help, so she paid Willie Lee to help her clean Oral's house of blood and death. They carried the heavy furniture to the dumpster, including Oral's favorite chair, which couldn't be salvaged, the braided rugs that Raven used to lie on as a child, the bedroom door that Lovelle clubbed his way through with the adrenaline of a madman and a scythe he had found among Oral's gardening tools.

She ignored Billy Ray's comment and went on with the story she was telling in the first place.

"Willie Lee said that someone called crying about a maggot infestation. They had no idea where they were coming from. When Willie Lee got there, he pulled up the floorboards. There they were, squirming in the congealed blood of the homeowner's dearly departed loved one. True story."

"I can't believe you let that dimwit in here," Billy Ray said.

"Don't be too hard on him," she said. "Willie Lee's trying to make up for what he did."

"You mean killing all those animals and messing up a murder investigation?" Billy Ray said.

"He's trying to make amends," she said. "Can we get back to the house?"

"Be my guest," Billy Ray said.

"Most of the drywall had to go because of the blood." She looked up. "The cast-off even reached the ceiling beams. Those cost a fortune to replace."

She walked Billy Ray to the master bedroom, their footsteps loud and hollow in the empty house.

"This was the hardest room," she said. "Everything had to go, the floors, the drywall, the furniture. Oral had this antique four-poster bed with a feather mattress. I'm trying to find one just like it. That's why I'm still sleeping on an air mattress."

"Where's the door?" Billy Ray asked.

The door as it was during the crime scene flashed through Raven's mind. It was an old-fashioned, heavy brown door that Lovelle made short work of. When she and Billy Ray examined the crime scene it hung from its frame as useless as tissue paper.

"I decided to leave the door off," Raven said. "It's just going to be me here, after all."

She led him to the kitchen.

"You didn't replace the cabinets?" Billy Ray asked.

"Of course, I did," she said. "Every single one. You think I want to be staring at the same cabinets Oral saw as he lay dying?"

"Huh," was all Billy Ray said.

They returned to the living room, where Billy Ray stopped and folded his arms across his broad chest. His eyes swept the bright yellow walls, the new floors. He peered back toward the kitchen with its replaced cabinets.

"Place is huge, Raven," Billy Ray said.

She said nothing. She waited.

"I know you want me to tell you that you're doing the right thing," Billy Ray said.

"It's clean, Billy Ray. No more blood. No more terror," Raven said. "Professionally done by the book. That was the condition when I asked Willie Lee to help me."

"That's not what I'm saying," he said.

"What are you saying?" she said.

"You got time to sit and talk?" he asked her.

She led him outside of the house. They both took a seat on the porch, he on the top step with his back leaning against the porch railing, and she on the second step. It was going on two a.m. on a summer morning thick with heat. A yellow Byrd's Landing moon hung fat and low in a sky of black velvet. A sweet, musky scent from the wisteria gripping the pergola perfumed the air. All of it, the dark, the young morning, the whispering branches of the one-hundred-year-old pecan orchard that had seen much but told nothing made her uneasy.

Billy Ray regarded her for a few moments with his dark brown eyes unblinking, a look she'd seen him give to countless suspects, one that would force them to confess every single transgression from birth to that moment. He said, "You got any beer?"

"Are you kidding? That's the one thing I got is beer."

He stood and went into the house and returned with two open bottles of Abita. He sat back down on the porch, not talking, not drinking.

Raven took a long swig of the beer. "Just say it, Billy Ray."

"Say what?" he asked.

"You don't think I'm doing the right thing."

"That matter to you?" he answered.

She tipped the bottle to him and took another long drink.

"It'll hurt my feelings," she said. "Seriously, you don't know how much it would mean to me if you thought I was doing at least one thing right."

He grunted. "I told you how I felt about you moving into this house before you and Willy Wonka cleaned it up," he said.

"Willie Lee," she corrected.

"Whatever," he said. He ran his index finger along the keloid scar. She knew that it hurt sometimes. At one point he told her he thought it was still growing.

"I don't see how you can be friends with him no how. Not after all that shit last year," he said.

"Everybody deserves a second chance," Raven said.

"Everybody except you?" he asked.

She scoffed and turned her face to him. She tried to read him by moonlight to no avail.

"This is my second chance, Billy Ray," she said.

"Why can't you get your own house?" he asked.

"This is my own house. Oral left it to me," she said.

"He also died in it," Billy Ray reminded her.

"That's in the past."

"Your daddy in the past, too?"

Floyd 'Fire' Burns was dead. He died in prison, not the way the state wanted, but the way he wanted, by slicing his own throat. He did it in front of his accusers, in front of God, in front of everybody. As the years passed the image of him dying sharpened and layered blood and gore over her daily life.

"He's dead and gone," she said.

"Dead but definitely not gone. You still hearing his voice in your head?" he asked.

"What are you, my shrink now? Besides, the old man had some good advice on the last case," she said.

"That ain't funny," he said.

Raven decided not to respond. He paused for a moment, and then said, "The place looks fine. But I don't understand why you keep running to things that make you sicker."

She stared at him. "You really do think I'm crazy?"

"Last year you were seeing things that weren't there," he said.

"Like what?" she said.

"That priest," he said.

She hadn't realized she was sitting bolt upright until he had said that. She sank back against the porch railing. He was right. She had gone a little crazy during the Sleeping Boy case last year. She knew that now. After Lovelle killed Oral and almost killed Billy Ray, Raven chased him across three states and put him down like the animal he was. Taking him out and getting away with it had left a mark on her soul. And besides that, something was coming to make her pay up. There would be a reckoning.

"My mind may have called the priest up a few times, but I'm telling you I didn't make him up," Raven said.

"A priest who looked like your father? Stalking you all around Byrd's Landing?" he said.

"I'm telling you that he's real," Raven muttered.

"How does a real guy appear out of nowhere in the middle of a back road you just happen to be driving? How is he at the place where…"

"You mean the place where Lovelle beat the tar out of you and set you on fire?" Raven prompted. "That place? The old shotgun where you used to live on Peabody?"

He sighed, took a long swallow of his beer and let out a soft laugh.

"God, I love the bitch in you," he said.

"I can't just run away like you did. Police work is the only work I know. Making Oral's house right is the only thing I can do to erase what Lovelle did," she said.

"I thought you killing him erased what he did," Billy Ray said.

"Now who's being the bitch?"

"I want you to think about something," Billy Ray said, pointing to the screen door. "The crime scene from the house the day Oral died? Your head was so far up your ass that you could've shat out of your mouth. All terror. Zero professionalism. You forgot you were a cop."

"I was in shock," she said.

"You do realize that when you showed me the house today you took the same route as you did through the crime scene. The things you replaced in there may be new, but it's not changed." He started counting on his fingers. "The floors are the same, the walls are painted the same color, and most of all..." He stopped.

"Most of all what?" she asked.

"The kitchen cabinets are the same color, make and model that Oral had. They may not be the ones with blood on them, but they're the same cabinets. Even the drawer handles are the same," he said.

She sucked in a breath. No, she hadn't realized.

"And for the record I didn't run away. I walked away on purpose to open Chastain's Creole Heaven because a restaurant was something my daddy wanted to do but never got the chance. I'll tell you one thing near dying did for me. It made me realize that life is too short and ridiculous to be afraid all the fucking time. We all gone end up the same way, might as well do what you want while you're here."

"You telling me that you're happy slinging gumbo and baking cornbread?" she asked.

He took another swig of beer. "Happier than when I was chasing perps all the livelong day," he mused. "So, yeah, I guess I'm happy. Are you?"

She didn't say anything. She didn't have to because Billy Ray knew. His cell phone rang, an old zydeco tune in homage to Buckwheat Zydeco, music Billy Ray loved and was always trying to promote in his restaurant. He answered and then pointed the phone at her.

"It's for you," he said.

"What do you mean it's for me?" she said.

"The chief," he said.

She took the phone from his outstretched hand and put it to her ear.

"Where your phone at, Burns?" Chief Early Sawyer said like he owned her.

She pictured her own Android on the card table in the kitchen. She had forgotten to bring it to the porch with her.

"Why do you care where my phone is? I'm off tonight," she said.

"Not anymore."

"Check the schedule, Chief," Raven said. "Breaker is on tonight."

"Breaker took the night off. Kid's sick."

Raven waited. The chief continued, "We got three bodies in the Old Bottoms part of town. I'm giving it to you and Stevenson. Meet him over there."

"You won't be there?" she asked.

"It's a drug hit," he said. "Y'all don't need me. But get over there before it gets too late."

"Late for what? You said bodies, right? You afraid they'll get up and walk into the afterlife before we can process the scene?"

The chief hung up on her after calling her a smartass.

She handed Billy Ray's phone back to him. He gave her a hard look. "Like I asked before, you happy?"

Chapter Two

Raven punched the address to the Old Bottoms into her Android's GPS before getting on the road. She was surprised that she wasn't familiar with the place. She thought that she and Floyd had walked every inch of Byrd's Landing when she was a little girl and he was still topside. As she pulled her red Mustang out of the driveway, she thought about how fast Billy Ray had left. It was as if his shoes were on fire. She knew it was because he didn't want her talking him into going with her to the crime scene.

He would have been welcome.

The chief was so short of detectives that he had hired the likes of Delbert Stevenson. No one knew Stevenson was a homicide detective when he appeared in Byrd's Landing last year during the Sleeping Boy case. He claimed that he was a location scout looking for a place to shoot a movie. In reality he came to Byrd's Landing with only one obsession. He wanted to prove that Raven sniped Lamont Lovelle while he crossed the street for lunch at a Quiznos in a California town a lifetime away from Byrd's Landing.

He hadn't come close. Desperate, Stevenson went a step further. He pretended to be interested in a romantic relationship. Raven was tangled up in her own obsession after the Lovelle killing. She longed for a normal life. A life without bloodshed where there was a boyfriend, a boring job, friends like Billy Ray, and family like her brother, Cameron. Stevenson caught her just at the right moment and she fell for his ruse.

She put memories of Stevenson's betrayal out of her mind. Though she would be the last to admit it, they hurt too much. And with pain usually came her daddy ready to absorb it as if it gave his ghost a chance at life and breath. As she navigated the dark backroads of Byrd's Landing, she could not only hear her father, she could see him. Her gray matter showed Floyd sitting atop a milk crate. He wore a suit with a matching fedora so white it appeared to sparkle like the clothes in the old detergent commercials. The only bit of color on him was a silky peacock feather glowing neon green and blue in the hatband. He cracked pecans one after the other with his rat teeth before slivering out the meat with a long pinkie nail. She knew that as long as the smell of blood and pain stood on the air, Floyd would continue to sit inside her skull.

Billy Ray was right.

As long as she lived in Oral's house, Floyd would be there sniffing around trying to catch the last whiff of blood her mop buckets and scrubbing brushes missed. *Now, don't be like that, Birdie Girl*, Floyd said. *You know you like keeping company with me, especially when we lived on The Hill and you drew me baths in that pink clawfoot tub.* Floyd's voice made her heart jump. It tugged the string on a faint memory that she knew would destroy her if opened. She shook her head until the phantom of Floyd dissipated along with the smell of his Stetson cologne.

The dirt road unraveled before her in the light of the Mustang's high beams. Billy Ray's zydeco ringtone coming from her Android brought her back to reality. Hearing it called to mind newly paved roads with bright yellow dividing lines, of live music at Chastain's Creole Heaven, and laughter. She pushed the answer button on the Bluetooth.

"You want to come out and play with the big kids?" she asked.

But it wasn't Billy Ray. What came next destroyed the solid reality she thought she had gained from banishing Floyd's ghost. The Mustang's speaker emitted a sound that was a cross between the tail of a rattler and a long, deep breath.

"Billy Ray?" she said in the dark.

He didn't answer. Instead, two more sounds filled the secluded cabin of the Mustang before the line went dead.

Maybe she was mistaken. Maybe she had been doing so much wool gathering that she only thought she heard Billy Ray's ringtone. She pressed the 'all calls' button. A list of calls made to her phone appeared on the screen. There it was, Billy Ray's number. She pressed the dial button.

"What up?" Billy Ray said.

"Where are you?" she asked.

"Home. Where do you think I am?"

"Did you fly?" she asked.

"Why you calling, Raven?" he said. "I was just about to fall asleep."

"Did you just dial me with your butt?"

"Nope, my butt is in bed trying to get some rest. I got to be at the restaurant in a few hours."

"How did you answer so fast?"

He laughed. "This you trying to get me at the crime scene? How do you think I answered so fast? Being a cop for years makes you speedy."

"You must have rolled over on your phone. You snore?" she said.

"I'd like to be snoring, but someone is not letting that happen. You want to know who that is?"

"Sorry," she said.

He hung up, which was fine by her. No time to argue with Billy Ray. That man didn't like to admit when he made a mistake. She had let the Floyd nonsense and the dark backroads get to her. She'd have to do better, especially if she was going to work this job and live in that house. It didn't help that darkness claimed every inch of road not touched by her headlights. It was as if she were moving through black silk. She had brought Oral's house back from darkness by scrubbing away all the blood that had been spilled by Byrd's Landing's second-most ruthless serial killer. The first had been Floyd, her father. Now, driving through the palatable dark, she felt herself slipping back into the hell she had so recently washed away.

⋆ ⋆ ⋆

It wasn't long before she saw the bright lights from ambulances and cruisers. Spotlights illuminated a muddy yard splayed in front of a derelict church with a leaning steeple. Silver needles from a soft rain fell in the glow of the artificial light. She parked the Mustang and cut the engine. Stevenson was across the street all decked out in a white jumpsuit and a pair of booties. He glared at her with both hands on his hips as she opened the car door. She knew as well as she knew the sun came up in the east that there was a muscle jumping in his jaw. His initial reaction every time he saw her was hostility.

He blamed her for the downward spiral of his career. It wasn't because his cover was blown. Stevenson did that willingly enough himself in an attempt to trick Raven into a confession. But Raven found out that Stevenson had gone rogue. His boss was in no hurry to finger a cop who put down a serial killer. Stevenson traveled to Byrd's Landing on his own dime to find evidence that his boss couldn't ignore. The only thing that saved his career was that the chief was so desperate for detectives that he hired him. Now Stevenson was Raven's partner. *And how's that for a laugh riot,* Floyd said in her head.

"Seriously, Stevenson?" she said as she got out of the car. "In the rain? Jumpsuit?"

"Chief's rules," he said.

"Booties?" she said, taking her time to survey the scene.

"They're waterproof," he said. "And don't let us rush you. It's only a triple homicide."

"Got here as fast as I could," she said.

"We're keeping a lot of people up waiting for you," he replied.

"Rita here yet?" Raven said, referring to the medical examiner as well as trying to prove a point. She hadn't seen the medical examiner's van.

"She's on her way," Stevenson said. "Coming from some party."

"Bet she's not happy," Raven said. "How long you been here?"

"About an hour," he said.

The uniforms had roped off the crime scene. Yellow tape twirled around a busted light pole and several spindly trees. They had rightly encircled the perimeter of the entire churchyard and sidewalk.

"What about out back?" she said, pointing to the crime scene tape.

"They taped that off, too, the best they could," Stevenson said. "But I don't know if our guy got out that way."

Raven said nothing. Stevenson always made assumptions like that, as if 'our guy' couldn't be one pissed-off female.

"Just Tim here?" Raven asked.

Tim, BLPD's one-man CSI team, would have quit a couple of years ago but a shiny new CSI mobile unit with all the trimmings caused him to reconsider. It was the corner office in the BLPD station house that Tim turned into a laboratory that finally clinched the deal. When he was in the field Tim would corral a few patrol officers to help gather evidence. That didn't stop the detectives and patrol officers from calling CSI 'Just Tim' even though it sent the little man into spasms.

"Use your eyes, Detective," Stevenson said. "You see the tarps."

She did see the tarps. But Stevenson talking about the case was better than him pronouncing judgment on her. Two blue tarps had been erected in the churchyard. One lay about twenty feet diagonally from the other. Another tarp kept the officers guarding the crime scene dry.

Tim, in a white jumpsuit, snapped pictures of the bodies.

"Two tarps?" Raven asked. "Bodies weren't together?"

"One of them ran. If you'd been here earlier, you'd already know that," Stevenson said.

"Are you going to spend the rest of the night being a walking pain in my rear end?" Raven asked.

Stevenson let out a sigh and wiped rainwater from his face. Raven reached into a jacket pocket and gave him a handkerchief. She had recently started carrying linen handkerchiefs with her initials on them, not admitting to herself that they were a holdover from Floyd. Stevenson wiped his face.

"Why is it that every time I'm being an asshole, you choose that exact moment to be kind?"

"I do it to make you feel bad," Raven said.

"You ready for the walk-thru?" he asked.

"I was born ready," she said.

He handed the handkerchief back to her before leading her to the guard station. A uniformed officer was there with a clipboard so they could keep track of who entered the crime scene. Raven took the clipboard from one of the officers without looking up, not even a by-your-leave, or as Floyd used to say, a dog-kiss-my-foot. Her mind was elsewhere. She was thinking about living in Oral's house, wondering if Billy Ray was right. Instead of running away from the gore, she appeared to be inviting it to take a seat next to her at the dinner table.

"Hey, Raven."

Raven looked up from the clipboard where she had just finished signing in. Marna stood there looking stout and capable in her uniform. Her dark skin was slick with rainwater, which told Raven Marna had been taking her uniform cover on and off during the time she had been on scene, an old nervous habit of hers. *Must be bad*, Raven thought.

"Marna," Raven said, and smiled. "Or should I say, Sergeant? Congratulations."

"Couldn't have done it without your help," Marna said.

She and Marna used to run together in grade school and then high school. No, that wasn't quite right, was it? They were good friends. Cameron, her brother, accused Raven of making a career out of pushing her close friends away. She may have pushed Marna away, but she could never forget her, not the girl whose daddy was Byrd's Landing's postmaster, and whose mama was a first-grade teacher and always smelled as sweet as candy. The woman wasn't stingy with hugs, or sleepovers, or the extra lunches she packed for Marna to give to Raven. Marna always had enough sense and kindness to give them to Raven when no one was looking.

While Raven was chasing Lamont Lovelle all over northern California, Marna had gotten married. Raven had been to the house a few times. Marna had her obsessions, or as her new husband, Newell, called them, weaknesses, too. Weaknesses because they were making them broke. It was barbecue. The woman had three Kamado Joes and a Blackstone. She honed her techniques with YouTube videos and went to a high-priced butcher in town. Her favorite videos were from some place called the Meat Church. At one of those dinners, one which Billy Ray attended, Newell laughed about how Marna had even convinced the butcher to let her help cut up a steer. *Last time*, Marna had laughed, and said, *I enjoy cooking but butchering pushes cooking and death much too close together for my liking.*

It wasn't until she looked nervously at the churchyard and swallowed that Raven understood why Marna appeared so troubled.

"You got the first call?" Raven asked. "Discovered the bodies?"

"I did," Marna said. "Somebody reported gunshots, but I along with everybody else was on a burglary call over in Bayou Lake Estates, and we didn't have anyone else to send."

Raven understood. BLPD was so short-staffed that the chief prioritized folk in the big, bright houses on the other side of the Red River over gunshots heard in the poor neighborhoods.

"I would've been here earlier, but the homeowner wanted to talk, I mean scream for forty-five minutes about how helpless BLPD was. Even called the chief, who came over so fast you'd think I'd stole something. I left for this call when he got there."

So that's why Chief Sawyer wasn't at this crime scene, Raven thought. He needed to stay to calm the Richie Riches down.

"How long between the first shot and when you got here?" Raven asked.

"A couple of hours," Marna said.

Raven looked at Stevenson in amazement.

"Couldn't believe it myself," he said. "But hey, that's how you all roll in Byrd's Landing."

"Anything changed since you first got here? Aside from the tarps? Anybody move anything?" Raven asked.

"Left as pristine as when it first happened, Raven. Nothing changed except Tim put the tarps up to keep us dry and preserve the evidence, and we roped off the area," Marna said.

Raven grabbed a flashlight from the table where patrol had set up as a command center. It was much sturdier than the portable one she carried in her jacket pocket. She flicked it on and off to make sure it was bright enough for what she needed.

"Come on with us, Marna," Raven said.

"You sure?"

"Yeah, I'm sure. You earned it," Raven said.

"I'm not sure going on the walk-thru is much of a reward," Marna said. "I hate this shit."

"I know you do, but you need to get used to it or die trying," Raven said. "It's our cross in this godforsaken town," she added, but only loud enough for the night to hear.

Chapter Three

Even if the rain hadn't already washed the evidence away, Raven was sure they wouldn't have found much, given the terrain. The churchyard was made of dirt. And even in the unusually fecund Byrd's Landing, it was a dirt where nothing dared to grow.

She looked around the neighborhood where the church stood. Leaning shotguns, vacant lots, boarded-up houses choked in kudzu.

The light rain had turned the mud slick, or as Billy Ray would say, slicker than owl shit. Marna tried to lead them to the body, but Raven resisted.

She liked searching around the body first for context, starting out in a wide spiral and then circling in with smaller spirals. Stevenson called it her vulture thing. She would quip back by asking if he missed that day of class at the academy. The best thing to do was go around the body first and then spiral into it.

Besides, no matter how much you prided yourself on staying detached from death, running straight to the body triggered something primitive. The primitive called on the emotions and the emotions clouded the judgment. The gaping mouth of a gunshot victim, or the half-lidded eyes of someone who had just been beaten to death could cause you to miss a handprint, or a scrap of torn fabric, perhaps a shoeprint. She flicked the flashlight on and angled the yellow light at the ground, hoping it would reveal what the darkness wanted to hide.

But the light told her nothing – no footprints, no torn fabric, no drag marks. The killer had even picked up the shell casings.

She directed the flashlight toward the sky. She hadn't forgotten about the third dimension of the crime scene, and the church looming over her like a ghoul the entire time compelled her to look up. The church was a multistoried, humpbacked building, the tallest part seeming to shoot up and up. Cracked windows leered from each floor on the way to a crumbling tower, then a belfry and next a sharp, deadly spire. On top of the spire was a cross. Raven moved her flashlight toward it for a better look.

"What in the tarnation is that?" she asked.

"What in hell is what?" Stevenson said.

"That cross. Is that thing made of nails?" she asked.

"I've seen crosses like that before. It's to remind us that Jesus died for our sins," Stevenson said.

Raven turned to look at Marna. "What is this place?"

"Didn't you grow up here?" Stevenson asked.

"I guess I didn't get around enough," Raven answered.

"You'd know if you were native," Marna said. "We don't like to talk about this place too much. When we do, we call it the Old Bottoms. It's where the poorest of the poor live. Folk with lots of problems and absolutely no money, you know. Addiction, all kinds of disease, including mental illness. They use the shotgun shacks for shelter. It's like a homeless camp you see on the side of a freeway but just tucked away out of sight."

"Why isn't it on our radar?" Raven asked.

Marna shook her head. "Shit, Raven. Nobody cares about these people. You see how long it took for us to even respond to a call? They mostly police themselves."

"Police themselves?" Raven asked. "How does that even work?"

"Well, if you get killed here, too bad. They might pray over you, might tell your kin, but in the end they'll just throw your corpse in a grave. Then they'll find the person who did it and throw them in right after you. Stealing will get the shit beat out of you, and you don't want to know what'll happen if you bold enough to rape somebody," Marna said.

"That's the craziest thing I've ever heard," Raven said.

"It's Byrd's Landing."

"What does the chief say about all this?" Raven asked.

"Have you met the chief? As long as the homeless aren't using the doorways of Byrd's Landing businesses as motel rooms, he doesn't care." Marna said.

Yes, she had indeed met the chief, but this still surprised her. In her heart she knew, though, that Chief Sawyer wouldn't care about these people until they started voting. His office was an appointed one, but his job depended on his friend, the mayor, staying in office.

"So, they have rules," Raven said. "That must mean someone is in charge. Who is it?"

Marna gestured at a tight crowd that had formed on a porch across the wide street from the crime scene. Raven knew immediately who she meant. A man in a white t-shirt and what looked like black sweatpants stood in the middle of the crowd. He was so much taller than those around him that Raven wouldn't have been surprised if he topped the church with the cross of nails himself without a ladder. From what she could see in the low light, his face was broad and flat, and his chest as wide as a wheelbarrow.

"You mean the giant?" Raven asked.

"That's him. The one who looks like he eats a bowl of nails with moonshine for breakfast. Folk call him Papa. Name's Lucien Toussaint. He's judge, jury and executioner here," Marna said.

"But they called the police tonight?" Stevenson said.

"Or did one of the victims call?" Raven asked.

"We don't know, yet. I wouldn't be surprised if someone from the neighborhood called in the shots. Papa tries to control the gun thing, don't like people bringing them in," Marna said.

Raven looked at other members of the crowd. Young men, some in dreadlocks, others in braids or in do-rags, watched them with their arms folded across their chest, and their faces obscured by the dark. No women. She took note of what the men were wearing. Sweatpants without shirts on a few, four or five in pajama pants, and a couple of them fully dressed in basketball shorts or jeans and t-shirts, like the man Marna called Papa. Raven waved Tim over.

"Try to be discreet," she told him. "Get some pictures of the crowd. I'm especially interested in those fully dressed."

"Why?" Marna asked.

"They may have been up at the time of the murders," she answered.

"Or they got dressed while they were waiting for the po-po," Stevenson said.

She didn't answer him. *No sense talking to stupid*, she heard Floyd say in her head. Raven didn't believe that they dressed after the commotion. Why would they? They would have been too busy looking for those who fired the shots.

"What about statements?"

Marna chuckled. "We got them, but they aren't saying much. I'm thinking we should come back when it's daylight. Maybe they'll be more forthcoming. We did tell them detectives may be following up."

Raven looked once more at the hostile crowd. "Oh joy," she said. She turned her attention back to the church.

"Do you have someone on tap to canvass the neighborhood tomorrow?" Stevenson said.

"We do," Marna answered.

"Make sure they do it in pairs," Stevenson said, eyes on the crowd.

"I ain't stupid, Detective," Marna said.

"Nobody saying you are," Raven answered for him, wanting to stave off an argument. They already had their hands full.

"Can you take me through what you're thinking, Stevenson?" Raven asked.

"Drug deal gone bad, my guess," he said.

"They don't allow guns, but they allow drug deals?" Raven asked.

"Papa can't control everything," Marna said.

"Go on, Stevenson," Raven said.

"Two shots execution style, and the other you need to see," Stevenson said.

"Not yet," Raven said. "How do you think the killers escaped?"

"Killers, plural?" Stevenson said. "You thinking more than one perp?"

"With three bodies? It wouldn't surprise me, but I wouldn't bet the whole pot on it. How do you think they got out of here, Marna?"

"Gunshots? My guess is that they had to go fast," Marna said. "Or the entire neighborhood would have been down on them."

Raven tried to imagine the place without the lamps the BLPD erected and the headlights from the many police vehicles illuminating the scene. It would be dark as purgatory. With her mind's eye she visualized the people in the Old Bottoms, unused to the sound of gunfire, leaping out of their beds and bolting out of their houses, perhaps yelling at each other, trying to figure out what to do. Would they have remembered flashlights? Smartphones? Did they even have smartphones? The perp would have heard the ruckus. While the neighborhood patrol tried to get themselves together, he would have had two, maybe five minutes to get away. Not a lot of time, especially if the perp was unfamiliar with the neighborhood and wasted precious seconds retrieving the shell casings. Her gaze wandered back to the church.

"Could they have gone in there?" Raven asked. "Anybody been inside to check it out?"

Stevenson shook his head. "Place is falling down. It's not safe."

"Plenty safe if someone's running," she said. "Marna, did you check?"

"I don't agree with Stevenson on most things, but I do that. Place is a death trap," Marna said.

"Huh," Raven said contemplatively.

"I'm not going in there, Raven," Stevenson said flatly.

Marna looked at Raven.

"You talked me into some crazy shit when we were little, Raven, but I'm telling you, not tonight," Marna said.

Raven didn't answer. Maybe they were right. She began another search on the right side of the church. Stevenson and Marna followed in her footsteps. Raven knew that Marna was trying to be respectful of her process. Her partner showed his disdain by whistling old Satchmo's 'What a Wonderful World'. She knew that he was doing so just to get on her nerves. At first, she didn't want to give him the satisfaction by responding, but soon she just couldn't take it anymore.

"Could you please put a sock in it?" Raven asked him.

"Why?" Stevenson asked.

"Because it's annoying as hell and I'm trying to concentrate," Raven said.

He stopped. But regardless of being set to music or silence, their search yielded no evidence. Raven caught Marna's eye, held the gaze for half a second, and then peered at Stevenson. After a moment she sent the flashlight's beam in the direction of the church.

"Raven," Marna breathed.

Stevenson shook his head. "Not only is it not safe, it's not necessary. Nobody's been in there in years."

"You know that how?" Raven asked.

"Look, if you really want to go in there let's get the building or fire department out here first so they can make sure it's safe to enter," Stevenson said.

"And keep all these people from their nice, soft beds while letting a killer get away?" Raven pressed.

"I tell you right now, Evel Knievel, if you go in there, you're on your own," Stevenson said.

Evel Knievel. Raven laughed a little. She knew from dating Stevenson that this cautious man had been fascinated with daredevils since he was a boy. She'd catch him watching videos of base jumpers, zip-liners, and elite surfers who were willing to put their lives on the line for a thrill that only lasted as long as it takes to spit in the wind. Taking what he called dumb risks was something he'd never been able to or willing to do, except when it came to trying to put her in jail over Lovelle's murder. And to him, that wasn't a risk, but justice. Evel Knievel, long dead but known as the man who put the dare in daredevil by jumping over a mile of cars, was his favorite. Raven looked at him standing there in his white jumpsuit and waterproof booties wondering how he ever got up the nerve to become a cop. Then she took another look at the building. The place did appear as if one stiff wind would knock it down. She didn't know if anybody in their right mind would risk it. But what if they weren't in their right mind?

If I'm running from somebody, Floyd whispered in her head. *If I used up time picking up them shell casings, I'd give hiding in that church some thought.* His raspy voice with its assumed Southern accent made the decision for her. Never mind that the last time he gave her counsel of any significance entailed her jumping into the Pacific and swimming until she became too tired to make it back to shore.

But still. Something in that church pulled at her.

Chapter Four

The bloated church door hung slightly askew on its frame. It made a scraping sound when Raven pushed it open.

"Good, sweet Holy Mother of God," Marna said, her fist against her nose. "What's that smell?"

"Probably animals crawled in here to die," Raven said.

"Fuck," Stevenson said for what seemed like the fiftieth time.

"You could have stayed outside, Stevenson," Raven said. "Waited for the fire chief to hold your hand."

"You're crazy, Raven," Marna complained.

"Both of you could have stayed outside. I didn't ask you to follow me in here," Raven said.

"Somebody has to look out for you," Marna said, sending Stevenson a nasty look.

"I can take care of my partner," Stevenson spat. "If you're such good friends with her, Marna, maybe you can convince her to leave."

"Come on both of you," Raven said. "Stop being such fragile flowers."

She stepped into the pitch black. The flashlight had been acting up in the rain. She thumped it against her palm to get the light to turn back on. By some instinctual agreement between the three of them, Raven went to the right. Above her was a long balcony on the verge of collapse. She stepped carefully around the debris scattered over the floor, with an occasional glance at Marna and Stevenson.

Marna chose the center aisle, her flashlight pointed at the altar. The light crawled over the pallid flesh of a bloody Jesus wearing a crown of thorns. Stevenson cut left, making his way toward a Wurlitzer piano on its side. Raven couldn't imagine a force big enough to flip the instrument. The light from Stevenson's flashlight traveled over the torn floor surrounding the piano. He stared down through a tangle of floor planks to the exposed subfloor.

Except for the water dripping hollowly from the ruptured ceiling, the place was eerily quiet, so quiet that Raven felt like an intruder into a place that was not only abandoned by God, but everyone else, a place never again meant for the breath of a living thing. *Especially not a little Birdie Girl*, Floyd said, his voice clear as a bell in her head.

Raven had to admit that this place scared her. She had the overwhelming urge to run. *What do you always tell your lil' Shirley Temple ex-boyfriend?* Floyd said of Stevenson who had left the Wurlitzer and was walking toward Marna. She had jumped onto the altar. *Suck it up, buttercup*, Floyd finished.

"I don't think anybody's been through here," Stevenson said. "We could hardly get in the front door. What you doing up there, Marna? Praying?"

"Looking for footprints," Marna said. "If he did use the church as an escape route, he'd probably come up here looking for a back or side door, the one the preacher usually comes through."

"That's crazy," Stevenson said.

"We here now," Marna responded. "Might as well do the job."

Raven wasn't so sure that the altar led to the way out. She was looking at the balcony that twisted along the bulging north wall of the church. She was drawn to a door and what looked like a flight of stairs at the end of a long hallway. Sturdy stairs, stairs that could sustain the weight of a person running.

Raven heard Stevenson trip over something. He cursed. "There's nothing here," he said. "This is stupid."

"You're stupid," Raven mumbled under her breath, feeling like a twelve-year-old and enjoying every moment of it.

"What?" Stevenson said.

"He ain't wrong," Marna called from the altar. "No footprints up here, and the debris doesn't look like it's been disturbed in a long time. Even the graffiti ain't fresh."

No disturbed debris down where you are, Raven thought. She retrained the flashlight on the staircase that had so gripped her attention. Something flashed by near the stairs so fast that she questioned if it was real.

"Hey, you guys," Raven called.

Marna and Stevenson started toward her. They came too slowly for her liking. They had to hurry. She didn't know why but they did.

"Raven, wait," Marna said, now stepping fast.

Stevenson was soon jogging beneath the twisted balcony, trying to catch up with both Raven and Marna.

"Slow down," he urged.

One of the boards that had been teetering from a hole in the floor above fell right in front of Raven. She would later swear that it was so close that it scraped her nose before crashing to the floor. She sneezed from the resulting plume of dust that compromised her view of the stairs. But she kept going.

And then a sound from the balcony.

"Did you hear—" Raven started to ask.

Stevenson tackled her before she could finish the question. He knocked her down while at the same time dragging her from beneath the balcony. Marna was running and jumping over torn-up boards in front of them. Stevenson and Raven reached Marna just when the entire balcony released from the wall and went crashing accordion-style behind them.

Marna fell. Stevenson stood from a crawling position. He pulled Raven along with one hand and tried to grab Marna with the other. The bulk of her uniform kept him from getting a good hold on her. Raven slapped his hand.

"Get Marna!" she yelled amid the noise. She didn't need Stevenson teaching her how to run.

The balcony kept clattering down along the entire length of the wall. If Raven hadn't known better, she would have sworn that the thing was chasing them. It felt like it took forever to reach the foyer. But soon the three of them exploded through the front door and tumbled down the front steps. Tim, as well as a couple of uniform officers, ran toward them.

"Y'all hurt?" Tim asked.

Raven groaned. She felt mud along her back and jeans. Her jacket sleeve was torn and a gash on her arm burned like fire.

"Marna? Stevenson?" she coughed.

"Fine," Marna said. Was Marna laughing? "Nothing like almost being killed that makes you feel alive. Thank you, Jesus."

"I'm alive, no thanks to your stupidity," Stevenson said.

"Good, I'm glad all's right with the world," Raven said, and passed out.

Chapter Five

As Raven opened her eyes, light slid beneath her eyelids like cracked glass. She sat up, jerked her forearm across her face. Rita was there shouting, telling someone to move back. Marna was yelling at the officers guarding the crime scene about not anyone in this Podunk town knowing how to do their job.

Stevenson, in a very Stevenson-like way, was saying, "Turn off that damned camera and get the hell out of here before I arrest both of you for obstruction of justice."

"You go ahead and do that," a voice said. "And I'll publish the video of the three of you being spit out of that church like God tasted something nasty. I'm just trying to do my job."

Raven closed her eyes and flopped back down to the ground. She didn't know how long she was out, but it wasn't long enough. That voice belonged to Imogene Tucker, Byrd's Landing's intrepid news anchor and investigative reporter. The light was most likely from the cameraman who followed her around like an extra limb.

"I know you're awake, Raven," Imogene said. "You might as well get up and face the music."

There was no way around it. Raven opened her eyes and attempted to stand up. Her head spun for several seconds while she tried to focus on Imogene's red-blonde hair extensions framing her perfectly made-up face, the pale-as-dusk pink blouse, and the pencil skirt encasing her round behind. She was also wearing sky-high stilettos. What evidence the rain didn't destroy, Imogene's shoes surely would.

"Easy now." It was Rita, the medical examiner, talking and trying to steady Raven. "I'm going to have the paramedics check you over. You were out for a minute or two."

Raven waved her away. "I'm fine." She turned to Imogene. "You know you aren't supposed to be back here. How do you always manage to slither your way into my crime scenes?"

"They let me through," Imogene said, pointing toward the now-empty guard station. The two rookies who were supposed to be guarding the entrance were now standing behind Imogene.

"Sorry, Sergeant," the tall one said to Marna. "She zigged when I zagged. I couldn't catch her in time."

"Too late now," Marna said. "Get your sorry asses back over there. Useless as tits on a bull."

"Don't worry," Imogene said. "I followed the path into the crime scene just like I learned from you, Raven. I didn't mess anything up."

"Great, maybe we should deputize you," Stevenson said.

"Imogene, I swear on everything that's holy..." Raven started.

"Just give me a statement and I'm out, I swear," Imogene said.

"Like I haven't heard that one before," Raven responded.

The cameraman raised his camera but lowered it again at the look on Raven's face.

"Come on, Raven," Imogene whined.

"One statement? And you swear you won't put that video on the ten o'clock news for all of Byrd's Landing to see?"

"I swear," Imogene said, a sharp number two pencil poised over a memo pad.

"You got a deal," Raven said. "The statement is 'no comment'. Marna, escort our guests back behind the yellow tape."

Chapter Six

Rita insisted on the paramedic. They found a deep gash on Raven's arm that needed cleaning. They tried to get her to the hospital for stitches, but Raven refused. They settled on closing the wound the best they could with butterfly strips.

"Nice tuck and roll," Rita said when they were done.

"I try," Raven said, as they ducked beneath the tarp over the two bodies, and knelt.

"Sure you don't want to get your hard head checked out? You fainted," Rita said.

"I didn't *faint*," Raven said. "I don't *faint*. I just blacked out for a few seconds, that's all. Please don't tell the chief. I thought you were at some big shindig. Where's your princess gown?"

"It was my sister's wedding. Her fourth one," Rita said. "For every single one she stuffs me in organza and ruffles to match her tactless white wedding gown. I was glad somebody got murdered so I could get out of that thing."

"You're as sick as Raven," Stevenson said, standing above them. "People are dead."

"See you still with the second string," Rita replied without looking at him.

"It's my albatross," Raven said. "Who's the mouse?"

She pointed to a slight red-headed girl in jeans carrying an iPad almost as big as she was.

"Intern from the college. Name's Augusta," Rita said. "Over here, small fry."

Augusta stuffed the iPad inside her jacket and walked over using the same path they'd all taken to the bodies. After Rita introduced Raven and

Stevenson, the young woman said, "Call me Gus." She took out her iPad again and asked, "Mind if I take notes?"

"Knock yourself out," Raven said.

"Just don't post it on Facebook," Stevenson interjected, frowning.

Gus rolled her eyes. "Are you kidding? Facebook is deader than these guys."

"Or Twitter," Stevenson said, unwilling to concede the point.

Gus rolled her eyes so hard that Raven wondered if they were still in her head.

Rita chuckled. "Albatross indeed."

Gus wasn't the only one who needed to take notes. Raven took a moleskin notebook from inside her jacket pocket and turned her attention back to the dead men. White light spilled on the two victims. Both of them were face down with their hands zip-tied behind their backs. Raven shivered at what must have been going through their minds as they waited for the bullet. Did they think the cavalry would show up, the killer or killers would change their mind, that God would reach down from his heaven with a hand made of lightning to save them? She looked at the crumbling church before her, the cross made of nails. *Not bloody likely*, she thought. Not in this place anyway.

Starting at the tips of their tennis shoes, Raven scanned the first body, and then the second, examining arms, legs, and hands. No cuts or defensive wounds were clear. She worked quickly, sketching the scene, including the positions of the two bodies in relationship to each other. As an afterthought, she then scribbled down what she thought she saw in the church, that flash of movement. She wrote it down even though she knew she'd not forget it.

"Tim, did you get all the pictures you need?" Raven asked.

"Yes, I did. I'll hang around in case you want me to get anything else."

Raven looked over her shoulder at the church that had almost eaten them alive. "Get some of the church too," she said.

"Already did that, and street signs, and a view from across the street. I photographed every place that needed it before you came on scene," Tim said.

She grinned. "I don't think the church's the same. You got the before, now we need the after. Get some more of the front door, steps and on both sides. Don't go in, though." She looked at Stevenson. "It's dangerous," she said, still grinning. "Alternate light source on the bodies?"

"Yes," Tim said. "When they were lying face down. Didn't find anything. I'll do another pass after you roll them."

She turned back to Rita, leaned close to her until their shoulders were touching.

"Talk to me, Rita," she said.

"Why don't you tell her, Small Fry."

Gus knelt beside them. "Well, we got some lividity on both bodies," she said. "So, I'd guess they've been dead several hours. Killed here, not dumped."

Rita looked at Raven. "That match your timeline?"

"Pretty much," she said.

"We'll get temps to make sure," Rita said. "At least we can get a pretty good estimate."

"Entry wound back of the head," Raven said.

"Yep, on both of them," Rita said. "Thank God water can't wash away stippling. It's around both wounds. The gun was close. Somebody went Russian mafia on these boys."

"Mind if I check the pockets?"

"Go ahead." Rita sighed. "I'm not going to find out much more out here anyway except for the fact that they're doornail dead."

Raven tucked her notebook back into her inside jacket pocket. She wiped her hands on her jeans the best she could before taking a pair of blue latex gloves from another pocket. She pulled them on, reached over to the man nearest her. She turned him gingerly, just enough so she could slide her hand into a front pocket. She came away with a Steelers wallet that had a state ID and a wet ten-dollar bill.

"So, our friend here is Marcel Thibodeaux," she said. "Late thirties of 4965 Lavender Lane, Apartment 888D."

She gave the wallet to Tim, who had been hovering. He placed it in an evidence bag. In the man's other pocket Raven found a small memo pad that some detectives still carry around. Billy Ray used to carry one like it when he was still a cop. He got them ten for ten dollars at Staples office supply. She wanted to open the memo pad but it was wet. She feared that it would disintegrate in her hands. She handed it to Tim, who carefully placed it into a plastic evidence bag.

"I saw writing," Raven said. "You think we'll be able to read it?"

"I'll try my best," Tim said.

Raven glanced at Rita.

"Oh no," Rita said. "That's your 'can I roll him' face."

"Well, can I?"

"Be my guest but let Gus help. She needs the training."

They rolled him, and then the other victim. He also had a state ID. Raven held it in her hand for a moment, studied the face and said, "Lionel Williams."

It was becoming a ritual for her to look at their faces and say their names.

Rolling the bodies told them nothing more about why their life ended here. The rain had taken it all.

Chapter Seven

Raven left Gus and Tim with the two bodies beneath the tarp. Gus would wrap the hands and feet in plastic bags on the off chance they'd find more evidence. Drug hit, the chief had said. Raven was feeling that. Two dead execution style. The killings were horrific but all business.

The body beneath the second tarp blew that theory away like dust on a strong wind. She squatted next to the hand of an arm that appeared to be reaching for something alive to touch before oblivion. Wearing a fresh pair of gloves, she brushed the back of the doomed hand. Not understanding the reason she did it, she whispered to this latest unlucky, "Hey you, I'm so sorry. We're going to get this cretin. Don't you worry about it."

She took his hand in hers and examined it.

"Nails are torn all to hell. He fought," Raven said, this time loud enough for Rita to hear.

Rita grunted an agreement. "Don't see any bullet wounds, either. See the gashes in his shirt? This one was stabbed."

"A lot," Gus said, walking up to them.

Raven glanced at the men she had recently visited. Two morgue assistants lifted one of the bodies onto a plastic sheet near a black body bag. A gurney waited beside it. *Coming for to carry me home*, Floyd sang in his high, sweet voice inside her head.

"Intended target?" Stevenson said, breaking into her thoughts. She hadn't noticed him walking up.

"Has to be," Raven said. "Those two over there could've been just in the wrong place at the wrong time."

"Or maybe this one tried to run and pissed off the killer," Marna interjected.

"What is this?" Raven said. "An Al Green concert? Y'all know that it's one detective at a time with the medical examiner at the body. Remember the chief's new rule?"

"You funny talking about rules," Stevenson said.

Raven shook her head, let it go.

"Could be that the killer or killers were angry because this one tried to run," Raven said, acknowledging Marna's earlier point, but she didn't think that was it.

The rain had turned the victim's blood rose-pink. The color touched another dark memory that Raven slammed down with the practiced ease of a champion ping-pong player.

"He fought like an angry bear," Raven said.

Gus stooped so close to her that Raven could feel one bony shoulder pressing against hers. A flash from Tim's camera above them threw the hand in stark relief – knuckles abraded and bloody, nails torn off on a couple of fingers, broken to the quick on the others.

"Marna, you know what to do," Raven said.

"Already did it," she said. "The minute I saw the body I got patrol calling the hospitals looking for anyone who came in with cut-up arms or hands."

"You check his pockets?" Raven asked.

"Only checked to see if he was deceased," Marna said. "Didn't put my hand on him, otherwise. I know better than that."

"Tim?" Raven asked.

"All done," he said. "Just getting a few extra photographs."

"Should we roll him, Rita?" Raven asked.

Raven hoped that Rita saw in her face that she wasn't eager to roll another body tonight. She was glad when Rita took on that chore with Gus. They carefully turned the body over until it lay face up. This victim's throat had been cut. Stab wounds peppered his upper torso. But his face was only touched by death.

Raven doubled over as if she had been sucker-punched. She heard Marna scream, *Goddamnit, no! no!* Tim grasped Marna's forearms and started walking her backward from the scene. Raven was still doubled over, her hands on her hips, trying to keep the sobs racking her insides from escaping her body. Stevenson kept saying *What is it?* over and over like a whiny child and good God she knew that she would soon clobber him if he didn't shut up. And there was Rita's voice, faint but audible. *Raven* she was saying in a sob. *Raven*. Raven wanted to answer her but couldn't find her voice. She knew – no, Rita, Marna and she knew the man staring up at them with dead eyes, speaking to them through a gaping throat.

His name was Ezekiel Riverton. They all called him Zeke. At one point in time, many years ago, Raven would have laid her body in front of a train for him. Raven hadn't seen Zeke in a year or more, but she knew he, Rita, and Marna hung out, bowled, and shot the breeze at Chastain's often. They may have forgone the train sacrifice, but knowing how loyal they both were, Raven knew that they would have at least pulled the handbrake.

Chapter Eight
Floyd

Floyd soon tired of lingering over a kill. After it was done, it was done. Why, if someone were brave enough to ask him, he'd say a kill was like a real good meal. You'd eat until it was gone. You'd suck the last bit from your fingers and lick the plate clean. The memory of how much you enjoyed the food may flow through your mind every now and then like a cool breeze on a blistering day, but you really don't give it too much thought. He thought it was right foolish to return to the scene of the crime, read the newspapers, or keep tabs on the investigation. It wasn't like he wasn't proud of his work, but he'd just had his fill. And Floyd 'Fire' Burns didn't like feeding on scraps.

But Mrs. Jefferson was different. She was close. His Birdie Girl had taken a liking to her. After Mrs. Jefferson went off to her meeting with the Lord, the police put yellow tape all around the woman's house and over the door. They searched the woods, questioned the boys who found her for so long the morons started making things up just to get it done and over with. Cops walked up and down The Hill, knocking on doors, asking questions. Most folks slammed the doors in their faces.

What got Floyd, though, was that the trouble from Mrs. Jefferson's death entered into his own house as bold as you please. It sat at his kitchen table uninvited. It explained to him what grief tasted like. Grief scrubbed the flavor out of the food. The canned soups and stews that Raven heated up for him reached Floyd's dinner table cool and tasteless. Even the color of the eggs she used to make so good paled, the yolks runny and thin as pus.

And on occasion, grief compelled a body to move. Raven started running away. Sometimes she didn't come home until he dragged her home. At first, he'd go looking every time, but one day, he decided to see what would happen if he didn't. It was raining something fierce. When she finally dragged herself back to the house she was soaked to the bone.

But that didn't stop her from running.

She kept on until one day a cop brought her home. Now that was a situation Floyd just couldn't abide. He decided that he was going to need to get his own body moving or he'd end up getting caught, not just for Mrs. Jefferson, but all the other good meals he ate from California to Louisiana. Of course, he knew it wouldn't last forever, but he just wasn't ready to stop eating high off the hog.

Not just yet.

He and Raven would have to get off The Hill, go live someplace where folk weren't looking into his mouth the whole time. He could then erase ole Mrs. Jefferson from Raven's mind. He'd make it so that the woman was like a dream so foggy that Raven wouldn't know how to tell it. Every time she would say, 'Miss Ruth', he'd answer back with, 'Miss Who?' When Raven grew up, she wouldn't know that a body named Ruth Jefferson ever walked this earth.

Chapter Nine

Well after the sun rose Rita's team loaded two of the bodies into the coroner's vehicles. They had to use an old beat-up, green station wagon because the van couldn't hold all three bodies. Sweat trickled down Raven's back as she watched the station wagon carry Zeke's body away. He was gone but she'd never forget how he was lying in the barren churchyard, his mouth open in accusation. He had been calling her for weeks, leaving voicemail, sending texts. She was always too busy to reply.

And now this.

Raven felt guilt bloom in her gut. Did she have something to do with Zeke being dead? Why was he calling her in the last few weeks? If Billy Ray were here, he'd tell her to stop it. Not everything led back to her. Besides, it wasn't unusual for those who grew up with abuse to think they were to blame for everything. That kind of guilt was unnatural, he would tell her. Write it down. Burn both ink and paper and don't think about it no more. She would heed his advice. After all, she had a killer to catch.

Still, she wished with everything in her that it was Billy Ray now crossing the street while she leaned against the back bumper of Miss Jean, the name of the red Mustang she bought long ago in honor of her slain stepmother. But it was Delbert Stevenson, her new partner and old lover, crossing the street toward her. He thankfully kept his trap shut when he reached her. He simply turned and leaned his well-formed behind against the bumper before folding his arms across his chest and mimicking her position. His arm brushed against her shoulder. She didn't break the silence, was in fact all right with it. That's what she liked about him when they were dating, his ability to just be there when she was hurting. He didn't try to take away her pain. He just sat with her while she was in it. That's what had tricked her.

"Crime scene?" she said.

"Yeah, Marna is going to keep uniforms on it. Set up some shifts. They'll do a grid search now that it's daylight."

"I also want a thorough search of the woods out back, and around the church itself," she started but he cut her off before she could finish.

"Not inside?" he said.

"No," she said. "You and Marna were probably right about that, but I still want the building department to check it out, to see what caused that collapse. Also interested to see if they find any evidence that someone had been there recently."

He shook his head like it was a waste of time.

"Just to be sure," she said.

Raven let the silence stretch out between them again.

Finally, he said, "You knew the victim?"

Raven turned to him with a blank look on her face. "What gave it away?"

He shifted his weight on the bumper. "Stupid question," he conceded.

Raven watched him for a few seconds before her gaze returned to the place where Zeke's body had been. She imagined his blood lingering in the wet soil.

"Are you going to run and tell the chief that I knew Zeke and get me thrown off the case? Is that what this feigned concern's all about, Mr. Goody Two Shoes?" she asked.

He took a deep breath, let it out slowly. "I know you hate me," he said.

"At least you know something," she said.

"But like I said before, I did come to care for you."

"Just answer my question and save the rest for St. Peter at the holy gates," she said.

"I'm not going to say anything to the chief. I'm just concerned about you. You took that hard."

She nodded. Raven did appreciate his companionship at that moment. Some part of her was glad that he was there. She realized she should have told him then only after it was too late.

"Can I at least say I'm sorry?" Stevenson asked.

"You can say it."

Raven straightened into a full standing position. She rubbed both palms of her hands against her eyes until they hurt. She hoped the pain would help keep her from crying.

Stevenson matched her stance. "What's next?" he asked.

"I need to tell Zeke's mama," she said.

"A patrol officer and I can do that," Stevenson said. "You go home, clean up and get an hour or two of rest. Process this and meet me back at the station."

"I don't need to rest," Raven said. "I need to do. He was my friend, I can tell his mother that he's dead."

"You still have to clean up," he said, indicating the sleeve of her torn jacket, the blood.

"I'll swing by home first," she said. "Probably be over there in an hour or so."

"You knew Zeke, and know his mother. You have any idea who their pastor is? What church they go to?"

"Church?" she asked.

"Yes. It might be a good idea to have her pastor meet us over there," he said.

"How do you know she'll cotton to a preacher darkening her doorstep? What makes you think she believes in the same fairy tales you do?" she asked.

He stood straighter as if his puppeteer had tightened his strings.

"They aren't fairy tales, and I know most people in the South are religious," he said.

"You've been watching too much TV," Raven said. "Zeke's mama and God haven't been getting along since her husband left her with two kids to raise, and a bad attitude that knows no bounds."

* * *

Raven's red Mustang traced the backroads home. She shed her jacket and tossed it into the kitchen garbage can. She wondered if Zeke dying on the same day she thought the house was ready for living in meant anything. She wasn't surprised when Floyd responded in her head. *Naw, Birdie Girl. Don't mean nothing. Just lousy timing. We'll see,* she thought.

The dirt from the abandoned church had invaded every part of her body. She felt the grit in her hair, mouth, under her fingernails. She stripped her remaining clothes and stepped into the shower. She tilted her head beneath the faucet and let the water run over her hair and down her face. She prayed that the water would cleanse her inside and out. But it was slimy, warm as spit even turned all the way to cold. She didn't feel at all clean, not even after she soaped up, rinsed and toweled off.

Someone filled with rage had murdered Ezekiel Riverton. The gut punch she felt when she saw Zeke's body returned, and her breath hitched as if she had been physically struck. It was her job to find out who killed Zeke. But first, she had to tell Zeke's mother. She didn't know how she would be able to look that woman in the eye.

Raven pulled from her closet a duplicate of the black blazer now gracing the bottom of the kitchen garbage. She tossed it on the air mattress. After underwear, she dressed in dark blue jeans. She reached into her top dresser drawer to retrieve a white t-shirt that sat atop five other perfectly folded white t-shirts and pulled it on. She complemented her outfit with an ankle holster with a newly acquired Gerber Ghostrike six-inch knife, a shoulder holster that carried her own personal Glock 19, and a .22 revolver tucked in a holster at the small of her back. You can never be too careful in this hellhole of a town.

Once again outside, she stood next to the Mustang and took a deep breath. Pecan trees stood all around her. She listened hard for Oral's voice, hoping that he would send a whisper along the leaves that he had her back. But she knew that wouldn't happen. He would never talk to her like Floyd. Oral hated that she was a cop, never approved of what she did for a living. She'd never feel his presence again, living or dead. She squared her shoulders and dialed a number by heart, one that she should have forgotten long ago. She wasn't at all surprised when he answered on the first ring.

Chapter Ten

Stevenson beat her to 1232 Coral Road, where Zeke had lived with his mother. This duplex shotgun house, what the locals called a double-barrel shotgun, was nothing like the falling-down shack that Raven and Floyd occupied on The Hill. Instead of peeling paint and snaggle-toothed steps, Zeke's house had drop-lap siding painted sunshine yellow, and lacy Italianate corner porch brackets that Floyd used to call curly-cues.

Stevenson's bald head and broad shoulders were visible through the front windshield of his gray Toyota Camry. Raven could see him through the front windshield because she had parked opposite him, front bumper to front bumper on the wrong side of the road. She smiled as he scowled. Aggravating the piss out of him were moments she lived for. His driver's side door clicked open. He shut it hard.

"Nice parking job," he said. "You ready?"

"I was born ready," she said, looking at him with a little grin. "But where's your preacher?"

He looked startled.

She laughed and shook her head. Before he could ask more questions, she strolled past him to a gold BMW two-door coupe slowing against the curb. The driver parked behind Stevenson's vehicle.

"Who the hell is that in the Black Man Wagon?" Stevenson asked.

Who the hell indeed? The man now shutting his car door wasn't tall like Raven liked them. He was around five seven and heavily muscled. In the old days when they were teenagers he spent as much time in the gym as she did. She had a distant memory of him saying, *The only thing you can control, right?* From what she saw now, he hadn't kicked the habit. His skin was dark, blue-black. His long dreadlocks were gathered in a band at the back of his neck.

It didn't matter that he was too far away to touch her. Raven could feel his hands on her as she drew closer. She shook the memory away. His being here right now had nothing to do with their past. She kept her face immobile as she approached him. But she could do nothing about her beating heart, or the lump in her throat, or Floyd's voice saying, *And in walks the man who could have changed your life if only you'd let him. Glad you didn't. I'd been bored to tears.*

"You sure picked a shit time to call," he said. "And a shit reason."

Raven apologized. She introduced Zeke's brother, Diamond Riverton, to Stevenson.

"What happened to him?" Diamond asked Raven.

"Someone killed him," she said. "I know it's him, but I need you and your mama to come down to identify the body."

"You told me that on the phone. I'm asking for more details. What happened to my brother?" Diamond asked.

"We've given you all the information we can at this time," Stevenson said. "It's an active investigation."

Diamond flicked his eyes over Stevenson like the man was a fly shitting in his gumbo. He then turned and walked toward the porch without looking back.

"I guess you know him too," Stevenson said dryly as they followed him up the steps to a front door painted a glossy purple.

A tall, big-boned woman answered the door. She was clutching the collar of a silk peacock-embroidered kimono. Maybelline Riverton's dark eyes landed on Raven, who she knew well, moved to Stevenson, a man she didn't know at all, and then to Diamond, the estranged son who she hadn't spoken to in years. When her eyes settled back on Raven, Maybelline's shoulders slumped. The large hand on the collar of the kimono loosened, but it didn't fall open.

Raven read the look on the woman's face as clearly as if she were reading a newspaper. This was a visit that Zeke's mother had always dreaded even though he had beaten his addiction. Trouble would always find him, no matter what. Maybelline stood there for several long moments. When she finally spoke, she said one word: "Goddamn."

Chapter Eleven

Floyd

Miss Maybelline Riverton.

She's the reason that most of Byrd's Landing's shotguns didn't end up beneath some developer's backhoe. This is how it happened. Mrs. Jefferson and Mrs. Riverton were cousins. Not real cousins. Folk in the South will claim you as a relative not because you share blood, but because you and them get along so well. By mutual agreement you decide to be relatives even if God didn't set it up that way. Both of them ladies lived on The Hill when they were girls. Mrs. Riverton left the neighborhood when she married up. Mrs. Jefferson? Well, ain't no use rehashing what happened to Mrs. Ruth Jefferson, or as others called her, Miss Ruth. But when Mrs. Jefferson died, Mrs. Riverton went stone crazy and decided to preserve Byrd's Landing's shotgun houses. She thought it'd take her mind off the pain because she enjoyed so many good times up there with her dearly departed pretend relative.

She pestered banks all over Louisiana, from the top of the boot to the tip, so she could buy them old shotgun houses. She bought so many that you'd think they were filled with gold. Her husband finally left her because she tried to make him cash in his retirement. It wasn't that Mr. Riverton was looking to wipe his ass with dollar bills, he just knew that you can't get no care when you're old without money. He skedaddled. Nobody blamed him.

The other thing she did was speak up for them houses at City Council meetings. The way she talked you'd think those falling-down shacks were her kin. There was this one meeting where all the Black folk were in an uproar because of this policeman who was terrorizing poor folk and wasn't nobody doing a thing to stop it. Ain't nobody remembered what they said, because Mrs. Riverton got up and shat all over their complaining.

First is the way she was dressed, all in Kente cloth from the turban on the top of her head making her look seven feet tall to the slippers on her big, barbell feet. And here it was hot enough to boil grits on the sidewalk, and the air conditioner clunking out way before the meeting started. The whole crowd was plenty fanning themselves with advertisements about the word of God from First Baptist and the crawfish sale at Boones and Sons Market. While everybody was sweating rivers, Miss May, who looked like she rolled herself up in a tablecloth and stepped out of doors, didn't shed nary a drop of sweat.

She strolled up to that podium like they put it there just for the glory of her six-foot-too-tall queenly self. She stared down the mayor, who had this rabid fear of being called a racist. She eyed that Black woman who owned a perch fish hatchery out on Heron Road, the only one up there who had any sense, and that Black man who wanted every shotgun in Byrd's Landing crushed into the dirt like them houses done something evil to his Black body. And I had to give it to big, tall, and ugly because she had them folks' attention like they were listening to the Sermon on the Mount.

"You didn't want us in the White neighborhoods even when we had money in hand," she said. "You just told us to get and we got. We had no choice but to move into the Bottoms."

"Mrs. Riverton," the mayor said, her face red, her wig looking like a cocker spaniel had died on her head. "I want to state for the record that none of us up here are responsible for that. It was oh, so long ago."

"I'm telling it because I want you to understand the history, because what y'all are trying to do relates directly to that," Mrs. Riverton said.

"How?" said the woman who owned the perch fish hatchery. Her voice was dry as a piece of paper.

"By turning it into pulp," Mrs. Riverton responded.

"Come on, now," the shotgun-hating man said.

"Let her have her say," the mayor said.

"We moved to the Bottoms on land nobody wanted. We did that." Here she paused for effect before starting up again. "We formed a community. We took care of each other."

"Those places were so ganged up even St. Peter wouldn't walk the streets without a bodyguard," the perch farm lady said.

"Don't blaspheme, Emma," the mayor said. "Go on, Mrs. Riverton. You've got about five more minutes."

"Then you go and label that place a police-free zone. You invited drug dealers, prostitutes, and a bunch of thieving motherfuckers to come in and set up house."

The crowd shouted so many 'amens' you'd think they were all at church.

"Next thing we know folk building whorehouses, strip clubs, bars selling stuff that'd make you blind. And young girls walking up and down the street in cootie shorts." She paused for breath. "Still, you know what we did?" When nobody answered, she said it louder. "Do you know what we did?" and someone in the crowd yelled, "Tell it!" which got other folk yelling 'tell it'.

"Three minutes, May," the perch farm lady said. "Dinner's waiting."

"We still took care of each other," someone from the audience yelled.

"That's right, we did. In our shotgun shacks we brought over from Haiti and West Africa. We made food in our kitchens and sold it on the street to make a living. We had our rent parties, and when the young ones needed watching, the old folk sat on the porch and watched them. We were a community."

She slammed her big ham-hock fist on the podium again. The mayor and the businessmen jumped high, and whew doggie, the tater tots hit the fan then. The folk in the audience, already hot on account of the broken air conditioner and mad over that crooked policeman, smelled blood.

"Let me tell it, May," one of the old women who had been amening said. "White folk started coming over to the Bottoms to foment addiction, prostitution and fortification. They started to get themselves into trouble. Y'all couldn't have that now, could you? You called it an emergency."

"Now hold on," the mayor said. "Ain't nobody up here did that."

"So, you had the raids," Miss May said, not letting herself be interrupted by nobody. "Sent the cops down there to run out the gangs. Closed down the whorehouses and cleaned up the drugs. Everybody would've been satisfied with that. But not you."

"They sure wasn't!" someone yelled from the crowd.

"You sent our young men to Angola on trumped-up charges. You went after legitimate business. You drove us out!"

"Now, May, that's just not true," the mayor said. "People still living in shotguns all over the city."

"But not the Bottoms. The Bottoms are gone," May accused.

"The Bottoms ain't gone. Those houses are still there. And those real estate practices you talk about were fixed decades ago," the mayor continued. "Y'all can buy anywhere you want now. Stop talking like that stuff happened Sunday before last."

"The arm of history is long, but hits hard," Mrs. Riverton said. "It's still knocking us around today. You stole our neighborhood and now you want to steal our history. Well, I'm here to tell you that I will protect every standing shotgun with my very body, every single barrel, double barrel, camelback, or north shore. I'll protect them as if they were made of flesh and blood and bone instead of nails and wood and copper. I will protect them if only to remind you of what this town did and to also remind us of how we came together despite it. Are you sorry we didn't crumble like those houses are crumbling today, Madam Mayor? Are you sorry that you can't pound us into dust like you want to do with these houses?"

"Oh, for heaven's sakes, May!" the mayor said.

But it was done. That night Miss May won. She developed some sort of historical society to save them houses. She wrote people for money, and they obliged. She got folk believing in something that never happened – fantasies about good times in desperate circumstances. The city backed off. Most were left in the hands of Mrs. Riverton, except for the Bottoms. Somehow that speck of land on the edge of town escaped her initial designs. But Miss May didn't give up. All she have to do is see a thing she want to get it. She's the kind of woman who could sell salt to a snail.

Chapter Twelve

Miss May led them to a living room filled with deep comfortable furniture on a hardwood floor painted a slick black. The wood still smelled of the trees that died to produce something comfortable enough for her to walk on. She sat in one of two matching armchairs and showed the couch opposite to Raven and Stevenson.

"Di," she commanded without looking at him. "Put some coffee on."

"That's not necessary, Miss May," Raven said.

"It's necessary for me," Miss May snapped.

"Ma," Diamond said as he started to the back of the house toward the kitchen.

"It's okay," Raven said. "I'm good."

"You're a country mile from good," Miss May said.

Raven kept her face still, like Floyd did when he needed to hide his evil. No one ever knew what he was thinking until it was too late.

"I could go. Detective Stevenson can tell you the details," Raven said.

"No. Stay. Do your damned job. They'd need to put me in my grave if I'm no longer able to handle your stupid ass," Miss May said.

Diamond came back from the kitchen with four mugs on a tray. May leaned over to take a cup and then sat back. She blew at the white steam rising from the hot liquid. Raven didn't move toward the tray though the smell of black coffee made her long for a taste. She left it on the table. She was thankful when Stevenson did the same, a show of support she needed.

Miss May sipped before placing the cup on the end table between the two chairs.

"What are you doing here, Di?" she asked.

Diamond hadn't bothered to sit down. He leaned instead against the doorframe leading to the middle room.

"What do you think I'm doing here? I'm here for you. You still my mama and he's still my brother," he said.

"Even after you abandoned us?" Miss May said, her eyes glittering.

Diamond walked fully into the room and sat in the matching leather chair next to his mother.

"I didn't abandon you. I went to college," he said.

"You went to college out of state. Louisiana not good enough for you?" Miss May said.

"I went to college out of state like a lot of other kids," he said.

She leaned over the little round table between them. She got into his face. "You left us."

Diamond flung a hand at the pictures on the wall, the leather strap of a necklace he wore beneath his shirt lifting as he did so. No pictures of him or Zeke graced Miss May's wall. Oh, she had them, Raven knew. Those pictures just weren't wall worthy. Instead, the photos and drawings chronicled the history of Byrd's Landing. Black and white photos of tired men next to tall cane, some of them missing fingers, color photos of restored plantation houses, tobacco fields from the old days, the Catholic church downtown, the Baptist church out in the country, in fact all kinds of churches and churchgoers, of Black women in tall shoes, and pearl-adorned satin skirts with matching jackets, with big showy hats decorated with flowers or feathers or a combination of both. Photos of shotguns interspersed throughout, exterior photos of houses with peeling paint and crumbling porches. Others restored and pimped out with shiny paint and stained glass.

"Why would I stay? You had plenty of company. You've plastered your walls with the only thing you care about, not me or Zeke. But this town. This crazy place with its history of lynchings and its crime and its isolation. This town is a prison, Ma, a prison where the inmates are willing."

"You were fine with it until you met her," Miss May said, pointing a brown finger at Raven.

Diamond's eyes moved toward Raven then darted away. He stood muttering something about not being able to do this. Raven intercepted him on his way to the door.

"Stay. She's going to need you, Diamond. Sit down. Please," she said.

He sat back down.

"Miss May," Raven asked. "Can you tell me where your son was last night?"

"Why you ask that?" Miss May said.

"Or if anyone wanted to hurt him?" Stevenson asked. Stupidly, Raven thought.

There was plenty of time to ask that question. He'd been her partner for months, but their interactions had no elegance when questioning a witness or suspect. They bumbled, stepped on each other's toes. They walked away with little that would help solve the case.

She remembered how interviewing a witness was with Billy Ray. The dance. It was like performing the Lindy Hop while Duke Ellington blared from an old record player. Billy Ray knew when to swing out. He knew when to connect or disconnect. Raven knew the exact moment to step aside, to slide. Without speaking, they knew who was going to leap or twirl, and the perfect moment for the flip. She'd ask a question, and Billy Ray would encourage an answer with a sympathetic nod, a hand on a shoulder. She'd make a stinging comment. Billy Ray would follow up with the comforting rejoinder. The interview resulted in the suspect trusting at least one of them enough to tell all. Conducting an interview with Stevenson was like stomping grapes.

"What do you mean if anyone wanted to hurt him?" Miss May said.

"You know why we're here, right?" Raven said.

"What happened to my son?" Miss May demanded.

Stevenson gaped at Miss May as if the elderly woman had just graduated kindergarten. Diamond's muscular body seemed to fold in on itself. It was as if he wanted to crawl into a hole.

"What was I supposed to think?" Miss May asked. "What conclusions was I supposed to draw?"

And then Raven got it. The woman didn't think that foul play was involved in her son's death. She thought that they were there to tell her that Zeke had passed away of some natural cause or an accident. Raven didn't waste time trying to sugarcoat anything. She never did. "Your son was the victim of a homicide," she said.

A wail as old as time left Miss May's lips. Diamond went to her and she fell against him.

"Maybe we should come back later," Stevenson said.

"Hell no," Raven said in a low voice.

"Mrs. Riverton is in no condition—" he started.

"I'm in plenty good condition," Miss May said, the words pushing through her sobs. She shoved her son away, not hard but away, and stood up.

"I just need to put some water on my face," Miss May said.

She left the room without looking at any of them.

★ ★ ★

Raven first met Zeke Riverton in the ninth grade. He was a soulful boy with luminous eyes that appeared to soak up light. He had a smile that could coax a chicken bone from a pregnant stray dog. And he had this spirit.

The memory stopped there. She didn't know how to adequately explain Zeke's spirit. Once when she was visiting Floyd in prison, she told him about Zeke. And Floyd said something that she would never forget; he said, "Looks like God done sent y'all a sponge."

"A sponge?" Raven asked.

"Darn right," he said. "Built to soak up sin and grief from the troubled, and provide comfort in its place. That boy ain't gone last long. All that grief he sopping up gone kill him."

Raven on the other hand couldn't imagine Zeke's charmed life. She was ostracized in high school. She crept down the linoleum hallways like she was haunting the place. Zeke's locker was next to hers. One day, whistling as he always did, he dug into his own locker. He stopped whistling when he noticed Raven standing there staring at a drawing someone had taped to the front of her locker of a stick figure murdering another stick figure. Much black and red ink was fashioned into screaming mouths and separated body parts. Zeke reached above her head and tore the picture down. He crumpled it up and threw it into his own locker.

"Bastids," he said, not *bastards*, but 'bastids'.

She wanted to tell him to mind his own business, but he gave her a smile that made a body want to tell him everything. And she eventually did.

They stayed friends throughout high school, going to house parties, fishing for perch in the Red, heading out of town across the bridge for a football game or a carnival. People talked, but they weren't dating. They were just salves for the pain in each other's soul. Raven for the crap her father did, and Zeke for a mother who cared more about old houses than her own kids.

"It's all the lawsuit stuff," he told her. "That's all she thinks about, those stupid shotgun houses. She's even talking about moving into one. And she's going after the city for a strip of land that she says they stole from us and sold to developers."

Even with his own troubles, he could talk down a suicide or help a friend come out to their parents. And all the while he was cheerful, carefree as ever with remedies and love for those who needed them. No one thought about Zeke's own pain until he had descended so far into addiction that he couldn't be lifted out. By that time, Raven couldn't help him if she wanted to. Besides, she knew she had to get out of Byrd's Landing before the town gobbled her up. She would never be able to tell him that she was sorry now that he was dead.

Chapter Thirteen

Raven didn't realize she had closed her eyes when thinking about those early days with Zeke until she heard Miss May's voice. "My son's dead and you sleeping."

"Just waiting for you," Raven said.

"How did he die?" Miss May asked.

"He was stabbed to death," Stevenson said.

"Like somebody hated him." Miss May shuddered. "Where was he killed?"

"In the Old Bottoms," Raven said.

"What in the hell was he doing down there?" Miss May asked.

"We don't know," Raven said.

"Drugs?" Diamond asked.

Raven leveled her eyes at him. "Too early to tell," she said.

"He wasn't on no drugs. He was clean!" Miss May shouted. "There was no reason for him to be down in that hole with that devil. Mostly criminals and cultish no accounts."

"You mean Lucien Toussiant?" Raven asked.

"Calls himself Papa," Miss May said. She sat down in the chair she had recently vacated, bent at the waist and folded her arms over her knees.

"You know him?" Raven asked.

Miss May blew out a breath and nodded. She was about to speak when Stevenson interrupted with another question.

"Can you tell us about the last time you saw Zeke?" he asked.

"Yesterday evening after he got home from work," she said. "He was going to stay at his girlfriend's house."

"Girlfriend?" Diamond asked.

"He had a life," Miss May spat back. "Everything didn't stop when your ass left."

"What's his girlfriend's name?" Raven asked.

"Lois Wareham," she said, a sneer in her voice.

"You don't like her?" Stevenson asked.

"Man, she don't like nobody," Diamond said.

"Shut up, Di," Miss May said. "Nobody asked you."

"I told you not to call me that. It's like you're telling me to shut up and die. You wishing I would have died instead of Zeke?"

"It's your nickname. You didn't mind it when you was little," Miss May said.

"You didn't give a shit about what I minded when I was little," Diamond said.

Miss May straightened. She picked up the coffee cup and took a long swallow. Seeing this, Diamond left the room. He returned with a bottle of Gentlemen Jack, opened the cap and swirled a good amount into her coffee cup. She didn't protest.

"Glad you still remembered where I kept it," she said before putting the cup to her lips and drinking deeply. She leaned her head against his arm and closed her eyes.

"Please, Miss May. I know this is painful, but if we're going to find out who killed Zeke, we need you to focus for just a little more," Raven said.

"Zeke," she said without opening her eyes. "Not EZ like y'all used to call him. EZ Rivers. Stupid."

"You don't like Lois?" Stevenson prodded gently.

"Not a lot of people do. She's a whacked-out root worker always trying to find meaning in numbers and old slave remedies instead of a proper doctor or the word of the good Lord. She isn't a good girl. She's been sucking up to Zeke for years. Probably after his money."

"Money?" Stevenson replied.

Raven gave him an I'll-tell-you-later wave.

"What time did Zeke go over to Lois's?" Raven asked.

"Around eight or so, I think," Miss May said.

"Can you think of anyone who would want to hurt your son?" Raven said.

"No, he was an angel. And here you are asking me like you don't know him or who he was. A mixed-up angel, but my boy had wings always. You know that," Miss May said.

Raven stood. They wouldn't get anything else out of her. Before she could say *thank you* and *I'm sorry for your loss*, Miss May said, "You know he been calling you for the last couple of weeks? He said you were ghosting him."

Raven didn't try to defend herself. The slightest hint of a defense would keep Miss May spewing poison. Son dead? Doesn't stop mama of the year from finding butts to kick and joys to kill. Like many high school friends, Zeke and Raven had drifted apart over the years, but they had managed to meet up once or twice a year to catch up, especially after he had gotten clean. Sometimes she took too long to answer back, but she eventually did. He was always there, waiting.

"Calling and texting but you just couldn't be bothered," Miss May said.

Stevenson also stood, stunned into silence by the hate rising from Miss May.

"After he carried your broke ass all though high school," Miss May continued. "I'm not talking about money broke, though you was that, too. I'm talking broke in spirit. You poisoning him with all that your daddy did and him sucking it up. Where did you think all that would go? He wasn't strong enough to handle all the trash you told him. He started drugs just to deal with it."

"Mama," Diamond said.

"Don't you mama me. Because this bitch not happy with ruining one son. She took you too, turned you against me and your brother."

Raven was at the door now and so was Stevenson. If she were as cruel as her father, she would have accused Miss May of stealing her own son's soul long before she, Raven, came along. Diamond placed a hand of comfort on Raven's back.

What Raven's father did to people was horrific, no getting around that, but the pain a mama like Miss May can wrought without lifting a knife was equally horrific. These children were forced to live with scars. Some of them passed their hurt onto others. Some become killers like Floyd.

"Diamond, stay with her. I'm fine," Raven said.

"I tell you what," Miss May yelled as Raven stepped outside. "I bet you that he was trying to help your ass when he was killed. Always trying to help somebody, even people that don't deserve it."

Her words tailed off as Diamond closed the door. Raven felt sorry for him, left to deal with a woman who spewed bitterness instead of carbon dioxide on every exhale.

⋆ ⋆ ⋆

Outside of Zeke's house the sun was the color of an overboiled egg yolk. Its blistering heat cut through a thick haze of humidity. Sweat trickled from Raven's hair and into her ears. She couldn't help but think that this case would be bigger than the three bodies in the churchyard, maybe another serial killer. All the signs were there. This heat, this sun and yes, Floyd blooming like a corpse flower inside her skull. Stevenson walked beside her, his pace slow. He was careful not to make eye contact as if she were a mangy dog he was trying to rescue.

"I can do the next one," he said, meaning Marcel Thibodeaux, the victim found with the notes in his pocket.

"Don't be stupid," Raven said. "I can handle it."

"It's been a rough morning," he said.

"Yes," she agreed. "I've had my share. Do we have an address for Mr. Thibodeaux's next of kin?"

"Yes, a cousin. Justin, but he goes by Rock. He works construction. Probably at work now." He gave her the address.

"Meet you over there," Raven said in a voice that brooked no argument.

Chapter Fourteen

Some parts of Byrd's Landing were dying off like necrotized limbs while others flourished. Rock Thibodeaux worked a job paving the roads for a new subdivision going in by Big Bayou Lake. Developers uprooted the alligators and snakes, ruined the habitats of the blue herons and filled the swamps to make room for cookie-cutter houses that no one could afford unless they were rich or willing to hedge their bets with balloon mortgages or ridiculous interest rates.

Raven sat in the car watching the construction. She needed to get her head right. Three bulldozers drove in circles to grade the new road. The place smelled of dog crap and dirt. A tall, thin man in an orange vest watched the bulldozers with the pathological attention of a supervisor trying to wrest every bit of work he could from his subordinates. Something was familiar about him, but his white hard hat obscured his face. It didn't help that he was in profile. Stevenson was already talking to him. Raven could tell by the man's posture that Stevenson's badge or business wasn't enough to move the man to action. Raven adjusted her own badge around her neck. She opened her blazer to reveal the shoulder holster, and to make it clear that she wasn't about to cotton to any craziness. She got out of the car and walked toward them.

"Raven," Stevenson began as she approached.

"You got to be shitting me," Raven said, cutting him off.

"Hey, I thought you didn't cuss, Ray Ray. And here you are with the nasty words like a busted sewer," the man said.

He was right. She didn't like cussing mostly because of Floyd's training. The man who liked gutting people and setting them on fire couldn't stand hearing or saying the 'F' word. She knew it was stupid, but it was a hard habit to break.

"Wrong," Raven said. "When the occasion calls for it, I cuss up a storm. And right now, this moment is an occasion."

It was none other than Willie Lee Speck, the frenetic, greasy-haired man who used to own a crime cleanup service before the entire town discovered he was as crazy as a bag of cats. He became known not as the irreverent crime scene cleaner who would do anything for a buck, but as one who stole the neighborhood pets so he could dissect them in his backyard shed.

He was also a hoarder.

Long before Raven found the piles of dogs and cats in the corner of the shed, and a possum still carrying her babies on his dissecting table, his wife took the kids and left. But for the entire Sleeping Boy serial murder case last year, Willie Lee pretended that he and his wife, Suzy, were together. Every time he and Raven met, he would talk about his kids and how JoJo was doing in Little League. Over the course of the investigation, Raven learned that Willie Lee was a decent person deep inside, but the trauma he had buried cleaning up after some of the worst crime scenes in Byrd's Landing undid him. And his being a town pariah just like her made her feel a sick sort of kinship. She spoke up for him at his trial and lucky for him a word from a cop still meant something, even if it was coming from her. He didn't get jail time. She got him help with his hoard and he cleaned it up as best his anxiety would let him. She even hired him to help her make her new house livable again. The last she heard he was getting better and trying to woo his wife back.

"What are you doing here, Willie Lee?"

"What you mean what I'm doing here?" he said. "A man got to eat. I go where the work is now this crazy town won't let me clean up crime scenes."

"But here," Raven said, "on a construction site?"

"Now don't be like that, Rave Girl," Willie Lee said.

Stevenson interjected with, "Rave Girl?"

"Don't call me that," Raven said.

"Okay, Detective, then," he said, drawing the word out for emphasis. "I played around with working construction back in the day. The union took me back on a probationary basis. Sometimes they let me fill in for the sickies. Today, I'm filling in for the bossman of this here site. I don't mind saying that we're behind schedule. I can't have you interrupting my workers. Time, as they say, is money. Every minute you standing here, that cha-ching the cash register makes gets quieter and quieter."

Raven sent a glance Stevenson's way. She did so to keep from popping Willie Lee in the mouth. That was his God. The mighty dollar bill, or as he liked to call it, the mighty green machine. She remembered him once at a crime scene smiling like a cat who swallowed the last of the cream. He had caught a suicide who used a shotgun. "More mess equals more time equals more money," he told her. Never mind that somebody had lost their baby. She thought he had changed. But now, here he was, after all that had happened, proving her wrong.

Raven looked at him for several moments, the blue jeans slick with wear, the faded black t-shirt stuffed into the waistband, the work boots covered in dirt. At another crime scene he joked that he had to use a soup ladle to scoop up the remains of an elderly woman who had died alone in her sleep. She hadn't seen that Willie Lee in a while, only the pitiful one who needed kind words for a judge, and a little work to get back on his feet. Now that he had both, he was back to his true self.

"I told him why we're here, but he said we're going to have to wait until Justin goes on a break," Stevenson said.

"Who's Justin?" Willie Lee said, looking from Stevenson to Raven.

"Justin Thibodeaux," Raven said through tight lips.

"Oh, you mean Rock," Willie Lee said. "Well, like I told this one, if you want to see him, lunch will be in a few hours. You can talk his head off then."

"We don't have that long," Stevenson said. "His cousin is dead. We need to notify him."

"I know you're Raven's boss..." Willie Lee started.

"He's not my boss," Raven said.

"But if Rock's cousin is dead, he's going to stay dead. He'll be just as dead at lunch. You can tell him then on his time. This is my time."

He splayed his fingers and tapped his skinny chest twice. She was surprised he didn't knock himself over. Raven noticed that his fingernails were yellow, his nails thick and lifting from some type of fungus.

"I'm dealing with a deadline," Willie Lee continued. "We all up against it. This road got to get built so these houses can go up."

"Get him over here," Raven said.

"What?" Willie Lee replied.

"You deaf? Justin Thibodeaux. Rock. Whatever you call him. Interrupt him."

"Now?" Willie Lee whined.

"Is he driving right now? Tell him to stop and get over here," Raven said.

"Y'all can't make me." He stopped at the look in Raven's eyes. Floyd peered through them as if he were staring out of a window. *I hate them pencil-pushing-penny-grubbing-clock-watching-booby-crats*, Floyd said in her head. *The only thing they good for is killing. Tell him I said it. A message from me.*

"We can make you do anything we want. We're the police. This is America," Raven said. "And if you don't move with a quickness, I can arrest you for obstruction of justice, take you down to the ground right now and say that you hit me. I can even shoot you if the mood strikes me, and I'll most likely get away with it. It's not right, I know, but that doesn't change the fact that I've got all the power here plus trigger-happy genes from my serial killer daddy. Plus, I'm losing my patience. Get him."

Willie Lee grumbled and walked a few steps away before pulling out a walkie talkie from his jeans pocket. She looked up to see Stevenson studying her.

"What?" she said.

"Is the mood striking you now?" Stevenson said.

"Like you wouldn't believe," Raven said. "I misjudged Willie Lee. Should have never helped him. Once a jerk, always a jerk. People like that don't change."

"Don't agree with you there but I'm too tired to fight. Besides, I was asking him nicely. You didn't have to go all Floyd on him."

"Shut up, Delbert," Raven said.

Stevenson laughed briefly, lifted his hands in surrender.

Chapter Fifteen

A short, Black man in a hard hat and blue jeans much cleaner than his boss's lumbered over to Raven and Stevenson. He had taken off his leather gloves and was tapping them against his palms as he made his way toward them. Soon Raven stared into a pair of brown eyes that were so light that they looked golden. But those eyes were narrowed. His full lips were set in a hard line. *You need to tell him that he better be careful*, Raven heard Floyd say in her head. *Keep making that face and it'll stay that way*. But Raven thought the man standing there glaring at her and then Stevenson had missed that opportunity. He looked like the type that stayed mad.

"Are you Justin Thibodeaux? Rock?" Stevenson asked. "Marcel Thibodeaux's cousin?"

"You know I am," he said. "Or I'd be working instead of standing here."

"When was the last time you saw your cousin?" Raven asked.

"Couple of nights ago," he said, looking at her again.

"I thought he lived with you," Stevenson said. "And the last time you saw him was a couple of nights ago?"

"I ain't his jailor," Rock said, tugging at the leather-strap necklace around his neck. "He come and go when it pleases him. I learned not to ask questions."

"Why?" Raven asked.

"I don't like being disappointed," Rock said.

"Sounds like you two didn't get along," Raven said.

"We were close when we were coming up, but now he just a pinked-lip drunk taking up space in my house."

"Well, you don't have to worry about that anymore," Stevenson said. "He's dead."

"I know that," Rock said.

"How?" Raven asked.

"Facebook," Rock said. "News travels there faster than you do."

Stevenson gave Raven an I-told-you-so look. Then he turned his attention back to Rock.

"Your cousin's dead and you don't care?"

"I care as much as he deserves," Rock said.

Stevenson turned his back on him. But Raven kept her eyes on the man now tapping the leather gloves against his thigh. She knew a soothing activity when she saw one.

"Was he acting strange the last time you saw him? Did he say anybody was after him?" she asked.

"No stranger than usual, but we don't talk like that anymore."

"Did you have a falling out?" Stevenson asked as he turned back around.

"Not like you thinking. Not a big falling out or nothing. He just started going his way, and I started going mine. A drift. That's all."

And everything, Raven thought. Now that his cousin was dead, he would never be able to fix it.

"Yet you still stayed roommates?" Raven said.

"Had to make the rent. Sometimes he was good for it," Rock said.

"Did you notice anybody new hanging around with Marcel?" Stevenson asked.

"No, not new," he said, his voice sullen.

"Do you know why he was in the Old Bottoms?" Raven asked.

"Probably to score a hit," Rock said.

"I thought they didn't do drugs down there?" Raven said.

"You think what you want, but them people down there are crooked as a mountain road," Rock said.

Raven was about to ask another question, but Stevenson chose that exact same moment to blow up.

"Look man," he said. "We're trying to find out who killed your cousin. Can you be more forthcoming?"

"I don't know what you mean," Rock said. "I've told you what I know. Be nice if you let me do my job."

Raven followed his gaze to Willie Lee. Hat off, Willie Lee was running his hand through his greasy hair at rapid intervals.

"We appreciate that, Mr. Thibodeaux. We're almost done," Raven said. "Did Marcel have any friends or associates you think we should talk to?"

"Call me Rock. His only friends were Zeke and Lionel. But I hear they dead, too. We ain't got no other family. That means I'm the one who has to bury him."

They stood there while the other two bulldozers spun the road from under their wheels. Willie Lee was audibly cursing now to anyone who cared enough to listen.

"Can I go now?" Rock said, his face turned toward the flattening earth. "I have a road to build."

"Sure," Raven said, flicking her card at him. He took it. She laid a hand on his shoulder. "If you think of anything, call me. I'm real sorry for your loss. We are going to find who did this."

She watched him walk over to his bulldozer and swing into the driver's seat. It beeped loudly as he turned on the ignition and backed up a few feet. He ran the sleeve of his blue chambray shirt over his eyes before putting on a pair of goggles. He sat motionless for a few moments and then drove forward, his shoulders slumped.

Imagine knowing that your blood was the last of your family's blood on earth.

"What are you staring at?" Stevenson said. She knew that he was taking his anger out on her.

"Nothing," she said in a flat voice.

Raven looked up at the hard-boiled sun beating down on them and wiped her face with a handkerchief. *Grief is a changeling*, she thought as she walked back to the Mustang. It never shows up the same way. If you blink, you just might miss it.

★ ★ ★

The last notification wasn't any easier. Like Rock, they already knew. Social media had accomplished its number-one mission to spread misery like wildfire. Unlike Rock, the wife of Lionel Williams was more demonstrative in her grief. Screams, cries, and a mother-in-law who had to scoop her from the floor while at the same time trying to stay upright herself. All the while the smell of a cold breakfast hung in the room, *Blue's Clues* blared from the TV and two little girls with gold beads in their French braids kept asking 'what's wrong' over and over again. The chaos prevented any type of interview.

Raven asked one of the little girls if she knew anybody they could call. The girl ran from the room and returned with her mother's phone. She unlocked it and handed it to Raven. Raven punched the call button for a contact named My sistah and told her what was happening. Both she and Stevenson stayed until the woman, who was already on her way, arrived. She was so prayed up that every other sentence was an *Oh Lord* and *He has a plan.* She eventually took everybody's hand, including Raven and Stevenson's. She said a long, meandering prayer that knocked the wind out of everybody. By the time Raven and Stevenson left, he was swearing up a blue streak and rubbing his forearm across his wet eyes.

"What are you doing?" she asked him as they reached her Mustang. He was tugging at the handle of the passenger-side door.

"What do you mean what am I doing. I'm riding back to the station with you," he said.

"What about your car?" she asked.

"I'll have Marna send a patrol officer to get it for me," he answered.

"Drive yourself. I want to be alone," she countered as she unlocked the Mustang.

"Well, I don't," he said and snatched the door open.

Raven got in on the driver's side and watched him for a few seconds. Then she put the car in gear and pulled onto the main road heading toward the station. At the light, she glanced over at him. He was cradling his face in his hands as if he were trying to keep it from falling off.

"Deep breathing," she said as the light changed from red to green.

To her surprise, he did. He took two long, deep breaths, sat up, and breathed again. She hadn't gone a quarter of a mile before he started punching the dashboard.

"Hey, hey, easy, easy on Miss Jean," Raven said to remind him that the car wasn't any old car, but a shiny red beast in honor of Jean Rineheart, her stepmother whose wardrobe always included patent leather, bright red shoes. Her stepmother, that is, until Floyd murdered her.

"I have a daughter that age," Stevenson said.

"I know," Raven said. "You told me when you were pretending to be my boyfriend."

"I told you that I didn't mean for that to happen. I was just doing my job. I got too close. I slipped."

"Water under the bridge," Raven said.

It wasn't, but Raven was disinterested in some long, emotional conversation, especially after notifying three families that they would never see their loved ones again. Besides, they already had that conversation at the big reveal when he tried to get her to confess to Lamont Lovelle's murder. She grinned thinking about how horribly he had failed.

"What on God's green earth could you be grinning about?" Stevenson asked.

"Nothing," she said. "You better now?"

"I don't know," he said.

He stared out the window as the bones of the town flew by – Liberty High School, Boones and Sons Market, and the Snack Shack. Raven pulled into the Perc Me Up, a local coffee shop they used to frequent when they dated. Without fail Raven would nudge him and say, "Perc Me Up, you get it? Huh? Perk me up." He'd groan and call her a fool. But those days were over.

"Tell you what," she said as she parked the car and unclicked her seatbelt. "Let's go in and get some coffee. It's been a rough morning. We deserve a break."

"I hate it when you're nice to me," he said.

They walked into a wide air-conditioned room with a wooden coffee table surrounded by neon blue and green chairs. Stevenson sat down at one of the small round tables. He didn't tell her what he wanted. She knew. He wanted candy coffee with lots of cream and sugar. She ordered one for him, and a black coffee for herself. The barista took her order with a grunt, a bag on a leather strap around his neck swinging against his skinny chest. She had been seeing leather-strap necklaces all over Byrd's Landing lately, and wondered what new fashion trend she was missing. Back at the table, she sat opposite and pushed his coffee to him.

"When was the last time you talked to your wife?" Raven asked.

He and his wife had separated when he traveled from Louisiana to California on his ill-fated, rogue undercover mission. Raven believed that's one of the reasons he – what did he call it? Slipped. Got too close. He was an emotional mess who should've been taking time off to repair his marriage instead of working. But that was one of the reasons his wife kicked him out, wasn't it? His obsession with the job.

He laced his fingers together and pressed them to his lips. "A couple of months ago."

"The kids?" she asked.

"Longer," he answered.

"Call them," she said.

"Raven," he said, ready to protest.

"You know how this works, Stevenson. Your ego has to take some risks if you want your wife back. Call them. Today."

"I've already tried. She won't talk to me," he said.

Raven took a sip of her own coffee. It was hot, strong, but full of flavor. That's what she liked about these little out-of-the-way coffee shops.

"Maybe she won't, but you don't know that. Call her and be sure," Raven urged.

"Maybe," he said, and then more sure, "I will after this case."

"Today. When we get back to the station," she said.

He drank more coffee, nodded and sighed. She didn't know if he would follow her advice but decided not to let up until he did. Stevenson loved his job, she knew that. He loved putting things right. He couldn't see that the only thing he was doing was laying a thin veneer of order over chaos. He needed a tether, or he would lose his mind. He looked up at her. Their eyes met and she said once again in a firm voice that brooked no nonsense, "Call her today."

He didn't agree or disagree. Instead, he said, "What's next?"

"We could go back to the station, set up the command center, get ready to update the chief," she said.

But he was shaking his head before the words got out of her mouth. "The mother said Zeke was at his girlfriend's last night. We should go talk to her."

"Right now?" Raven said.

"Yes, I want to get to her before she has time to make something up," he said.

Raven spread her hands in surrender. "Like Willie Lee said, you're the boss."

"No, I'm not," he said. "You just happen to agree with me for once."

She smiled. "Well, finish up your coffee then and let's get to it."

Chapter Sixteen

Raven opened the door of Lois Wareham's beauty salon, which was called Rooted in Hair and More. It was located in a strip mall next to a liquor store with bars on the window. The bell on the door jingled as the door swung closed behind them. Raven could tell by the smell that the 'more' in the salon's name meant hair relaxers. The place reeked of lye as an old woman plastered an even older woman's hair with relaxer white as cream. The cost of this tortured homage to assimilation was high in dollars. It also included alopecia, uterine fibroids and in some cases cancer. Allegedly. The jury was still out on that one.

A young woman in a hijab glanced at them as she braided the afro of a light-skinned young man. He looked at Raven and Stevenson with a serious side-eye. The shop itself was long and narrow, the baseboards lined with thick grime. Faded pictures of Black women in braids, afros, and lustrous, straight bobs graced the walls.

In the beauty shops Raven visited with her stepmother Jean, these pictures would have been radiant with color. The shop would have been full to bursting, especially on Saturdays, with women waiting all day to get their hair styled while sharing gossip most profane and teasing those who couldn't hide their embarrassment. The metallic clank of Marcel curling irons and the sizzle of hot combs would meld with the R&B playing low in the background. If Raven were lucky, the candy man would come around with his cart full of gummy bears, Bit-O-Honey, peanut patties, and sometimes jerky he bought from an old man who lived in the swamps. All candy man transactions were cash. No receipts. If Miss Jean was too involved in a conversation to buy her something, another of the women would pick something off the cart and say to Raven, "Here you go, baby."

But this shop was nearly empty, the posters curled at the corners. The salons of Raven's childhood were alive. This one was dying if not already dead.

"May I help you?" said a tall woman with dreadlocks spilling from a blood-red headwrap.

Her silky striped pants rippled as she braided extensions into the hair of a chubby, round-faced girl who couldn't have been more than fourteen. Watching them the entire time, she touched the girl's shoulder. The girl passed her strands of purple hair she had draped over one palm. The woman's nails clicked as she braided the extensions way past the girl's shoulders. It wasn't lost on Raven that the woman had an old rag wrapped around her right hand.

"Yes," Raven said. "We are looking for Lois Wareham."

"Wear-em," the woman corrected. "Like shoes. You put them on to wear 'em."

Her eyes slid over Raven. She had unusual eyes of gold and green, and light gold-brown skin.

"You that cop," she said.

"Depends on what you mean by 'that cop'," Raven said.

"That cop EZ knows. That cop with the killer father," the woman said.

"I take it you're Lois Wareham," Stevenson said, a note of annoyance in his voice.

"I am," Lois said.

She touched the girl's shoulder with her knuckles. More strands of purple rose and Lois took up the strands with her long, slim fingers, her nails click, click, clicking as she braided the hair all the way down.

"But I already know what you're going to tell me. I read it on Facebook. No need to waste your time. I've got work to do."

"Your boyfriend's dead and you got work to do?" Stevenson accused.

"Can't pay the rent with grief," Lois said. Another shoulder touch, purple strands lifting, fingernails clicking.

Raven walked up to Lois. The clicking was driving her crazy. She placed her hand over Lois's hand, the one without the bandage. Raven could tell from the smell that there was some funky poultice wrapped within the brown rag.

"We need to talk to you in private, Ms. Wareham," Raven said, taking care to pronounce her name correctly.

The woman flashed her a look, those golden eyes as cold as her hand felt.

"I told you I already know about EZ," she said.

"Zeke," Raven corrected.

"Zeke to you, but EZ to me and the friends he has now. I don't need no privacy. These two know how to keep my business to themselves," she said, nodding to the other two stylists.

"We have some sensitive questions for you," Stevenson insisted.

"And I need to work, so ask your questions," Lois said.

"Why are you people so damned rude in this town?" Stevenson said. "Is it in the water or were you all just brought up this way?"

Lois stared at him for a few moments.

"Come on to the back before Mr. Man breaks down," she said.

She bent down and whispered something in the girl's ear. She told the woman in the hijab to holler if anyone needed anything she couldn't handle. She led them to an office across from a bathroom. The office was surprisingly large with two bookcases stuffed with books. Those that didn't fit were stacked on the floor and along the walls. Most of them looked like poetry, and other classics that Raven had read in high school. Right across from the desk were built-in shelves with dried plants and roots. An old-timey logbook lay atop a podium near the shelves.

Lois sat behind her desk. She moved some magazines aside. She indicated two cheap chairs for Raven and Stevenson to sit.

Stevenson glanced around as if he was trying to find the origins of a nasty smell only he was aware of. His eyes landed on the shelf.

"What's all that shit in the jars?" he asked. "You some sort of witch doctor?"

"It's not shit," Lois said. "It's part of my work."

Lois picked up a pack of Camels on the desk, tapped out a cigarette. She lit it and inhaled.

"My healing work," she said, looking at Stevenson.

Stevenson laughed. "What? You into homeopathic healing? That cigarette doesn't look like it's part of the program. Neither did that lye your stylist is slathering all over that old lady's head."

Lois leaned back in her chair. She blew a long stream of smoke at the water-stained ceiling. Raven noticed that she clutched a small bag hanging from a leather strap around her neck. Another victim of fashion, Raven thought.

"To each their own," Lois said. "I give my help to people who want it. And others, like Miss Thelma out there who wants her hair straightened? She pays me and I make it straight. I'm not her mama. Y'all want something to drink, some water? I got some sweet tea in the kitchen fridge."

"We're fine," Raven said.

"Can we just get on with it?" Stevenson said.

"I'm waiting on you," Lois said, and took another drag of her cigarette.

Raven placed a hand on Stevenson's arm in warning. He needed to stop antagonizing her. They needed her open, not guarded.

"When was the last time you saw Zeke?" Raven asked.

Lois pulled a heavy amber ashtray closer to her. She tapped ash from the cigarette into it.

"The night he died, as I'm sure you know," she said.

"Why would you be sure we knew?" Stevenson asked.

"I'm sure you notified his mama first. I bet she couldn't wait to tell you where he was last night," Lois said.

"She did. But we want to hear it from you," Raven said.

"He came over at seven forty p.m., ate, left at eight twenty-two. I thought he was going to stay the night, but he said he and his boys had some business to handle," Lois said.

"That's precise," Stevenson said.

She stabbed out her cigarette into the heavy ashtray. "In my line of work, both lines, precise is the only way you can be. Or you end up burning someone's scalp off or sending them to Jesus before their time."

"Did he say what business he had to handle?" Raven asked.

"At first, I just thought he needed to talk some addict off the ledge. It wasn't weird for him at all to get a call in the middle of the night and jet," Lois said.

"Would he usually go help somebody with his friends tagging along?" Stevenson asked.

"He usually did that shit by himself," Lois said.

"You didn't ask why he was taking friends with him?" Stevenson said.

"Wasn't none of my business," Lois said.

"Can you look at me when I'm talking to you?" Stevenson demanded.

And she did, straight at him. She looked him in the eye and said, "Why? You my daddy?"

Stevenson pushed his chair back. Raven felt it coming. He was going to go into a preaching tirade with phrases like 'don't you care' and 'obstruction' and 'why don't you cooperate'.

"Stevenson," Raven said. "Why don't you go outside."

"Yeah, Stevenson," Lois said. "Why don't you go back to your car and turn the AC on. Smash your face against it until the sweat quits sliding off your bald head like a river."

Stevenson gave Raven an incredulous look. Raven jerked her head toward the door, hoping her face told him in no uncertain terms that she wasn't playing. He stomped out, slammed the door behind him.

"He looks like joy on stilts," Lois said.

"It's hot, he's just in a mood. What kind of relationship did you and Zeke have?" Raven asked.

"He minded his business, I minded mine. We got along fine that way," Lois said.

"Did you know the friends he was referring to when he said he had to do some business with them?"

"I did figure he was talking about Marcel and Lionel. They hung out all the time. I thought they were going to get together, have some fun, you know. Stuff like that. They'd go to strip clubs occasionally. Guy things."

"And that didn't bother you?" Raven asked.

"Now you sound like tall, bald and agitated," Lois said. "Why should it bother me?"

"Would you say you were in a serious relationship?" Raven asked.

Lois shrugged. "As serious as we could be with no money and always worrying about how the bills were going to get paid."

"But I thought he had money?" Raven said.

"He had money. Me." She pointed a hand to her chest. "I'm broke. Make my way by cobbling two or three gigs together. And he didn't know how to act with money no how. He still worked talking about wanting to come by his living honestly with his own two hands."

"And the last time you saw him was around eight last night?"

"Ain't that what I said?" Lois asked. "Or thereabouts."

"Just confirming," Raven said, noticing how unprecise she now was.

Lois leaned over the desk and looked at Raven.

"Look, no matter how many times you ask, how many ways you ask, how you fix your mouth to ask, EZ or Zeke as you call him left my house around eight last night to meet some friends. What they were up to, I don't know. I just thought it would be EZ's way of hell-raising, or maybe helping some lost soul. But I'm telling you that I'm not and won't be the last person who saw him alive," Lois said.

Without taking her eyes from Lois, Raven said, "Get a piece of paper and write down the places you'd think Zeke might have gone last night."

As Lois was writing down places on a notepaper she had found in a drawer, Raven said, "One more question."

"Make it quick," Lois responded and slid the note to Raven.

"Were you two fighting on or before the night he died?" Raven asked.

Lois's eyes flitted away from her. "No," she said, and stood. The interview was over.

"We're not done," Raven said when Lois's hand touched the doorknob. "What happened to your hand?"

"My hand?"

Lois's confusion looked genuine. She brought her hand to her face and stared at the rag bandage as if she had never seen it before. She chuckled. "I burned it. Occupational hazard."

"And exactly where is the burn?"

"On my palm. Where did you think it would be?" she asked.

"Can I see it?" Raven asked.

"Hell, no," Lois said.

Raven couldn't tell if the refusal was from irritation or guilt. "Ms. Wareham, we can compel you to come down to the station to take some photos of your hand," Raven said.

"Compel through my lawyer," Lois said.

Raven tilted her head to the side. "You have a lawyer?"

"Not yet, but I can sure as hell scare one up to keep from being harassed," she said. "Now, get out."

⋆ ⋆ ⋆

Raven didn't bother to acknowledge Stevenson as she climbed into the driver's seat and buckled her seatbelt across her chest.

"That's one cold bitch," he said.

"Don't call her that." Raven put the car in gear and backed out of the parking lot.

"She's lying," he said.

"Yep," Raven agreed.

"That's all you have to say?" Stevenson said. "We need to look into her. A deep look."

"You sure you're not just mad because she hurt your feelings, Daddy?" Raven teased.

"Stop it," he said. "She didn't hurt my feelings."

Raven grinned at him, stepped on the gas as the red light turned green.

"Mark my words," he said, in that sulky voice she had grown to hate, "she's in this all the way to her hideously long ratchet nails."

Raven slammed on the brakes as an old Sienna van turned left in front of her. It was close. She could have laid on the horn or presented the errant driver with a one-finger salute. But that wasn't her way. After the car was all the way across, she pressed the gas again.

"She may be a liar," she said. "But that doesn't make her a killer."

Chapter Seventeen

When Floyd decided to add a young Raven to his list of victims, Chief Early Sawyer saved her life. Now, sitting across from him in his BLPD office ready to give an update on a case, she felt what she always felt. Glad to be alive, and grateful to him for being there. Yes, he had betrayed her in the past, but she forgave him because he was that BLPD rookie officer in the crisp uniform who made her feel safe in the face of Floyd's madness. She owed him her life and her career. His eyes staring at her as he twirled the baseball into the air of his corner office told her he would never let her forget it.

Stevenson, who sat next to her, didn't have this dysfunctional relationship with the chief. He just thought of Early Sawyer as his boss, a person who deserved respect by the virtue of his position. By the chief's grace Stevenson was able to do what he longed for: put away bad guys while preaching to Raven to be better.

"Y'all telling me this all you got?" the chief said. "Three bodies and some grieving families?"

"We're only hours out from the murder, Chief," Raven said.

"It was raining," Stevenson said.

"Now you giving me a weather report?" the chief said.

Raven sucked in a deep breath. What she wanted to send out on the exhale would have probably gotten her sidelined. She toned it down a little.

"The bodies spent hours in the rain," she said in a calm voice. "You know what that does to evidence."

Sawyer held his hand up in a so-what gesture. "Still may be some larger fibers or hair you can find on the bodies. Tim use a UV light at the scene? They dried up at some point, didn't they? They find anything at the autopsy?"

Raven checked her watch. They were wasting time. "Tim didn't find anything at the scene. Rita hasn't gotten to the autopsy, yet. That might not be until tomorrow morning."

"Except for Zeke Riverton," Stevenson said, "the murders were clean. Execution style to the back of the head. Zeke was stabbed."

"Who did Zeke piss off? Anybody following that up?" Chief Sawyer asked.

"You know the family, Chief?" Raven asked.

"Me and Zeke's mama go back some," he said. "I know what you're thinking, that she didn't get along with her boys. But I don't see her killing two men execution style and then slitting her son's throat. You get that idea out of your head right away."

"Maybe she had help. Paid somebody. Zeke did have some money from his part in the lawsuit," Raven said.

"What lawsuit?" Stevenson said.

"Miss May sued the city to recover some land she said they unlawfully took from her family. That was when the father was still around. She won, got quite a bit from punitive damages, but Daddy made her split the money between the sons as part of the divorce settlement. It wasn't a small amount, about a million or so, I heard. Enough for a motive for murder," Raven said.

The chief pointed at her. "That woman doesn't have it in her to kill her son. Do some real detective work, Raven. No wild goose chases like I've seen you do in the past. Stay focused. Maybelline had nothing to do with this."

Stevenson spoke before Raven could reply. "His girlfriend, Lois Wareham, maybe. We know she lied about the last time that she saw him."

"How do you know that?" the chief asked.

Raven laughed. "Because she didn't do grief like Stevenson expected. No keening or tearing out her hair."

"We're right back at it. No more Miss Nice Girl," Stevenson said.

"I've never been a nice girl, Delbert. I'm not convinced that the girlfriend had anything to do with Zeke's death. Too early, way too early," Raven said.

"But not too early for the mama?" the chief said.

"I'm just saying that we shouldn't fixate on Lois Wareham when we've hardly started investigating. Stevenson didn't like her because she puts her faith in roots and gods plural instead of the one God Almighty," Raven said.

"What do you know about root work, Raven?" the chief said, laughing a little.

"I know enough from being Black and having Floyd as my daddy. He sometimes had to doctor himself when he was running. He said he learned how to do it from my mother. I don't remember a lot."

"You mean before he killed your mother," Stevenson said.

"Cut that shit out, Stevenson," the chief said. "Y'all partners. You need to support each other."

"And I still want to personally talk to the witnesses at the scene," Raven said.

The chief sat back. He curled his dark hand around the baseball and rested his chin on his knuckles.

"You mean witnesses in the Old Bottoms," the chief said.

"Yes, I mean witnesses in the Old Bottoms," Raven said.

"Didn't the uniforms take statements?" the chief asked.

"Yes," Raven said.

"Marna has some uniforms out recanvassing as we speak," Stevenson said.

"Use whatever they get," the chief responded. "I don't want you messing around down there."

"What if they still won't talk?" Raven asked.

"Wouldn't be surprised," the chief said. "People over there don't like police."

"I want to find out what that place is about, drive back over there and do some door-to-door myself. Whatever they're into could have something to do with the murders," Raven said.

"By yourself? Or you mean with your partner?" the chief said, looking at her pointedly.

The skepticism on Stevenson's face didn't help her case with the chief.

"I'm fine with Marna and her team going down there. But I don't want you going back for another round. Could look like harassment. Besides, y'all need to follow up on this Wareham character," the chief said.

"Numb nuts can follow up on that one. He's itching to do it. Didn't like being called Daddy. I want to talk to the guy who runs the Old Bottoms," Raven said.

"You talking about Lucien Toussaint?" The chief gripped the baseball as if he were trying to crush it.

"I think it'd be a good idea. He was eyeballing us through the entire thing, all of them were. But since he's in charge, he's the one I want to talk to," she said.

"I told you that they don't like police. Besides, curious people don't necessarily mean they have something to hide." The chief looked over at Stevenson. "Do you think it's worth it to rattle Toussaint's cage right now?"

Stevenson's expression revealed that she was about to regret the 'numb nuts' comment. He said, "I think it'll be a waste of time at this point. Patrol took statements at the scene. I talked to Toussaint before Raven got there. He said shots woke him up, and he and his men…"

"His men?" Raven asked.

"…went out to investigate. They didn't see or hear anything. The next thing they heard was sirens."

"That's a load of crap," Raven said. "We already know that BLPD didn't get there until at least two hours after the shots were fired. What were they doing all that time?"

"Next doesn't necessarily mean fast," Stevenson said.

"And you believed him?" Raven asked.

"Didn't give me a reason not to," Stevenson answered.

Raven knew that she needed to keep her mouth shut or she was going to be on the chief's bad side again. The chief was small town, knew everybody and was involved in almost everything. He was Byrd's Landing through and through. More than one of his entanglements had ended up at the center of the other cases she had worked on. The chief, Toussaint, and Zeke's mama. Was that a triangle that would lead anywhere?

"Stevenson," the chief said. "Go get started on setting up the command center and choosing your team. Do some background digging on Lois Wareham. I want to spend a few minutes with your partner."

⋆ ⋆ ⋆

The door had barely clicked shut before the chief said, "Are you going to make me regret bringing you back?"

"You mean begging me to come back?" Raven said. "To a place that's eating me alive inside out from bone to flesh?"

"Now you being dramatic just like your old man," the chief said. "You belong here, Raven. Hell, you were born with a badge on. Your life will be better the moment you realize that."

He set the baseball back in the gold glove holder on his desk.

"Marna said that you went all Bruce Willis action star in the church at the scene," the chief said.

"Doing my job," Raven said. "That place needed searching so I searched it."

"Bullshit," he said. "You could have waited until we got somebody over there to make sure it was safe. You were seeking a thrill like you always do, putting yourself in danger. Is your life so cheap to you, Raven?"

"Never took you for my therapist."

"You never took me for anything, and now you taking me for a fool. If you're trying to take yourself out, give yourself the death penalty for all the shit you did and your daddy did, don't take my good officers with you."

She smiled. "Oh shucks, just when I thought you cared."

"Don't get it twisted," he said. "I do care. But you've been on a self-destructive path so long it's starting to wear me out. I can't let you put anybody else in danger."

"I didn't ask them to follow me into the church," she said.

"You didn't have to ask them. They went because they care about you, as fucked up as that is because you don't appreciate it."

"What are you saying?" she asked.

"I'm going to put you on notice. If your inability to take a breath causes harm to any one of my officers, or if I find out you're playing fast and loose with your own life again, you're out."

She stood and went to the door. Her hand touched the doorknob.

"I'm not finished," the chief said.

"I heard you," Raven said.

"One more thing."

She looked back at him.

"If I get even an echo that you've carried your fast ass over to the Bottoms again to question Lucien Toussaint, I'll kick you back to waitressing over at Chastain's faster than you can say 'how's the gumbo'," he said.

Be still, Birdie Girl, Floyd said in her head. *Don't do or say nothing.* But as usual, she couldn't help herself.

"More secrets, Chief?" she asked.

He turned on his computer and started tapping the keys to see how much misery he could cause on the internet.

"More than you know," he said. "Dead and buried. That's where they're going to stay."

Chapter Eighteen
Floyd

Floyd didn't slam his door when the cops came knocking on the account of Mrs. Jefferson's death. There were two of them. One was a tall, skinny young fella whose badge was almost wider than he was. His shiny, new name tag said Early Sawyer. He had another one with him, a big-faced cop whose square jaw, wavy black hair and widow's peak made him look like a movie star. His eyes reminded Floyd of the sky when it's all gentle and blue. This cop's name was Victor Broussard. There was something wrong with that man on the inside that the outside wasn't saying nary a word about. When Floyd first laid eyes on him, he thought about something he heard long ago – not all beasts wear terrible faces.

Even so, Floyd opened the door as wide as you please and invited them in. He teased the rookie about being named Early Sawyer. Made a joke about Mark Twain and that book everybody goes on and on about. The man didn't laugh. Floyd sat them right down on his couch. They had a time of it trying to get comfortable. They looked like giant crabs trying to sit on a sofa. Officer Broussard stuck his hands in his pockets, pulled out a bunch of keys and started fiddling around with a baby fox's tail hanging off them.

"I know it's hotter than the hell, and y'all been walking up and down this hill a while," Floyd said. "I ain't got no sweet tea, don't care for it too much myself, but I've got some grape Kool-Aid if you want. My girl can make it ice-cold for you."

Sawyer said no, but Officer Broussard told Floyd to bring it on. Floyd directed Raven to go get Kool-Aid for both of them, ignoring Sawyer's refusal. She didn't move a muscle. Instead, she gazed at the police officers under her eyes as if she was about to say something. She even stood a second or two longer than Floyd liked before going back for the drinks. The refrigerator door creaked open and ice jumped as Raven pulled the lever on the metal ice tray.

She came back into the room carrying two glasses of purple Kool-Aid. Officer Broussard dropped the keys in his lap and took hold of the glass. Raven stayed as far away as she could, like she needed to deal with that man with a long-handled spoon. Sawyer took his glass but set it on the coffee table.

Raven perched on an armchair like some sort of beauty queen, her eyes swinging back and forth between the sweaty-face rookie and his partner, who looked like he had a few more years on him, but not enough years to get him out of uniform and all the gear he carried like he was going to war instead of patrolling a neighborhood. And by the way he was acting, Floyd surmised that Broussard hadn't had the pleasure of being in many Black folks' houses. He kept looking around, like he was searching for germs that might do him in. He even tested the cold drink for something rotten with a long pink tongue. And here is ole Floyd being proud of himself for keeping a clean house, the floors so spick and span you could eat from them, the windows so clear you'd have to knock twice to be sure they were closed.

Broussard must have eventually noticed all that because he gave this little appreciative nod, like he was saying, "Good job, Black folk." After that the man pulled his tongue back from the Kool-Aid, and drank almost all of it before bringing the glass back down. He even shook the ice, drank up any sugar that had sunk to the bottom of the glass. Then he started talking.

"We're here about the Jefferson murder. I hear you knew her," he said.

"Yessir, I did," Floyd said.

"How long have you and your daughter lived here?" Broussard asked. "I've done a lot of patrols out this way. I ain't seen you."

"Why, we've been here going on some months," Floyd said, giving Raven a look that said *keep your trap shut.*

Truth be told they had been in Byrd's Landing almost a year. They hid out in the woods and the swamps. They only came out when Floyd thought it was safe. He put a toe out, told folks he was just passing through. Then he went out with Raven, and learned that not too many people ask questions in this town. Soon, he ended up at Al's Diner, where he met his girlfriend, now fiancée, Miss Jean Rinehart. In a month or two he planned to march right out of these shotguns into a new life with his sweetheart. Ain't nobody was going to stop him from that.

"Where you from?" Sawyer, the young one, asked.

"All over," Floyd answered back.

"You want us to find out who killed this lady or not?" Officer Broussard said.

"Sir," Floyd answered, "I don't see where I'm from having a dog's turd in hell to do with how Mrs. Jefferson came to her bloody end."

Officer Broussard grinned then with all of his bright, white teeth. He had Floyd's number, and Floyd knew it.

"Miss Ruth," Raven said.

She said it under her breath like she hoped the words would blow away before they reached their ears. And then she said again, louder but still soft, "Her name was Miss Ruth."

Floyd couldn't help but stare at Raven. She was growing up, taller than he remembered seeing her, her hair pulled back in a ponytail instead of the two pigtails she'd favored. His little Birdie Girl was also growing sharper edges even as young as she was. He thought he was in control of the two poop stains sitting on his couch. He was having right fun playing with them. Wasn't it something that the one thing he should be worried about was this little bit of a girl he watched come down the birth canal. Why, he was beginning to think that he raised up a rattle snake in his own house.

Chapter Nineteen

Sunlight slid through the blinds along the back window of the murder room. That's what the admin assistants called it. To the detectives it was just conference room C. Most of the evidence on their big cases landed here. Today it was the command center for the homicides in the churchyard. Stevenson stood up and snipped each blind closed as if they were building a rocket to Mars and Russia was on the lawn trying to peep in. Cameron, the one foster brother that Raven stayed close to after foster care, was picking up the photos of the crime scene, glossy eight-by-tens, and then flipping them over on the table.

"Don't do that," Tim said. "I had them in order."

"In order of what?" Cameron asked.

"In the order that I need them on the whiteboard," he said.

He pointed to Marna, who was dragging a whiteboard to the front of the room.

"What am I doing here, sis?" Cameron asked Raven. "Because there ain't no way I can look at this shit and maintain my ever-loving cool."

"Detective," Raven corrected. "And you are here because Rudy left last month, remember?"

"That dude didn't just leave. Y'all fired him," Cameron said.

"And since he's not here, you're it. Think of it as a bloody game of tag," Raven said.

"You as creepy as hell," Cameron said.

"I come by it honestly," Raven said.

"What you need me for?" Cameron asked. "You got a computer that won't boot up, a virus, a server that needs reformatting, I'm your guy. But not this murder shit."

"You are now, especially since you ran Rudy off."

"I ain't run nobody off," Cameron said.

"We need you on the team," Raven said.

"To do what?" Cameron said.

"Check the victims' social media. I also need you to pull and analyze the phone records—" She was interrupted by Stevenson, who sat heavily in the chair next to Cameron. Cameron rolled his chair away as if he were afraid of catching something.

"Been subpoenaed," Stevenson said.

Raven looked at Stevenson. "Good boy," she said.

Cameron and Marna stifled laughs. Tim's acted as if he hadn't heard. Raven spoke loudly before Stevenson could hurl a retort.

"Listen up. All of you are on the team. Marna, who's canvassing the Old Bottoms?"

"Newell's doing it with a couple of patrol officers," she said.

Marna went back to place a bright yellow magnet on the photo of the body of Zeke Riverton. Raven caught a glimpse of his face staring at her accusingly. She turned away.

"A waste of time, I say," Marna said. "Folk down there only talk when Papa Toussaint tells them to talk."

"What's up with this Lucien Toussaint guy, anyway?" Raven asked. "Everybody seems to be afraid of him."

"I ain't scared of nobody," Marna said. "Except Jesus when he's angry and the devil when he's being himself. That man's got a hold on the people who live down there, and some who don't."

"Marna," Raven said. "I'd rather you go down there, too. Knock on some screen doors with your husband. Flash those pearly whites, turn on that hometown homegirl charm and get some answers. I have faith in you."

"Your dime, because I'm expensing lunch," Marna said.

"What else, my Black queen?" Cameron said.

"Detective," Raven corrected. "See who else Zeke ran with, maybe check out some old cellmates."

"Cellmates?" Stevenson said.

Raven didn't say anything for a moment, because the words forming in her head were far from the Zeke she knew in high school.

"Zeke had a record. He was a drug addict. I'm sure he spent some time behind bars," she said.

"What about the other two?" Stevenson asked. "They have records?"

"I don't know about the other two," Raven said. "I left my crystal ball in my other jacket pocket."

"No worries. I checked them all out. Zeke did have a record. I'm having some patrol check out his old cellmates. The other two had none," Marna said. "They were clean. If they stole something, broke something or sold something to get drugs, they were smart enough not to get caught."

"I know Zeke worked at Heron House," Raven said. "What about the other two?"

"Same place," Marna said. "They all worked there."

"What about Diamond?" Stevenson said.

"What about him?" Raven asked.

Stevenson counted on his fingers. "Background check. Phone records. Insurance policies. Inheritances. Where does Zeke's money go now that he's dead?"

"You thinking the man killed his own brother?" Marna asked. "Diamond ain't like that."

"Murder likes it close to home, Marna," Raven said. "Check the mama, too."

"Now you thinking some old lady shot two men execution style and stabbed her own son to death?" Marna said.

"We need to clear them. We also need to check out Marcel's cousin," Raven said.

As they were talking, Tim, ever useful, was writing each name on the board. Raven's heart skipped a beat when he wrote Diamond's name under the list of suspects along with the others they had been talking about. Could Diamond really have the nerve to kill his own brother? Her first thought was absolutely not, but her second and third? They were estranged, and after all, Zeke was an addict. Addicts can turn people they are close to into someone you'd cross the street to get away from.

"Raven," Stevenson said, pulling her attention back to the room. "I said what about Lois? Put her name up there, too, Tim."

"Lois is all yours. Knock yourself out," Raven said.

Chapter Twenty

Raven left Stevenson digging into Lois Wareham's background to see a woman who, like Raven, dished out her own brand of vigilante justice. Edmée Crowley killed the man responsible for the death of her son. She beat Ronnie True near to death with a golf club before ending his life with an old-fashioned bolt gun that she and her cousin used on the farm. Unlike Raven, Edmée was caught, tried and convicted. But because she was married to money and tradition, the conviction resulted in two years' probation, mandatory counseling, and thousands of hours of community service. Already the owner of a boys' home and addiction recovery center, Heron House, Edmée was more than familiar with community service.

Years ago, using funds raised from donors and her husband's bank account, Edmée built Heron House as an oasis in the center of town. She snatched up buildings where she wanted to locate the home and watched with her arms folded as wrecking balls smashed them to splinters. A facility rife with high glass walls and right angles rose in their place. In the middle of the facility was a garden of pretty things to look at and practical things to eat. Purple and red salvia, yellow daylilies and black-eyed Susans swirled among eggplant and beefsteak tomatoes. Just as with the eclectic gardens, Edmée mixed the righteous with the fallen. Byrd's Landing residents attended the community workshops alongside the juvenile and adult recovering addicts who lived there. With each passing day, Edmée became more well-loved, well-respected, and ultimately forgiven. Since all three men who were killed worked at Heron House, Raven thought it was about time she and Edmée had a conversation.

She raised her fist to knock at Edmée's office door, but lowered it when she heard voices on the other side. One of them she recognized.

Without knocking she pushed the door open. Billy Ray was standing there with his arms around a sobbing Edmée.

"What the—" Raven started.

"Oh, Raven," Edmée said.

She released Billy Ray as if he had become too hot to handle, only to run to Raven. She threw her arms around Raven's neck and sobbed harder. Raven could feel the woman's tears on her forehead. She smelled of magnolia, the cloying perfume that always made Raven sick to her stomach. Raven gently pushed her away.

"You heard?" Raven said.

"Billy Ray just told me," Edmée answered.

"How did Billy Ray know?" Raven asked with a pointed glance at her former partner.

"What do you mean how did I know? It's all over the news," he said.

He perched on the corner of Edmée's glass desk, rested clasped hands in his lap. Edmée, her long black hair swinging behind her, walked to the opposite side, and plopped down into an ultra-modern white leather office chair. She pulled tissues from a Puffs box and blew her nose. *God*, Raven thought. How was it fair that someone could still be beautiful while shooting snot from their noggin?

Edmée had been using her good looks in an attempt to trap Billy Ray since she first met him at Chastain's Creole Heaven. They argued about the differences between Creoles and Cajuns, what delineated zydeco from bluegrass and why only barbarians used tomatoes in their gumbo. In other words, they got on like a house on fire. The only thing standing between them was Edmée's husband, Dr. Fabian Long, the CEO of Memorial Hospital, and the man who stood by his wife through the arrest, conviction and now her probation.

"We didn't release the names or say where the victims worked," Raven said, still standing.

"Marna told me where they worked. She was worried about Edmée," he said.

Raven made a mental note to talk to Marna about confidentiality and police investigations. Sure, Raven wanted to pull Billy Ray into the investigation in order to help, but he refused. And to Raven, if you were out, you were out. No popping back in whenever it was convenient.

"You could have called me, Edmée," Raven said.

Edmée waved her bejeweled fingers at Raven, the nails perfectly shaped and painted a liquid red. "I figured you'd be too busy with the running around. You know how you get after a homicide."

"What's the problem, Raven?" Billy Ray said. "This morning you wanted my help, but now you mad because Marna looped me in?"

"What makes me mad is that you hightailed it over here to compromise a witness," Raven said.

"Do shut your mouth, Raven," Edmée said. "Billy Ray is a friend. He wanted to tell me himself. He knew how upset I would be."

"I thought your husband was your friend," Raven said.

"He is my lover, my rock, my support, but for some things, not my friend. He made it very clear from the start that he wants nothing to do with Heron House."

Edmée waved her hand around the office, the grounds behind the floor-to-ceiling windows.

"Who do you think we found?" Raven said, going into cop mode.

"Where's your boyfriend, Stevenson?" Billy Ray asked.

"He's where I tell him to be," Raven said. "Also, fun fact. He's not my boyfriend."

"Please, you two," Edmée said. "You found Zeke Riverton and Marcel Thibodeaux and Lionel Williams. Tell me I'm wrong. In fact, please tell me."

"Do you have any idea if Zeke or his friends had a beef with anyone?" Raven asked.

Edmée shook her head and snatched another tissue. "All I know is that they were great friends. When you saw one you saw the others."

"What did they do at the House?" Raven asked.

"Well, Zeke was the head janitor. Wouldn't hurt a fly. One of the kindest people I ever met. You know how he was in high school, Raven. He was still that way, but happy, at peace."

"Was he clean?" Raven asked.

Edmée nodded. “Completely. I’ll never believe that he wasn’t. That man didn’t know how to tell a lie, not a good one anyway.”

“When he was drugging, he lied plenty,” Raven said.

“That was the sickness driving him,” Edmée said. “You know this.”

“Did you notice anything different about him during the last couple of weeks?”

That came from Billy Ray. Raven held her breath. The one good thing that could come out of his twisted relationship with Edmée would be his agreeing to officially help with the investigation. Then she wouldn’t give a crap what he knew or what information Marna gave him. That hope was smashed when he held up a finger and said, “I’m just asking. I cook food and play music. That’s it.”

“Yet you still manage to stick your nose in my business,” Raven said.

“He was…off,” Edmée answered. “Distracted. I saw him on the phone a lot. At first, I thought it was the girlfriend.”

“Why is that?” Raven asked.

“Because she was a little,” Edmée touched her temple, “free with her thinking. She was into root work and things like that. Zeke wasn’t religious, but I still think it bothered him. You know, wearing mojo bags, plants, graveyard dirt, brick dust and all that asinine shit.”

“Then you changed your mind?” Billy Ray asked Edmée.

“I did, because I saw them together. She came for lunch one day and I joined them in the cafeteria. She was odd but I could tell that Zeke cared for her.” Edmée sniffed and sighed again. “Do you know how Zeke came to Heron House?”

Raven didn’t answer. Neither did Billy Ray. Edmée went on, “I found him on the street.”

“I can’t see you spending a lot of time on the street,” Raven said.

“You’d be surprised. How do you think I get my residents? I like plucking those dying flowers right from the street. I go in my high heels, pencil skirts and cashmere wraps. Nobody bothers me. They know why I’m there and who I am. Except for that one time, and I handled it.”

Raven was sure she did. Once, the woman wrangled a snake in Raven's apartment, not to mention the bloody golf club and bolt gun in her past.

"I found Zeke in an alley, skinny as hell, nothing but rags. I brought him here, cleaned him up, and started to get him treatment. He repaid me by stealing my purse and a bracelet Fabian gave me, before running away."

"You mean escaping," Raven said.

"Stop with the drama," Edmée said. "I didn't kidnap him." She considered. "Not really. But he was clearly not ready. I canceled the credit cards and bought a new Prada. Fabian replaced the bracelet, of course. I didn't give up. I stalked Zeke. When I found him, I locked up my purse, left the jewelry at home, and brought him back again. Even put Marcel at his door to make sure he did no more shenanigans. In hindsight, I think that's how they became friends."

"He stayed?" Billy Ray asked

"No, of course not. He left again," Edmée said.

"So how did he get clean?" Raven asked.

"He died," Edmée said.

"Edmée…"

"I am so serious. He overdosed in the same alley where I first saw him. One of the paramedics that I'm friendly with alerted me. When I went to see him in the hospital, he was scared down to his bones. Said he had a bad hit, died with the needle in his arm. The paramedics brought him back."

"Did he get a taste of a little hellfire?" Raven asked.

"No," Edmée said. "When I asked him what it was like to die, I thought he'd say something about his life flashing before his eyes, or walking toward the light, or feeling this overwhelming sense of peace. But it was none of that."

"What did he say?" Billy Ray asked.

Edmée didn't look at them. She picked at the edges of the tissue box.

"I'll never forget his words. He says to me, 'Aww, Edmée, ain't no time passed, no time at all'. That is what scared him the most, being nothing and nowhere, to simply not exist. No light."

Raven and Billy Ray learned from Edmée that Zeke had worked as head janitor at the sprawling facility. Edmée finally admitted that Marcel started off as Zeke's jailer. His job was to make sure Zeke didn't use, steal, run or a combination of all three. But soon after Zeke returned to Heron House that last time, Marcel became Zeke's close friend and confidant. The residents nicknamed them macaroni and cheese. Lionel joined them after Zeke helped him get clean. He got young Lionel a job working on the janitorial team, and ever since that day, they were always together. No, she didn't know why anyone would want to hurt either one of them. As Edmée described their relationship in that overly dramatic way of hers, Raven imagined three friends walking off into the Louisiana mist.

After she was finished talking, Edmée said, "Enough with the stupid tears. I have a business to run. You two, go on your way."

Chapter Twenty-One

Raven rushed to catch up with Billy Ray in the parking lot. She had come to Heron House to question a witness in the homicides. What she was leaving with was a nagging worry that Billy Ray was about to be in trouble. Not just any trouble, but probably the biggest trouble of his life.

"What the hell are you doing, Billy Ray?" she asked when she reached him.

He had stood next to his '67 Buick Skylark, car keys in his hands. He was a big man, good-looking enough to have once been a model for a department store catalog. That was how he put himself through college. But all of it was for nothing. In the end he was a big Black man, imposing without trying. He scared people, and he knew it. He spent most of his life trying to make other people comfortable. He did so by driving a classic car, favoring bowling shirts, loose slacks and keeping his oh-shucks hands in his pockets.

But that was the old Billy Ray, and the car was the only affectation that he hung on to after leaving the force, if it was an affectation at all. When Lamont Lovelle almost killed him, it was as if the fire burned away the affable Billy Ray everyone liked to be around. Raven wondered who was the real Billy Ray: the man of the past or the new one who was now staring at her as if she had just taken a dump in the parking lot.

"She's married," Raven said. "Her husband is a powerful man, and not dumb. He won't even have to cut your balls off himself. He can hire somebody to do it."

"You accusing me of sleeping with Edmée?"

"She's after you, Billy Ray," Raven said.

"Well, someone has to be," he said.

"She's a suspect," Raven insisted. "You need to stay away from her."

"You can't tell me who I can be around," he said. "Besides, she didn't kill Zeke and them."

"Fine. Tell me who you think did," Raven said.

"I'm not getting involved," he said.

She flapped an arm toward the main building.

"You're already involved!"

He said nothing, and then, "Drug hit most likely. A buy that went wrong."

"Did you notice the guards at Heron House?" she asked. "They're armed."

"I did notice," he said. By the way he said it, the fact that they were armed didn't impress him at all.

"Edmée kidnapped Zeke off the streets. Three times," Raven said.

"I thought the last time was his idea," Billy Ray said.

"Kidnapped," she reiterated. "She had someone guard him. An armed someone."

"Marcel. They became buddies afterward. Were you not just part of the same conversation?" Billy Ray said.

"What if Zeke threatened her?" she asked.

"Why?" he said.

"I don't know," Raven said. "A falling out. Friends fall out."

"Like you and Edmée," Billy Ray said.

"We didn't fall out. Just grew apart," Raven said.

"You remember what happened the last time you accused Edmée of murder?"

She did remember. Edmée wasn't their serial killer in that case last year. But still, she was a killer, and it was Raven who had caught her.

"Do you remember how she saved your life?" Billy Ray said.

"I said thank you."

Billy Ray laughed. "Okay, let's play. How did they die? Tell me everything."

"Marcel and Lionel had two shots to the back of the head, execution style. Zeke was stabbed, throat slit. We think he was the target," Raven said.

Billy Ray's laugh reminded Raven of the pink tank Edmée was wearing in the office. Her arms and hands were on full display, including her perfect blood-red manicure. No cuts or bruises indicating she was a knife-wielding killer the night before.

Billy Ray signaled he had finally had enough by unlocking his car door.

"Don't forget about tonight," he said.

"Tonight?" she answered.

"It's my birthday, remember? Chastain's. Just dinner, and I'm not even closing the place down. Not a party like last year. Thought you all could help me audition a new bandmember. You don't remember?" Billy Ray said.

"For the zydeco band?"

"Is there any other kind of music?" he said.

Chapter Twenty-Two

Raven slammed the door of the Mustang in the parking lot of Chastain's Creole Heaven. A birthday dinner with Billy Ray and the gang, a new zydeco bandmember he was trying out, the place would be loud. Loud was just what she needed right now after the silence of the three dead men in an abandoned churchyard.

Earlier that day after her trip to Heron House, she discovered that Rita wouldn't get to the autopsy until early the next morning. As for the canvass, the residents of the Old Bottoms had handed Newell, Marna and the patrol officers a bag full of nothing along with a message to the chief. Lucien Toussaint directed Marna to tell the chief to keep his fucking shiny-shoes cops out of the Old Bottoms like they agreed or there would be trouble. Raven would follow up, but tonight she would let all that sleep.

Live zydeco music poured from the screen doors as Raven drew closer. This was no novice band. The music swallowed her up as soon as she entered the restaurant. It was the usual band with a man Raven had never seen before. He wore a black top hat, and a vest of velvet patchwork the color of midnight, blood red and purple against his bare skin. The bright lights illuminated a thick scar that started at his right temple and made a serpentine curve beneath his eye and over his nose. The twisted tissue ended just beneath his opposite ear. He strutted on the stage as if it were built just for him. He coerced every bit of joy, pain and taunting he could from the instrument strapped across his chest as the band rocked 'Someone Else Steppin' In'. He played his accordion so furiously Raven was surprised that the thing wasn't bleeding.

"What do you think?" Billy Ray said.

She was so busy watching the accordion player that she hadn't noticed Billy Ray next to her.

"Top hat?" she asked. "He's good. Where did you find him?"

"His name is Gervais Armstrong, says he's from here but just got back in town. Couch surfing, that sort of shit. Brother needed a break so I hooked him up with the band. Good, huh?"

Raven turned back to the stage. Gervais flashed a smile full of white teeth, tipped his black top hat at her. Raven responded with a jaunty salute.

"He's a showman," she said. "But I guess with everybody out there on the dance floor whooping it up he'll be invited back."

As the band moved on to 'Hot Tamale Baby', Billy Ray pointed Raven toward the bar.

Now that she was getting used to the music, she could smell gumbo fighting for air space with Billy Ray's special creole-inspired lamb stew. The word around town was that the soup was so good you'd slap your mama if that was what was required for seconds. As she made her way to the bar, she noticed that every table was packed and as usual, everybody was talking loud, laughing loud, and pounding the table when they got a bite of food that was too good to be believed, or heard a story that was too wild to be true.

A sound like a gunshot cracked through the noise. Before Raven could flinch, there came a loud 'Whoop' and a voice that had too much playful triumph in it to be a threat. "In your face, Anna."

Raven looked toward what had come to be known as the old folks' corner of Chastain's. Mr. Joe had just vanquished Mama Anna in dominoes. She was his regular opponent and the unofficial matriarch of Chastain's. They practically lived at the restaurant in their spare time, and had even helped Raven on a case last summer. Ever since Billy Ray opened the creole restaurant in the double-barrel shotgun house, this group of old folk claimed the only live-edge mahogany table in the place as their own. It surprised Raven when she first saw the table. It wasn't something that Billy Ray would normally do, buy a new, expensive table. He was Mister Recycle, Reuse and Renew, a 'respect the planet' kind of man. He served his creations on secondhand plates that didn't match. His guests ate while sitting in mismatched chairs. And then that table appeared. When she asked Billy Ray about it, he said something about always wanting to serve his shrimp and grits on a slice of Africa.

"Sit, Raven," Edmée gestured to a seat next to her.

In the meantime, Billy Ray had gone over to talk to the band, who was now in between songs. As if he could feel them watching him, Billy Ray turned and winked.

"Oh, he slays me," Edmée said as she swiveled back to face the bar.

"Easy girl," Raven said. "You're married, remember?"

"Married, but not dead," Edmée said. "Besides, my husband is in the restroom. What he doesn't see won't hurt him."

Raven stared at her. "You mean Dr. Long is here?"

"He insisted on accompanying me because he knew I'd be blue because of Zeke and the boys."

"Or maybe he had enough of you running after Billy Ray as if he had the last bottle of water in the Mojave," Raven said.

"Tell the bitch in you to calm down," she said. "I would never be unfaithful to my husband."

Raven laughed. "If I had my beer, I would have spit it out." She held her hand up at Edmée's flat stare.

"Get her a shot of whiskey to mellow her out," Edmée said to the bartender.

"No whiskey," Raven said. "Just a beer."

They sat in silence a few moments until the bartender slid Raven's beer to her.

Edmée drained her wineglass, and said to the bartender, "Another, please."

"Whoa," Raven said. "You can't get drunk now."

"Why not?" Edmée asked.

"You don't want your husband to see you misbehaving," Raven said.

Edmée looked to where Raven was looking. Fabian Long, a befuddled look on his face, weaved his way through the now gyrating bodies. The band had started playing again, this time without Gervais and his top hat.

"Poor baby," Imogene said. "A fish out of water."

"Oh, I wouldn't worry about him," Raven said. "He's been married to a shark for years and appears to be doing just fine."

"Darling," Edmée said, leaving her seat and running to Fabian. He picked her up and swung her around, tried to do a little dance step that made him look like an uncoordinated spider.

"Detective," Fabian said, extending a hand. Raven shook it, noting how weirdly long and bony his fingers were.

"How are you, Dr. Long?" she asked.

"Oh, please. In these quarters you call me Fabian. Bartender, may I have an Angel's Wing double? Neat."

He turned and leaned against the bar. He watched Billy Ray talking to the potential band member for a long moment, the man in the top hat and patchwork vest. Raven followed Long's gaze. What did Billy Ray say his name was? Gervais. He noticed them looking at him and a smile transformed his entire scarred face – friendly, easy, happy. Billy Ray noticed the attention, too, and waved all of them over.

"Who's this?" Edmée asked when she reached him.

"This is Gervais," Billy Ray said. "He's new to town."

"Not exactly new," Gervais said with that same winning smile. "I grew up here, left, but now I'm back." He then looked at Raven. "Don't I know you?"

"Everybody knows Raven," Edmée said. "She's famous around these parts."

"Shut up, Edmée," Raven said.

"Cop, right?" Gervais said.

"Guilty as charged," Raven said. "But tonight I'm just a customer. I heard you play."

"Well, I hope I did okay. I'm a jazz man myself, but Billy Ray got me into this zydeco shit."

"You can't tell from the way you work that accordion," Raven said.

"It ain't shit," said Clifton, one of the band members. He jumped down and clamped his hand on Gervais's shoulder. "This brother can look at an instrument and it get so scared it start shitting 'Jambalaya' all by itself."

★ ★ ★

Billy Ray's birthday dinner was family style in one of the back rooms with doors so heavy the music from the band, now playing without Gervais, sounded like echoes from a distant dream. Cameron sat at the other end of the table with Raven's nephew Noe. Her foster brother was as loud as ever as he told some story that had Edmée once again in stitches. *That girl would laugh at a joke older than Methuselah and lamer than a one-legged goat*, Floyd said in Raven's head. Edmée let out another peal of laughter. Gervais was down at that end of the table, too, talking loudly and laughing hard. Raven thought she heard the words 'Wu-Tang' and 'Fortnite'. Pretty soon Gervais and Cameron were exchanging elaborate handshakes and bro hugs. Her brother had found a new friend.

After spending time with Cameron and Edmée, Gervais made it to the end of the table where Raven and Billy Ray sat. Edmée and Dr. Long soon joined them. Gervais made it known that he wanted to sit next to Raven. He even sent her a warm, wide smile. In turn, Raven glared at Billy Ray. Was he seriously trying to set her up? Edmée, sitting on the other side of Raven, poked her with an elbow. Raven slapped it away.

"How is the new wing, Dr. Long?" Raven asked as the food started to make its way around the table. Fabian had been shooting daggers at Billy Ray all night but took his eyes away from him long enough to answer Raven's question.

"Splendid," he said, and ordered another double whiskey. "We will help a lot of people."

"Raven, Gervais is looking for a job," Billy Ray said.

"Aside from playing in the band?" Raven said.

"That don't pay rent, lil' sis," Gervais said. "Billy Ray has been kind enough to let me clean up around here, do a little of this and that. But it don't make ends meet. I need another gig."

Raven let the *lil' sis* go. The man did look older than her if only by a few years.

"You looking for work down at the station?" Raven asked him.

He laughed. "No, I don't like cops." He then considered and followed up with a perfunctory, "Present company excluded. I like Billy Ray and you just fine."

"Well, I'm glad," Raven said. "Now I don't have to break out my hanky."

"I do landscaping," he said.

"Landscaping?" Raven said.

"Yeah, you know, lawns, shrubbery, gardens are my specialty."

"Don't you need someone to dig out Oral's old garden?" Billy Ray said, before shoving gumbo in his mouth.

Raven laughed and sat back. "Whew," she said. "Here I was thinking you were trying to set me up, Billy Ray."

"Oh no," Gervais said, laughing. "No way. I'm spoken for."

"By who?" Billy Ray said.

"My music," Gervais said. "Music is my only girl."

"You lie," Raven said.

"Okay, I do," he said. "But I would never go out with you. You carry a gun."

"Raven, I wouldn't set Gervais up with you. I like him too much," Billy Ray said.

"Anyway, I'd love to do that job for you," Gervais said.

"I could use the help," Raven said.

They exchanged numbers while the waiter twirled merlot into Edmée's glass.

"You can help me with my garden, too, Gervais. My home and Heron House," Edmée said.

"Heron House?" Gervais shuddered. "Naw, I know too many people there, if you know what I mean." He laughed. "Besides, I'm not interested in a bunch of paperwork and interviewing. I need something that pays fast so I can get a decent place to stay."

"Fine, just let me know anytime you want to give me your services," Edmée said on a hiccup. Fabian covered her hand with his.

"Yes," Fabian said. "I'm afraid my wife has been a bit free with her…ahem…procurement of services from third parties."

Raven was reaching for her beer again. She stopped. Edmée's face went white under her makeup. She moved her hand from beneath her husband's.

"Seriously, Dr. Long?" Raven said. "You being that piece of butt filth?"

Billy Ray's voice belied the scowl on his face. It was languid, slow and friendly as if he were giving confused strangers directions and wanted to make sure that they understood. Otherwise, they'd end up in a dangerous place.

"Come on, man," he said. "Ain't no cause for all that. And I'm really not in the mood to stomp a bitch on my birthday."

Chapter Twenty-Three

The next morning Raven opened the door of Oral's house to Gervais Armstrong. It was early and Raven still had a piece of toast hanging out of her mouth. Gervais was no longer the accordion-playing fashionista from the night before. His instrument of choice was a shovel, which he held beside him like an accomplice.

"Ready and reporting for duty, ma'am," he said, and saluted.

"A sense of humor. I like it," Raven said.

"Most people do," he said and smiled. "I can meet you out back if you want."

"Don't be stupid, come on inside," Raven said. "I'll show you where things are."

Gervais stepped into the wide, empty living room. Raven closed the door behind him. Early morning light streamed through the curtainless windows and washed the dark wood with yellow-gold rays.

"Looks like you don't have any things to show me," Gervais said. "Did you just move in?"

Raven smiled, led him to the kitchen. She indicated a seat at the card table.

"I've been here for a while, but just got the place cleaned up," she said.

"Cleaned up?" he said. "Not remodeled?"

"A friend of mine got killed here," she said. "He left the place to me."

"That's fucked up," he said. "I'm sorry."

"Coffee?" Raven asked.

"You got tea?" he asked.

"No," Raven said.

"Then coffee it'll have to be."

Raven poured coffee into two mugs. She joined him at the card table.

"How long have you known Billy Ray?" she asked.

Gervais's cup was halfway to his lips, but he didn't drink from it. Instead, he placed the cup on the card table.

"You ain't just going to let me in your backyard to turn dirt. This here is an interview," he said.

She laughed. "I am a cop. Naturally suspicious, and not big on stupid. I don't know you, Gervais."

"So you say," he said.

"What does that mean?" she asked.

"What happened to any friend of so-and-so is a friend of mine?" he said.

Raven studied the man sitting across from her. Last night he was dressed like a star. Someone could have taken his picture and placed it on a billboard. People would have bought tickets to see him without questioning his legitimacy as a musician. And he played well, which is why Billy Ray thought he deserved a shot. But that was Billy Ray, not her.

"I don't give anybody access to my space without getting to know them a little first," she said.

He looked around, confused. "Maybe you scared I'm going to abscond with the drywall? The card table?"

"Billy Ray and I go way back. I trust him. That doesn't mean I'm not going to find out what you're about. I need to hear from your own lips. I saw you play the accordion. How do I even know you can garden?"

He considered. "I've already been in your backyard. Those weeds are as tall as me, at least six feet."

Raven guffawed. He topped five-eight, maybe less. He kept going as if he didn't hear her.

"And you got a morning glory vine going wild out there. Don't even get me started on the mint. If you want a real garden with peppers and tomatoes and all that shit, you need someone who knows what they doing. I know what I'm doing."

"How?" she asked.

"I've been on landscaping crews all over Louisiana. Temporary. I take those gigs when the music gigs are slow. I can show you pictures if you want. Plus, I know a little bit about everything – plumbing, electrical. I can help with that, too. Be your handyman if you want."

"You have a criminal record?" she asked.

"You know I do," he said. "If you don't, I know you will, because you're going to run a background check on me. I'm trying to turn things around. Second chances and all that."

"I see," Raven said, her mind turning to Willie Lee, who was about to blow his second chance. She dismissed the thought and got back to the conversation. "What will I find in your background check?"

"Not a lot," he said. "Petty theft, disturbing the peace. A few drug charges."

"Using or selling?"

"Both," he said. "But I was never addicted. You ain't going to find nothing big on my record."

Raven nodded. She believed him. And Billy Ray trusted him, or he wouldn't have recommended him.

"Besides, you ain't got shit to steal anyway," he said.

Chapter Twenty-Four

Raven left Gervais at her place, showed him where the gardening tools were and gave him a key in case he needed to use the bathroom or grab some water. Her Android rang as she walked through the glass doors of the Byrd's Landing police department. She answered without bothering to check the caller ID.

"Get naked," a voice said.

"I haven't even had my second cup of coffee. You waited all day yesterday. Can't you wait a few more minutes?" Raven said.

"Nope," Rita Sandbourne said. "Me and Gus have been here for hours. Already autopsied the two headshots, now moving on to Zeke."

Raven's heart sank. She didn't want to see Zeke slit up the middle, his organs removed, and his gray matter exposed. But she reminded herself that Zeke was long gone. What remained was just an empty shell, meat. She wished she was like some cops who didn't attend autopsies. They just read the reports.

Like Stevenson.

But Raven felt that she owed it to her victims to take that final step with them, to be there before earth or the crematorium claimed them. She stopped in the hallway by the window overlooking the parking lot. She realized that she was still holding the phone with Rita on the other end. She could hear her breathing.

"Can I get a pass on this one, Rita?"

"If I have to be here, so do you. Your scrubs are waiting for you in the locker room. Get there, get naked and put them on. You've got ten minutes."

Raven didn't answer.

"I will drag your ass," Rita said. "You know I will."

★ ★ ★

In the locker room Raven undressed and pulled on a pair of scrubs and long plastic gloves. She completed the outfit with a bonnet and a pair of booties. She left the rubber apron on the locker room bench. As with all the autopsies she attended, she didn't plan to get that close.

Raven had seen the aftermath of many killings, the floaters, the decomposed bodies of the elderly who were left to stew in their own juices. She always found a way to focus on the case, the why and who. But the smell of the morgue got to her – disinfectants and bile and guts and shit, an earthy muddy smell that wormed its way into your clothes, your hair, your mouth, the taste lingering for days after.

Raven was now walking toward Rita who was sitting on a stool next to a gurney with a body wrapped in a white sheet.

"Thought you'd never get here," Rita said, tapping on the screen of an iPad.

Raven noticed that the clothes from the other two men found alongside Zeke were on a white sheet covering an otherwise empty gurney. Rita saw her looking.

"I used a UV light on the clothes when they were dry. Thought I might get lucky, find some hair or fibers that the rain didn't wash away."

"You've been lucky before," Raven said.

"We've been lucky before," Rita answered. "You and me. Byrd's Landing's best cop and their most talented necromancer. Not this time. I got nothing."

Raven glanced over at Gus and another morgue technician, who were fiddling with a body in a black body bag. Gus had a Canon camera around her neck.

"Gus is doing the cutting today," Rita said. "She's excited."

Raven said nothing, but she knew Rita couldn't do the autopsy on Zeke as much as Raven couldn't bear to see it.

"Have they X-rayed him, yet?" Raven asked.

"They'll do it in a minute," Rita said.

"Then why did you get me down here so early?" Raven asked.

"Come over here, sunshine," Rita said.

They walked over to Tim where he had placed the pages from Marcel Thibodeaux's notebook onto glass. Most of the markings on the page were faded, almost gone. But on two of them the pen strokes were dark and legible.

Raven pointed at them. "Tell me that these pages were the last ones he wrote in."

"Maybe," Tim said. "But I don't see how they'll do you a lot of good. Can't understand any of it."

Tim was right. The pages they were looking at were filled with symbols and wavy lines instead of letters and punctuation.

"Not shorthand?" Raven asked. "And that has to be the funniest looking 'L' I've ever seen. It looks backward and upside down."

"Definitely not shorthand," Tim said. "My grandmother wrote shorthand, and it looked nothing like this. I compared this writing with other types of shorthand, and came up with nothing."

Floyd would have called Tim a speck of a man you could walk through without so much as a shudder. Tim wore black turtlenecks in the winter and light blue polo shirts with the BLPD forensics badge embroidered on them in the summer. He had to use a black leather belt to hold up his mom jeans on his kid-sized waist. His hair was blond, wispy like a baby's. At one point Raven thought he was going bald, but over the years his hairline hadn't budged. His eyes were light blue, his fingernails pink and clean. He lived alone with a big cat named Buster and had a longtime girlfriend who was a teller at the Byrd's Landing First Central Bank.

But just as Byrd's Landing wrapped scorpions in silk, Raven knew that you didn't want to get on the bad side of Tim. He was serious about his forensic work and could stare down the bloodiest crime scene without blinking.

"I remember this FBI case a while back," Raven said. "They had this murder victim who couldn't read or write the traditional way. He invented his own code for taking notes. The notes were on him when he died. The FBI couldn't make heads or tails out of it, but were convinced that the notes could lead them to the murderer. They even asked the public for help deciphering it, put it out on the internet, and still no one could break the code. True story."

"I'm not surprised," Tim said. "You need to find what the code's based on. It could be anything. It must have driven them crazy."

She stared at the now-dry paper on the glass and thought about Tim's comment. To break the code, you must have something to base it on. But how do you get inside the skull of someone who was dead? You start with the family, but Marcel had no family except for a cousin who pretended he didn't love him so he could avoid the pain of losing him. To complicate matters, the two men who knew him best were dead.

"Would it have driven you crazy?" Raven asked, smiling slightly, knowing how tenacious Tim really was.

A little smile tugged at the corner of his lips as he considered Raven's question.

"For a little while," was all he said.

"Can you crack it?" Raven said.

"Not without a key. It would take a lot of energy and time. Don't rely on this. Find some other evidence," Tim said.

"You telling us this is nothing but a bunch of useless gibberish?" Rita asked.

"I wouldn't call it gibberish just because we can't understand it. It meant something to him," Raven said.

Before Rita could answer, Gus called both Rita and Raven over so they could start the autopsy. Ezekiel Riverton was laid out on Rita's special porcelain autopsy table naked as the day he was born. But instead of being bathed in afterbirth, triangular wounds gaped open on his upper torso. His neck looked like it had been ripped open. Raven took a deep breath as she forced herself to keep her mind on the body, not the soul it once held.

Gus placed an alternate light source at an oblique angle over the body in another effort to find hair or fibers that had escaped the rain. Noticing the skeptical look on Raven's face, Rita shrugged and said, "Worth a try." She pulled a microphone out of the ceiling and started the recording. Raven slowly walked around the autopsy table with her own moleskin notebook open, ready to jot down notes even though she really didn't need them. It was just something to do with her hands. Rita said Zeke's name, age, gender, and circumstances of his death into the microphone. Then she gave a general overview, saying the victim had been stabbed and eviscerated. Zeke's guts were in a plastic bag on the gurney next to his clothes. Rita took out her iPad, punched the screen a couple of times, and handed it to Gus. Raven wondered about this slight girl with the red hair who could look death in the face without flinching. She was doing much better than Rita or Raven. Was it that she didn't know Zeke and didn't care that much, or was it because she didn't care at all?

Raven silenced her thoughts. Rita was talking again, detailing the wounds on Zeke's body, starting at his toes and moving up past his knees, and then his torso, where all the madness started.

"One, two, three, four, five…" Rita continued counting the stab wounds, saying what quadrant they were in, while Gus followed her making marks on the drawing of the man on the iPad. Rita stopped counting and said, "Interesting."

"How?" Raven asked.

Rita stepped closer to the body, bent until she was closer to the stab wounds on Zeke's chest. She stood up. "Not ready to say," she said.

"Well, when you're ready to say, I'm right here. You know, the detective, trying to find out who went crazy on this victim," Raven said.

Rita didn't mention that Raven was no longer calling him Zeke, but shot her a look that said, *Whatever you must do to survive, I'm not fooling with it.*

"Ten stab wounds, a clean-edged knife, most likely a butcher knife. A near-perfect stab wound. If I wasn't right in the head, I'd take a picture, frame it and send it to my mama," Rita said.

"What's that supposed to mean?" Raven said.

Rita smiled at Raven. "You've been with me on plenty of autopsies, Raven. Figure it out before we finish, and I'll buy you a drink."

"I don't know either, so how do I get in on this bet?" Gus said.

"I thought you were a nice churchgoing girl," Rita said. "Drinking and gambling."

"Me? A girl who likes looking at guts and dead bodies and dating conjure men," Gus said.

"Just pay attention to what you are doing, would you? If you and Detective Moody can figure this out before I tell you, I'll buy you both a drink. But for you, my dear, that drink would be a fizzy mocktail," Rita said.

"I'm over twenty-one, you know," Gus said.

"I still think that ID is fake," Rita said.

She grabbed a ruler from the instrument table and measured the perimeter and depth of each stab wound. She rattled off numbers. Gus tapped furiously on the iPad trying to keep up. Finally, Rita went to Zeke's head, which lay on a block. She spent a long time looking at his neck.

"What are you thinking, Rita?" Raven said.

Rita bit her lower lip.

"Come over here to me, Raven. Stop keeping your distance. If you can't look at his wounds, how are you going to watch Gus slit him the rest of the way open?"

Raven walked toward Rita and stood next to her. They both stared at the gaping wound for a long time. It didn't look like a knife wound. It looked like somebody ripped Zeke's neck open.

"What do you see?" Rita asked.

"Severed carotid arteries, trachea cut below the vocal cords. He wouldn't have been doing any screaming," Raven said, her voice clinical.

"You know, you scare the shit out of me when you do that. Not what your dumbass father would see. What do *you* see? What story does this wound tell you besides that it's probably the one that killed our friend?"

"Wound's not clean, it's jagged. He fought hard."

"Yep," Rita said. "His head was twisting all over the place. There are several starter cuts and the killer got blood all over his hands. That's why Zeke's face was covered in blood. The killer was trying to keep him still."

Gus came and stood next to them. She analyzed the wound with her head tilted to the side.

"He must have been strong," Gus said. "Fighting this hard after somebody just stabbed the shit out of him."

And then Raven got it. She looked back at the wounds on Zeke's torso, even the one that opened his guts. The wounds, though bright red, were clean all around. No tearing or jagged edges to suggest that Zeke twisted away from the knife. No swelling or bruises around the wounds, nothing.

"What do you like, whiskey, tequila, or that Abita beer you been drinking with Billy Ray lately?" Rita asked when she saw that Raven got it.

"I want whiskey, top shelf. A shot of Pappy's from Billy Ray's," Raven said.

"Looks like you want to break the bank, but hey, a bet's a bet," Rita said.

"I still don't get it," Gus said.

"Good, my bank account is your new best friend," Rita said.

"Are you two old broads going to clue me in, or have you already forgotten?" Gus asked.

Rita grinned. "See why I hired her? I love a smart mouth."

"The stab wounds are postmortem," Raven said crisply. "The son-of-a-biscuit-eater who did this slit his throat first and then stabbed and eviscerated him. That means it's not a rage killing like we thought. It was purposeful, intentional."

"That doesn't make any sense," Gus said. "Why?"

The air around them seemed to change. Raven couldn't put her finger on it. It wasn't like there was a chill in the air, but she felt something. Eyes staring at her, peering, taking in everything about her on both the inside and outside of her body. The eyes even found Floyd in his white suit and fedora sitting on his milk crate. This wasn't a rage killing. The two murders execution style, the slit throat, the stab wounds postmortem. The killer was sending them a message. Raven would need to find out what that message was if she was going to find him. She looked at Gus, wondering when the fresh-faced girl would regret taking this job.

"Nothing in town makes any sense. Haven't you learned that by now?" Raven said.

Raven's phone vibrated in the pocket of her scrubs. She dropped it while she was taking it out, inadvertently pressed buttons when she picked it up off the floor. A voicemail from the night of the murders played from the speakerphone. It was a butt dial from Billy Ray, one Raven must have missed. Rita paused when she heard it, and so did Gus. But it was Rita who spoke.

"Who was that?" she said. "If I didn't know any better, I'd say that was a death rattle."

Raven ignored her. She was done with Rita's banter today. She walked out of the room, pulling off her bonnet and scrubs. She had all the information she could manage right now. There was no need to stay for the first cut.

Chapter Twenty-Five

A week later Rock buried his cousin in a cypress coffin the color of wheat. Two women ushers in white dresses flanked the coffin in case grief compelled one of the mourners to throw themselves into the open grave.

"Like the pope," Stevenson whispered to Raven.

"What?" she whispered back.

"They buried a couple of popes in cypress caskets. Shows humility," he explained. "Reminds us that death comes for us all."

"Well, I do not approve," Raven said, thinking about a poem she read during her high school days.

"Of cypress caskets?" he whispered.

"Of death."

"I don't get it."

"Forget it. Forgot that the only book you read is the Bible," she said.

Marcel didn't deserve to be dead. He was gone too soon, and she would find who did this to him. His notebooks provided nothing in the way of evidence, but those writings meant something to the man lying in a coffin fit for the pope. She wouldn't throw the pages in the grave with him. Even though Stevenson said she was wasting more time they didn't have, she coerced him into attending the funeral to look for anyone else who might have known Marcel well enough to interpret his writings.

"Are you talking about a poem again?" Stevenson said. "I know some poetry. Is that Langston Hughes?"

"You giving me a headache, Stevenson," Raven said. And then, "Did you call your wife?"

He grinned, rocked back on his heels. "Yes," he said, smiling. "She talked to me."

Before Raven could ask more, a woman with calla lilies rising from a white hat perched on her dark wig turned and shushed them like they were in grade school. Raven moved away until she could barely hear the preacher drone on beneath the boiling Louisiana sun. Stevenson followed and caught up with her under one of the weeping willows at the edge of the graveyard.

"More people than I expected here," Stevenson said.

Raven thought so too, especially for a man with only one blood relative left. Raven tried to shake that eerie feeling that she knew some of them. Not Edmée and her husband, who had his arm around Edmée's waist, or Willie Lee, or Gervais. She of course knew them. She was feeling that she knew others there as well, or should've known them, like the woman with the calla lilies.

The graveside service started to break up. Willie Lee shook Rock's hand, gave him an awkward hug. Raven couldn't believe that Willie Lee had bothered to come to the funeral. Maybe he wasn't so bad after all.

The old woman with the lilies in her hat stumbled over to them on the uneven grass.

"I thought it was you," she said to Raven when she reached her. She pointed a white mesh-gloved finger at her. "I wasn't sure until I saw them eyes, green and blue like the Satan who was your daddy. I'll never forget you or him or them eyes."

Raven kept her face as immobile as a sheet of ice. Her voice was strong and unbothered when she spoke.

"I'm sorry for your loss," Raven said. "What my father did was what my father did. That wasn't me. He's dead, and I'm alive. I haven't killed anybody." *That didn't deserve killing*, she thought, but kept that part to herself.

"You don't know who I am, do you?" the woman said.

"I don't," Raven said.

"I lived on The Hill when you and your daddy moved in. Called himself Floyd Baxter back then. I always thought there was something weird about you and that man, but Ruth, she didn't listen. All she saw was an innocent child who needed tending."

"I don't remember too much about The Hill," Raven said.

"Don't remember or won't remember?" the woman said, her glare baleful.

"A little of both, I guess. It's all pretty hazy."

Before the woman could say more, Stevenson stuck his hand in her face and introduced himself. He promised the woman that he and Raven would bring Marcel's killer to justice. The woman softened a bit.

"I just hope you do," she said. "That boy ain't never hurt nobody for someone to do him like that."

"How do you know Marcel?" Raven asked.

"Like I said, I lived on The Hill right up until the time the city condemned all them houses," she said. "Marcel used to visit us there all the time. Ruthie took a liking to him. Read to him for all the good it done, fed him, tried to teach him some writing, but it didn't do no good. You telling me you don't remember him?"

Raven wasn't about to apologize. No, she didn't remember Marcel. She didn't remember the exact house she lived in. She didn't remember that woman Floyd killed. All she knew was that she and Floyd were there for a while and then gone once Floyd married Miss Jean.

"If you don't remember him, why are you here?" the woman asked.

"We found a notebook that Marcel had on him when he died. It had some writing on it, but it's not anything we can understand. We were hoping that we could find someone who could read it for us. Someone he was close to. May I show it to you?"

"If it'll help find them who done this you go right ahead."

Raven pulled out her phone and showed it to the old woman. The woman took the phone from Raven and brought it close to her face until it touched her nose. She then moved it back, and then held it down by her waist. Squinted at it hard.

"Why, this don't make no kind of sense," she said.

"You can't read it?" Stevenson said.

"It ain't Pig Latin?" the woman said.

Raven reached for her phone. The woman handed it back to her.

"We don't believe it is," Raven said.

"That's not what Miss Ruth showed him. Maybe that's the best he could do. Or he's playing some kind of game with all that chicken scratch," the woman said.

Raven looked back at the gravesite. Gervais was shaking hands with Rock before moving in for a bro hug. She had no idea that he knew Marcel. When he finished, he squeezed Rock's arm and said a few more words. Then he turned and jogged toward them. He kissed the old woman on the cheek when he reached them.

"Gervais," the woman said. "This here lady detective need help figuring out some stuff Marcel wrote."

"You knew Marcel?" Raven asked.

Gervais introduced himself to Stevenson as Raven's handyman. A one-thousand-watt smile lit up his entire scarred face.

"Miss Gladys," he said, taking the woman by her frail shoulders and pointing her in the direction of Marcel's cousin. "Why don't you go say hi to Rock? He's been asking after you."

The woman smiled broadly showing the wolf-white of her false teeth. She stumbled, straightened and started walking toward Rock. When she was out of earshot, Gervais said, "We used to play together when we were kids."

"You mean on The Hill?" Raven asked.

"We mostly played at my house cross town," he said. "I may have gone over there once or twice. I can't remember that far back. We lost touch in junior high. I haven't talked to Marcel in years. I know his cousin now better than I do him. Did you know him? I heard you and Miss Gladys talking. You lived on The Hill?"

"For a time," Raven said. "I don't remember much."

"What y'all doing here?" Gervais asked.

"Business," Stevenson said.

Gervais chuckled. "Cold. I understand, but still cold as hell. You still want me to help you move that furniture in on Saturday?"

"Please," Raven said. "I'm tired of sleeping on an air mattress."

"I get you," he said. "See you at the repast."

Raven watched him saunter off. When he was far enough away, she took out her notebook and wrote his name down.

"You've got to be kidding me," Stevenson said. "Talking about grasping at straws. Why don't you put the old lady's name down too?"

"When straws are all you have, the only thing you can do is grasp away," Raven said, only half-joking. "Let's just see if his alibi checks out. Then I'll leave it alone."

"He barely knew him," Stevenson said.

"That's what he said," she replied.

"Why don't you just check out everybody that came to the funeral? The chief is right, you like wild goose chases. We can't afford wasting time we don't have," Stevenson said.

"Once I find out his alibi is good, I'll move on," she said.

And she would. But something still gnawed at her about that entire interaction. She watched Gervais talk to various people at the funeral. He showed up at Billy Ray's, befriended her brother, and became her handyman within such a short time. He might be a good guy with the gift of gab, but Raven would keep an eye on him. After all, the old saying 'you can't be too careful' was a life-and-death rule in the town of Byrd's Landing.

Chapter Twenty-Six

When they returned from Marcel's funeral it was close to lunchtime. Marna was still at her desk holding an unlit cigarette between her capable brown fingers.

"I know you aren't smoking in here, Marna," Stevenson said.

"I ain't smoking, not yet, anyway," Marna said, not looking up from the file folder she had been perusing when they walked up. She handed the folder to Stevenson.

"Witness statements. Since you might not be smart enough to work on a computer, I printed them out for you," she said.

"You people have no respect," he said.

"Not for out-of-town gate crashers who tried to lock up one of our own," Marna said.

"I'm one of you now," Stevenson said as he took the folder.

"Doubt that," Marna responded.

"Why is it so thin? There must have been over two dozen people at that scene," Raven said.

"Thirty-two, to be exact," Marna said. "And all of them said they ain't heard or seen nothing."

"That's why I'm here," Raven said. "I need some intel on the Old Bottoms."

"No," a gruff voice said.

Raven looked up to see Newell, Marna's groom, strolling over to her desk. His big gut and red handlebar mustache reached them before he did. Newell never liked Raven. He only tolerated her because of Marna. It was a wonder that he didn't search her for stolen silverware every time she left their house.

"Hey, a party," Raven said. "What is it that Billy Ray always say?"

"If I knewed you were coming I'd baked a cake," Newell said. "We heard it, Raven, and it's old."

"No cause for all that," Marna said.

"Remember what happened last time you agreed to help her?" Newell said.

"She made sergeant," Raven said.

When Marna was working intake, she gave Raven unsupervised access to a murder suspect. That thirty minutes Raven spent with Willie Lee cracked the case, and Raven helped Marna study for her sergeant's exam in return.

"Tell you what," Marna said. "I'm due for a smoke break. Let's go out back and you can tell me what you need. You too, Stevenson."

Marna led them to the smokers' pit without saying goodbye to her husband. She sat at one of the stone picnic tables. Raven sat across from her. Stevenson slung a leg over the bench next to Marna and contorted his big body until he was facing the table. Primly, Raven thought, like a little private-school boy. Marna touched a flame from a Bic lighter to the cigarette hanging from her mouth.

"You sure you want to sit next to me?" she said, sending a sidelong glance Stevenson's way. "You're in the secondhand smoke zone."

"I'll survive," he responded. "But every drag you take on one of those things sends you one step closer to the casket."

"At least I'll go calm instead of raving like a bitch. The Marlboro Man steadies my nerves. That man staring at us from the window don't do nothing but tap dance on them from dawn to dusk. I need all the help I can get."

Raven looked toward the building. Sure as midnight, Newell stared at them from the window.

"You two have only been married a little over a year," Raven said.

"The hardest time of my life. Whew, that man smothers me. All this togetherness giving me a headache."

"The first years are the hardest," Stevenson said.

They both looked at him as if he had lost his mind. He went on as if he hadn't noticed.

"It's the adjustment, especially if you didn't live together before," he said.

"I thought you were divorced," Marna said.

"Getting a divorce. Not there yet. Still praying," Stevenson answered.

"Yep," Raven said. "Kiss it up to God. Are you going to tell me how that call went with your wife and kids?"

"Not terrible, but it was rough," he answered.

"What do you want to ask me about, Raven?" Marna said.

"The Old Bottoms," Raven said.

"What about it?" Marna said.

"Everything. How did it come to be? Who runs it. Who lives there and why won't the chief let us near the place?" Raven said.

"You're going to directly disobey his orders?" Stevenson said.

"We've got three murders to clear and not a shred of evidence," Raven said.

"So you want to spend time on a history lesson?" he said. "From what I heard this morning, you need to be looking into your own history. Find out why you can't remember a good chunk of your childhood. That's not normal, Raven."

Raven had dated Stevenson for a reason. His ways may have been ham-fisted sometimes, but she knew that at his core he cared. Sometimes, the more he cared, the rougher his advice became. And his actions. After all, that's why he was sitting here thousands of miles away from his family. He cared about justice. She learned to live with it when they were in a personal relationship. But they weren't in a relationship. Something in her rustled, an old stirring. If Stevenson opened his mouth one more time she'd put a bullet in him. She knew that he saw on her face that she was not only capable, but close. He jumped up from the table. Before he left, he called her a freak and reminded her that she was her father's child.

Marna gave a short laugh and said, "Now that's over, come take a ride with me, Raven."

Chapter Twenty-Seven

Marna drove Raven in one of the newer patrol cars, a Dodge Charger equipped with a Remington 870P shotgun. She guided the cruiser through downtown with the windows down, slowed to wave at people eating on shaded restaurant patios or strolling the bright sidewalks. She had known most of them all her life. In her younger days, she played stickball with some, or street games like Red Light Green Light and What Time Is it Old Fox. For others she ran errands when she was a girl. She got Mama Dale Spark Plug tobacco, and Mr. Elway's Milk of Magnesia from the Fast Mart. Others she arrested once she became a cop for BLPD, including the old man now dipping low in a respectable bow as they passed and the young man giving her a gangster nod. Mr. Robert spent the night in the BLPD jail for drunk and disorderly, the boy for shoplifting.

Once, a long time ago when Raven sat in the chief's office as he snapped that baseball in the air, he made it clear that he wanted Raven to follow in his footsteps. But watching Marna navigate the town she knew better than her own body, Raven understood that the chief had it all wrong. It wasn't Raven who should follow in his footsteps as chief. It was Marna. The only person who could protect this town was someone who belonged to it.

"Where are we going?" Raven asked.

"Just be patient, your highness," Marna said.

A few more miles and they were driving a country road. Eucalyptus trees, stands of birch, red clay and flat water whipped by as Marna picked up speed. She parked at a spot where Raven thought of as nowhere. The street signs were missing at this four-way stop. To the north were weeds and abandoned buildings with burnt-out windows and corners like knife edges.

"This is near the church where we found the bodies," Raven said.

"That's right," Marna said.

"What's with the show and tell?" Raven asked.

"You asked me for information. That's what I'm going to give you. As much as I can but in color."

Marna got out of the car, and Raven followed. Marna put her hands in the pockets of her uniform slacks.

"When I was a young girl before we knew each other, really young, when I thought a slice of Wonder Bread with a little oleo and sugar on it was the shit, this whole area was full of people living in shotgun houses. Black people. Good people lived here. But a lot of bad, too. You'd never see a taxi or a cop car in this neighborhood. They was too scared. And the smell. There used to be a slaughterhouse down here. The stench from offal was so thick you'd feel like you was eating it."

"What happened to the slaughterhouse?"

"Somebody burnt it down. Lot of animals died before they time, a lot of workers, too." Marna nosed the dirt with the tip of her shoe. "Bad people would come out at night, but those who were trying to make an honest living got up every morning and went to work. They'd walk to town or take the jitney. Some folk called it the jitlin."

"Jitney?" Raven asked.

"Think Uber without the computers. People used their private vehicles to give poor people rides to Weingarten's or the Social Security office or court. My uncle had this long green Cadillac that he'd use sometimes. He took me down here with him. I had to ride in the middle with my legs straddling the hump so I didn't take up any moneymaking space."

"Was that legal?" Raven asked.

"Chile, no, but nobody cared. The drivers were willing to risk it to pay for gas or the car note. That was mostly how people got around," Marna said.

Raven looked through the weeds on all sides of her. Even in the daylight they looked creepy as hell, invasive, greedy. "What happened to the houses, and the people here?"

"Before you and your daddy came to town, the city run most of them off. It was funny because the way the Bottoms started was like a controlled experiment."

"Controlled experiment?" Raven asked. "Like rats?"

"You think rats, I think Tuskegee," Marna said. "The city wanted to cut down on crime, so they created a police-free zone. Take the crime out of Byrd's Landing proper, they figured, and put it here where it would be controlled. Whorehouses, numbers runners, gangs, drugs, all legal as long as it's in the Bottoms. The city built that church, the one that almost killed us, thinking that maybe if they had some religion down here, too, it wouldn't get too wild."

"Is that what the chief is doing today?" Raven asked. "Trying to contain crime?"

"I don't know what the fuck the chief is doing. He doesn't check in with me before he does it. I'm just telling you how it was."

Raven nodded. "So, how did the experiment go for them?"

"How do you think? It was like trying to fence the sea. Crime was so bad that people were scared to go out in the dark. They scurried around like bugs from work to home and then back to work again."

"How do you know so much about it?" Raven asked.

"I had a cousin who lived in one of the shacks around here. She used to spend summers with us, but sometimes my mama would let me visit her. Her mama was so paranoid about a stray bullet hitting the house that she lined the walls by her bed with old refrigerators."

God, Raven thought. The depravity of those who tried to stop depravity by shoving people in a corner and hoping that they didn't kill themselves. What did that say about Byrd's Landing?

"How did they run everybody off?" Raven said, turning in a circle.

"When things got too hot, they shut the experiment down. Moved in and arrested everything that moved. Not on any petty charges, either. Big things. Racketeering, drug trafficking, conspiracy. Even the prostitutes were locked up for an inordinate amount of time. There were raids. People disappeared like cotton candy melting in the sun. Angola State Prison stayed busy. Soon it was just buildings and houses left standing.

But the city wanted to knock them down, claiming they were a haven for drug addicts. Saddest part was the kids."

"The kids?"

Marna nodded. "The kids of all the people they sent away. It was too much for Child Protective Services. A lot of them slipped through the cracks. There were a few people that took them in, especially along The Hill before the city condemned the houses there."

"You mean The Hill where I used to live?" Raven said.

"That's right," Marna said.

"What happened to the kids people didn't take in?" Raven asked.

"Most of them didn't make it," Marna said.

"They died?" Raven asked.

"Maybe that would have been better. They started getting mixed up in crime, getting arrested and sent away. It was like Angola was saving seats for them," Marna said.

"What you're telling me is that the cops cleared an entire neighborhood of its people?"

"No, not all. A few of them hung on, refused to leave." Marna stopped. "The mayor called them locusts."

"What happened? Did the city get them out?"

Marna stared at the sun for a few seconds and then started toward the patrol car. "They did. Most of them anyway. Some refused to go, laid low and dug in like crabs. The city tried to push them out, too, but failed."

"Why?" Raven asked, trudging behind her.

Marna just got in on the driver's side and started the engine. Raven got in on the passenger side, and asked again over the blare of the air conditioner.

"Hold your horses," Marna said, the tires of the Charger crunching over the road. "I'm too hungry to talk about this shit now."

Chapter Twenty-Eight

When they entered Chastain's Creole Heaven, Marna made a beeline toward the old folks' corner. Judging by the evil eye from most of the old heads around the table, including Mr. Joe, who favored Raven for what he called her 'hot bod', none of them were pleased by the interruption, especially when Raven loudly pulled out one of the empty chairs and sat down next to Mama Anna.

"Y'all ain't old enough to sit at this table," Mr. Bello said. He was a computer operator who used to work at Standard Oil. Being the youngest of the group, even his being at the table was tolerated.

"Especially dressed up like Marcus Garvey," Mr. Walter said, an old gray head with bushy eyebrows.

"I ain't dressed up like Marcus Garvey," Marna said. "I'm dressed up like a police officer for this great city."

"I don't like cops," Mr. Walter said. "Even ones whose diapers I've changed."

"Raven's a cop, and you used to let her sit here," Marna said.

"She's special," Miss Vera said. She fiddled with the gold cross around her neck, making sure it wasn't tangled with the leather-strap necklace she wore. "She used to work here."

"She gave us free food," Mr. Walter agreed.

"Besides, she got a nice ass," Mr. Joe said.

Marna looked highly offended. "I ain't got a nice ass?" she asked.

"Nobody can see your ass because of that damn tool belt you wear," Mr. Joe said.

"Why don't you go ahead and show us. We'll rate it one to ten," Mr. Walter said, cackling.

"Shut up, you ole dunderheads," Mama Anna said. "Leave these babies alone. They more than welcome to join us for lunch."

"We already had lunch," Mr. Joe said.

"Then they can watch me shellac your bony ass at spades. Again," Mama Anna said.

Marna ignored them. A young server came over with two menus, single pages on thick paper. Marna waved them away. She ordered two lamb stews and a diet Coke for herself. She told her that Raven was paying.

As Marna soaked up the last of the stew broth with the spongy ciabatta that was one of the things that made Chastain's special, she said, "This one wants to know about the Old Bottoms."

Mama Anna stopped shuffling cards. Miss Vera's hand left the cross she had been fiddling with since they arrived. Mr. Bello dropped the menu on the table as if it had bit him.

"Come on, now," Mr. Joe said.

"There are some things that just shouldn't be talked about," Miss Vera said as she adjusted her eyeglasses. "That man there is evil." She trembled as if he were in the next room.

"Evil," Raven said. "I heard he was helping the homeless."

"Keeping them prisoner, more like it," Miss Vera said. "When someone tries to leave, their body parts end up scattered all over town. I hear he feeds those he especially dislikes to the alligators."

"Cut it out," Mama Anna said. "Ya'll just slandering, now."

"I'm sure the chief wouldn't let that happen," Raven said.

Mama Anna choked on the water she had been drinking. Mr. Joe had to thump her on the back, Raven thought a little too hard. Probably trying to get her back for beating the crap out of him at spades.

"Fine. If you're going to make us talk about that clown Lucien Toussaint, call that waitress over so we can get some more food. Raven, you paying for this one, too. Get out your pocketbook," Mama Anna said.

Raven didn't bother to tell them that she didn't carry a pocketbook, or a purse. But she waited without saying a word or pulling out her phone while they all ordered from the appetizer menu. Most of them ordered water or soda, but Mr. Joe ordered a neat whiskey. He laughed while he did it, told the waitress to put it in a clean glass, not one of the secondhand ones that Billy Ray favors. Raven ordered a beer, not because she wanted it, but because she needed all the help she could get if she was going to hear a story from the old folk. The server left and soon came back balancing plates of fried green tomatoes, pickles and okra. A busboy trailed behind her with the drinks. She put the food down on the table, making a wide berth around Mr. Joe. No one talked until she left. They even remained silent as they dug into the food. Raven drank the Abita she had ordered.

"Drinking on the job?" Mr. Joe asked her.

"You'd be drinking, too, if you had my job. By the way, I'm not paying until you old people spill."

"You should have got the info first," Mr. Joe said.

"You ever heard of dine and dash?" Raven said. "I'll be out of this mother—"

"Hey," Miss Vera said. "The Lord is listening."

"Thought you didn't cuss..." Mama Anna said.

"...trucker," Raven said. "I was going to say mother-trucker."

"Just stop screwing around and tell her what you know," Marna said.

Mr. Joe leaned back and balanced his chair on the two back legs. He took a deep breath. "When Lucien Toussaint was born, he almost split his mama in two."

Mama Anna pushed his shoulder. The chair fell forward to the floor with a thump.

"You don't have to go back that far, you ole fool," she said.

Raven turned to Marna. "You hate me. That's why you brought me here."

"I brought you here because I was hungry and wanted a free lunch. I'm taking the second stew home for me and Newell's dinner. But listen up, they ain't finished," Marna said.

Raven stared at her, a good ole Floyd stare that usually drove people from the room. Marna wiped her greasy fingers with a balled-up napkin and laughed.

"Hey, I got a wedding to pay off. Meat to buy for my smoker. Newell's already climbing my frame about how much money I'm spending," Marna said.

"Y'all old people need to stop," Mama Anna said. "The gossip around that man's turning him into some kind of god. He's not. I have it on good authority that his mama was still in one piece after giving birth to him."

"How did he get to take over an entire part of town?" Raven asked.

"I'm getting to that," Mama Anna said.

"His mama and daddy were real good folk," Miss Vera said. "A praying people."

"His father was a deacon," Mama Anna said.

"They didn't want for money either," Mr. Joe said, pounding his chest to make the chunks of fried okra he had been stuffing into his face go down. He reached for his water glass only to find it empty. Then the whiskey glass, but not a drop was left. Raven had her beer halfway to her lips. He snatched it from her hands and drank it down, muttering something about an emergency.

"No, they didn't," Mama Anna agreed. "His mama was a teacher and the daddy had a good job. I don't remember where, though."

"They wanted to send him to college," Miss Vera said. "He got into Tulane or some such but got kicked out. Might as well had thrown his folks' money into a woodchipper."

"That's because he started smelling himself way too early. Thought he was grown," Mr. Joe said.

"Whatever, Joe. Anyway, he slinked back home with his tail between his legs but wouldn't get a job," Mama Anna said.

"Thought he was too good for one," Mr. Joe said after he finished off Raven's beer. She hoped he caught cooties from drinking after her.

"What?" he said, seeing how she was looking at him. He tipped the empty bottle of Abita at her. "You shouldn't be drinking anyway. You on duty."

"Lord have mercy, Joe. Would you stop interrupting me? You giving me indigestion. Anyway," Mama Anna said again, her eyes daring him to break in just one more time, "they put up with his pitiful self for as long as they could. Then his daddy kicked him out on the streets."

"I saw where that was headed," Raven said.

"It was when he killed somebody," Miss Vera said in a prim voice. "That was the real surprise, especially him coming from a good family and all."

"Aw hell, Vera," Mama Anna said. "He ain't kill nobody. He was just with the men who did it. Law said it didn't make no difference. They all went up to Angola together."

"That drove him the rest of the way crazy," Mr. Joe said.

"What do you mean?" Raven asked.

"He found God," Mr. Joe said, and winked.

"He's a religious freak," Raven said.

Miss Vera slapped both hands against the table. "The only religion that boy abide by is his own. What he preaches only has a passing relationship with the Bible. He's his own god and devil, if you ask me."

"Ain't nobody asked you," Mr. Joe said.

"Shut up, Joe," Mama Anna said. "I don't know what he does or doesn't believe in, but he sees himself as a leader of that community."

"Him and the two who got out of jail with him," Mr. Joe said. "Moon Pie and Cherry Bomb."

"Moon and Terry," Mama Anna said. "God bless it, Joe."

"So, he has a posse?" Raven asked.

"Yes," Mama Anna said. "They love Lucien so much that they'll lick his shitty drawers if he asked them to."

"Language, Anna!" Miss Vera admonished.

"So how did he take over the Old Bottoms?" Raven asked for what she thought of as the gazillionth time.

"When he and the other boys got out of prison, his mama wouldn't take him in. She said he wasn't her son. That he had traded places with her son in prison," Mr. Joe said.

Raven covered her face with her hands. She sighed deeply and let them fall in her lap.

She looked over at Marna.

"I know," Marna said. "It just keeps getting curiouser and curiouser."

"Her mind was gone," Mama Anna said. "She had Alzheimer's. Lucien moved into one of those abandoned houses down by the water.

In the daytime you'd see him walk up and down the streets all day long looking for a job."

"Excepting nobody would hire him because he's a murderer," Mr. Joe said.

"He ain't shot nobody," Mama Anna said.

"Might as well have," Miss Vera said.

Mama Anna rubbed her eyes and took a deep breath. "He took to preaching. I think to make a living."

Raven sucked in her own breath at hearing this. He took to preaching like her father, Floyd. His word though, not God's. But the difference was, Mama Anna was saying, that Toussaint was a street preacher who believed everything he was saying down to his marrow.

"What did he preach?" Raven asked.

"A lot of nonsense from what I heard," Miss Vera said.

"Like what?" Raven asked.

"Root work," Miss Vera said. "Hoodoo from Africa and slavery times."

"Even though hoodoo ain't a religion, he convinced some of the people living on the street to go down there to the Bottoms with him," Mama Anna said. "People who didn't have money to find a place to live, and others who didn't have the good sense God gave a goose. Pretty soon they hammering and nailing and planting and all of a sudden, it's a community."

"Why don't people like to talk about it?" Raven asked.

"It's embarrassing," Mr. Bello said, his voice deep and regretful. "We can't take care of our own, but some fresh-faced, hoodoo-preaching convict can? Besides, you can't throw a rock without hitting somebody who has a relative living over there."

"Well, if Maybelline has her way, he won't be there for long," Miss Vera said.

"What has Miss May got to do with anything?" Raven asked.

"Miss May loves to litigate," Mr. Joe said. "I calls her Miss May the Litigator. Lucien had convinced the city to rent him the place for a dollar a year, especially since he was taking care of a lot of folk. Miss May didn't like that."

"How so?" Raven asked.

"She likes houses more than people, or ain't you heard?" Mama Anna said. "She didn't cotton to what Lucien was doing to the houses. She hired a lawyer to get the place claimed an historical site. Said they should turn it over to her so she could keep it up. The city agreed, but wanted to give Lucien and them time to find another place to live. He got a year left on the lease. After that, the land, the houses, the gardens, everything goes to Miss May. And she was so proud of Zeke for getting clean, she promised that he could do whatever he wanted with it."

"That boy Zeke was trying to pull away from her, realized that she wasn't no kind of mama. She couldn't have that. It was a bribe, pure and simple," Mr. Bello put in.

Raven wasn't surprised at the new information. Her gut told her that Lucien was involved somehow in Zeke's death. Mama Anna's revelation put her one step closer to proving it. Raven leaned over the table.

"You say he's killing people who try to leave?" Raven asked.

"He ain't killing nobody," Mama Anna said. "That's just people being stupid."

"He seems to have this town wrapped around his little finger," Raven said. "Y'all don't talk about him unless somebody makes you. It's almost like he's a secret. What does he have on the chief?"

The table went quiet. Everyone stopped chewing. They looked away, except Mama Anna. She stared right into Raven's eyes before pushing the check toward her.

"We gave you information, you pay the check," she said.

Raven stared back at Mama Anna. The old woman's eyes reminded Raven that she wasn't from Byrd's Landing, just an interloper who came to town with a father who sowed misery on the regular. It didn't matter that Raven had spent most of her adult life trying to fix it.

"Lucien ain't killed nobody," Mama Anna said again. "I hear he's a harsh leader, but he keeps people safe. Some of those people are our families. We may joke around, say a lot of stuff, but that man is a hero. You should be throwing him a parade instead of trying to throw him back in jail."

Raven leaned forward, caught the old woman's gaze and held it. "And if he murdered three people?"

Mama Anna didn't move for a long moment. If anything, she leaned in closer to Raven as if to raise the stakes of the challenge. Raven knew the woman had daughters. She wondered for the first time what a younger Mama Anna was like, and how she responded to sass from her children. There was probably a raised hand, a quick slap, some pain involved. The server came to the table asking how everything was in a cheerful, sunny voice. The spell broke.

Mama Anna plucked a fried pickle from a sky-blue platter and popped it into her mouth. After she swallowed it down, she said, "Lucien ain't murdered nobody, even the one he done time for. Now go on, both of you. You giving me a headache."

Chapter Twenty-Nine

When Raven walked into the station a couple of days later, she nodded to the duty officer and grabbed two coffees from the breakroom. With the coffee in hand, she stopped by Marna's desk and handed one to her.

"Black?" Marna asked, accepting the cup.

"Is there any other kind?" Raven replied.

Marna took a sip. "Why you being nice to me today?"

"Why are you here so early?" Raven asked.

Marna grunted, but didn't say anything.

"Just stopping by to see if you checked out Gervais Armstrong's alibi," Raven said.

"I did last night while I was having dinner at Chastain's. I'm expensing it, by the way," she said.

"As you always do. What did he say?" Raven asked.

"He had jokes. When I asked him where he was when Zeke and them were killed, he said, 'Random much?' I tried to tell him that it was routine, but he blamed you for siccing me on him."

"I'm sure you covered for me, sis," Raven said, smiling.

"I told him that we were checking out all the folks from the funeral and I wanted to talk to known associates. I said that it was all me, and you had nothing to do with it. I know he's doing some work for you. Didn't want bad blood between y'all."

"So, did he have an alibi?" Raven pressed.

"He said he was at Chastain's with the band in an after-hours jam session. The band members vouched for him. Unless he can be in two places at once, he ain't had nothing to do with the murders. He's a smartass, though, with that scarred-up face and pretty smile."

Raven chuckled. "How do you mean?"

"He dedicated a song to me, Al Green's 'Let's Get Married Today'. Sang it A Capella in this sweet voice that'd make a weak person cry and say yes."

"But not you?" Raven asked.

"You kidding me? One husband is enough. Why you think I'm working late and coming in early?"

* * *

After she left Marna's desk, Raven walked past the windows of the command center on her way to Cameron's office. Through the murder room's window, she could see Stevenson jabbing a fist into the air in victory. She pushed down the temptation to see why he was so stoked because she needed to see Cameron.

She kept walking until she reached her foster brother's office, a space only slightly tidier than Ozy's junkyard on the rim of town. She opened the door and weaved her way past gutted computers and big dusty monitors that hadn't had a home since the nineties to Cameron's desk. He didn't hear her coming because of the expensive headphones clamped over his ears. He sang along to Wu-Tang's 'C.R.E.A.M.' while his eyes darted back and forth over the screen. He had no idea she was there standing over him like a ghoul. She pulled an earphone from one of his ears, and blew. He jumped a mile and almost fell from his chair. He ripped the headphones from his ears.

"Damn, girl!" he said. "What's that you said about being professional at work?"

She laughed, moved a pile of computer manuals from a wheeled chair and sat down. She spun around a few times, enjoying the spin and the playful mood Cameron always put her in.

"Whatcha got?" she said.

He looked at her with wide eyes. "You do realize that it ain't been long since you asked me for this shit."

"I know, and I also know you're amazing, and have a lot of friends. So, give it up, buttercup."

"There you go," he said. "With that creepy one green eye and one blue eye on me, looking like your bio daddy talking about giving it up. He still hanging out in your nightmares." He booed like a ghost. She slapped him upside the head but not so it'd hurt.

"Stop it. I got it all, okay?" he said.

"Gervais Armstrong?" Raven asked. "You check his social media and background like I asked you?"

"I don't see why you don't leave a brother alone," Cameron said. "Dude's not on social media. I did come up with some shoplifting charges and an assault from a fight in a bar over ten years ago. Stuff you should probably get a timeout for, not jail time."

"Good to know. Phone records for all three victims? Social media as well? Cell phones that pinged in the area?"

"Everything you requested, my Black queen. I had to beg, steal, and promise cheat codes that I don't give up lightly to a dude at the phone company. Not to mention a date with cross-eyed Kayla from Meta."

She slapped him again. "Ow! What was that for?"

"Kayla. I'm defending her from your smart mouth," she said. "What did you find?"

He wheeled around to face the computer. He waved her closer to him until she could smell sour gummies on his breath. He typed in his password and a web of lines popped up on the screen.

"What am I looking at?"

"A pattern analysis," he said. "See all the lines going to this point here? That number got action from all three of our vics."

"Victims," she corrected. "People with lives. You need to stop watching cop shows."

"You got it, sis," he said. "Marcel and Zeke and Lionel. Anyway, this tells me that all three of them called this number. A lot."

"A friend or killer. At least somebody that they were involved with. Who's at that other number?" she asked.

"It's a burner phone," Cameron said. "Whoever owns it knows his tech."

"What do you mean?" Raven asked.

"People get careless with burner phones. They return a message left on a burner using their known phone number. Or they might get a call on a burner, and then use their known phone to call another person involved in whatever shenanigans they are. They also carry around their burner with their known phone and they ping off the same tower. All those correlations can show up in the pattern analysis, and usually we can make a guess as to who owns the burner."

"But that doesn't happen here?" she asked.

"Nope, whoever owns that burner phone ain't stupid. Maybe he watches a lot of cop shows, too," Cameron said. "Instead of using his known phone number to call back, looks like he uses the same burner. Can't get a good correlation between the location of the burner and a real phone number, either. Dude's extra cautious."

"Do you know who the burner belongs to?" Raven asked.

"Used the name Ismael Reed for the burner," he said.

"The poet?" Raven asked.

"Yeah, that 'cowboy in the boat of rah' motherfucker," Cameron said. "The one you drove me crazy reciting all over the house when we were in high school."

"So you got nothing?" Raven asked.

"Not quite. There's our girl, Lois Wareham," he said. "Her phone was in the area. I already talked to the big dummy, your old boyfriend…"

"Stevenson?" Raven asked.

"Yeah, he called me before the sun woke up," he said.

That explained why Stevenson was punching the air earlier. That meant Lois moved higher on their suspect list. First the bandaged hand, then the lie, now her phone pinging off the tower near the murder scene. But Raven still wasn't convinced.

"There's other shit, Raven," Cameron said. Before he could continue, Stevenson burst into the room full of energy and purpose.

"Don't you knock, man?" Cameron asked.

"Did you tell her?" Stevenson said.

"Part of it," Cameron said

Stevenson looked around for a place to sit but couldn't find one. Cameron smirked. Stevenson sat on the corner of Cameron's desk.

"Man, get your ass off my desk," he said.

"I wouldn't have to sit on your desk if you'd clean this dump up," Stevenson said.

"This dump is going to save our lives one day," Cameron said.

"How's that?" Stevenson asked.

"When the singularity hits, and the machines decide to roll, I'm going to use this shit to fight."

"You're as nutted up as your sister," Stevenson said.

"Come back and tell me that when you can't start your car, get into your smart home, access your bank account, and you sweating your ass off when the machines won't turn on your AC."

"You serious?" Stevenson asked.

"He's messing with you, Stevenson, trying to get you to leave. Stop it, Cameron," Raven said.

"Still trying to figure out what you saw in him in the first place. Gullible as hell. So caught up in pleasing the man that I bet he still refers to Muhammad Ali as Cassius Clay," Cameron said.

"Cameron," Raven said.

He held his hands up. "Okay, don't shoot."

Stevenson looked mad enough to spit. Raven chuckled. Cameron picked up two file folders from his desk. He gave one each to Raven and Stevenson.

"What's this?" Raven asked.

"All the phones that pinged in the area during the timeframe you gave me," Cameron said.

"This has to be as illegal as hell," Stevenson said. "We don't even have a warrant, yet."

"Why do you think I'm only giving you hard copies?" Cameron said. "I'll take it back if you afraid it'll fuck up your already fucked-beyond-hope integrity. You being the same person who pretended to like my sister so you could put her in jail."

Cameron tried to snatch the printouts but Stevenson was quick enough to move them out of reach. "I already apologized more times than I care to count for that," he said.

Raven ignored them both. She skimmed the list. There was another name she recognized on it aside from Lois. Diamond Riverton, Zeke's brother. She looked up and caught Stevenson's eye. His face was as grim as she was sure hers was. And there was Floyd in her head saying, *Well, well, well, seems like you don't know a person until you know.*

Chapter Thirty

She wanted to meet at Chastain's Creole Heaven. Diamond insisted on Miss Molly's, a juke joint at night and restaurant during the day, a place where the prices went up when the rent was due or a bill needed paying. Miss Molly's shack was all but falling down, the yard weed choked and gravel pitted. The interior was dim and the tables small. Miss Molly's placed them along the walls to make sure one was not in hearing distance of the other. Her eatery was a place where everyone minded their own business so you could do yours in peace.

Raven stepped onto the porch and rang the buzzer. Miss Molly required visitors to her place to do so. Her living quarters were on the premises, and it was still her home, after all.

"Who that?" a voice crackled behind the door.

"Raven, Miss Molly."

The lock twisted and the door opened. The old woman waddled aside to let Raven in. The place smelled of bacon fat and biscuits.

"He over there," she said. She pointed a gnarled finger to a corner by the old woodstove. But Raven had already seen him. It brought back so many memories, even those that reminded her of why she left him. She left him because he was too full of ideas, of plans, of strategies and tactics to become somebody. He devoted every breath in his body to getting to someplace better, be it more money, more cars, more houses, more stuff, what the old folk called 'the getting place'. She left him because sometimes she was afraid that if she touched him too forcibly, he would burst like an overripe tomato from all of his ambitions.

"Come on in. Ain't got a lot of stuff cooked yet. Diamond already got coffee. You want some? Orange juice or soda?"

"No, I'm fine. How you doing?" Raven asked.

"I'm upright so I'm all right. Only thing is the hip's bad. Hurts some." She turned away before Raven could ask more questions.

Raven's boots made a hollow sound as she walked toward Diamond's table. He gazed at her as she sat down across from him. He looked dressed to kill. Floyd used to call it dressed for the grave. He wore a lavender suit jacket and a white shirt that glinted in the dimness of the restaurant. A thick gold bracelet encircled his wrist.

"You were at the crime scene," Raven said, as she sat opposite him.

"Good morning to you, too," Diamond said.

The buzzer rang. Miss Molly May shuffled to the door and said, "Who that?" before letting in two men in sanitation uniforms and work boots. She sat them at a table on the other side of the room, close to the kitchen and well out of earshot.

Raven watched them sit down and then returned her gaze to Diamond. "You lied. That makes you a suspect."

"I didn't lie," he said.

"Don't try that 'you never asked me' bull crap," Raven said. "What were you doing there, Di?"

"Lois calls me that. And my mama," he said. "I don't like it."

"You know Lois?" Raven said. "After claiming at your mama's that you didn't know Zeke had a girlfriend."

"I never said I didn't know," he countered. "She assumed."

"You didn't say anything, and you looked surprised. Even sounded surprised when I called and told you Zeke was dead. All that 'what happened to my brother' nonsense."

He hunched over his coffee cup, holding it tight with both hands. Onyx and diamond ring, fresh manicure, all that show but he hung on to that coffee cup as if he were afraid someone would try to take it from him.

"I hadn't, I mean I didn't know what to say. You called. I already knew, yes, but I was so surprised hearing from you that I just froze. By the time I had realized what I had done, it was too late to take it back."

"You mean by the time you shot Zeke's friends in the back of the head and then cut your brother's throat?" she said.

"You know me, Raven," he said. "I could never kill anyone, especially not Zeke."

"You do realize you didn't answer the question," she said.

"I didn't kill Zeke. Stop acting like you don't know me. We had something, Raven."

He reached for her hand. She pulled it away.

"You lied."

He choked out a frustrated laugh. "Yeah, I did. Lying liars gonna lie. Remember when you used to tell me that every single time I caught you in one? But that doesn't make me a killer."

"What were you doing there?" Raven pushed.

He told her that Lois Wareham had called him. "We knew each other before she started dating my brother. We have similar interests."

"Similar interests?" Raven asked.

"That has nothing to do with this," he said. "She said she was worried about Zeke but couldn't stay. She had some other business in the neighborhood that she needed to attend to."

"You mean business with Lucien Toussaint?" Raven said.

Miss Molly made her way toward their table. Her gait was slow, and one foot dragged across the uneven wooden floor. After a few words back and forth with Diamond, he ordered a breakfast of bacon, grits, fried eggs and more black coffee and ice water. Raven didn't order anything. Diamond answered Raven's question when Miss Molly left.

"I don't know if she had business with Toussaint, but I could tell she was worried about something, scared. I told her I would swing by to make sure Zeke was okay."

"Did she say who Zeke was meeting in the Old Bottoms?" Raven asked.

"She didn't know. She asked him but he wouldn't tell her. She thought it had something to do with you," he said.

"Me?" Raven asked. "How could it have something to do with me. I hadn't talked to Zeke in months."

"I know. He told Lois that someone was coming for you. He called you, texted. When you ghosted him, he said that it was up to him to make sure you stayed safe," Diamond said.

Raven looked up in time to see the loaded plates Miss Molly carried toward their table tumble from her hands. Ceramic along with food shattered against the floor. Miss Molly swore. A young girl with French braids ran into the room from the kitchen carrying a bucket. The sanitation workers flew out of their seats. They stooped and helped Miss Molly and the girl deposit the broken pieces into the plastic bucket. Diamond stood as if to go join them. Raven eyed him until he sat back down.

"That's nonsense," Raven said. "He was delusional. No one's coming for me. And if they were, how in the hell did Zeke think he could help me?"

"He knew a lot of people. Maybe he got wind of something," Diamond said.

But what? Raven couldn't fathom.

"What time did Lois call you?" Raven asked.

"Like I said, late," he said. "I had some things to do."

"Meaning you were on a date," she said.

"Yes. I called Zeke a couple of hours later. He didn't answer. I tried calling him a few times, really. When I still didn't get an answer, I jumped in my car and rolled out there."

"In your gold BMW," she said. "Nobody saw you?"

"I have another car I use for things like that," he said. "Less conspicuous."

"You sure you got the time right and you didn't get there just as you heard shots fired?"

"Why would I lie about that, Raven?"

"Maybe you heard the shots from the churchyard, knew that something bad was happening to your brother but was too cowardly to go check it out yourself. So, you called it in and ran."

He said nothing for a few moments. "Did you see my number calling 911 in the phone records?"

"Maybe you used a burner," she said. "You still like poetry, Diamond?"

He huffed a laugh. "What the fuck does that have to do with anything? You trying to throw me off? And why would I use a burner?"

"I don't know," she said. "You tell me."

"Look, Raven. By the time I got there, the place was surrounded by cops. Yellow police tape everywhere. Reporters. I saw the morgue van and then I knew it wasn't good, but I was holding out hope that Zeke was okay. I was genuinely surprised when you called telling me he was dead."

Raven used to know when he lied. But much time had passed since she had last seen him. She didn't know him anymore, and worse, she didn't know what to believe. She wondered about he and Lois's similar interests.

"Who gets Zeke's money now that he's dead?" she asked.

"You don't think I killed my brother for money?"

"Who? I'll find out anyway."

"Me and mama," he said. "And it doesn't mean a thing. I have enough money of my own."

"How much will you get?" she pressed.

"About a million and a half. From when we sued the city over the land they took from my family. And then there is the Old Bottoms, but I'm sure you already know about that."

"I do," she said. "Miss May will get that land once Toussaint's lease is up. Is that what this is about?"

"That land is worthless. Plus, I don't give a shit about those houses," Diamond said.

His left eye jumped, a nervous tic he had evidently not been able to conquer.

"You're lying again," she said.

He spread his hands. "I don't know what else you want me to say."

"Insurance policy?"

"Yeah, I guess. I mean, come on, Raven, you know Black folk. We'd ensure the dog if we could get his paw print."

She raised her eyebrow, waited for a real answer.

"I don't know how much, okay?" he said. "Mama has a policy on us both she took out a long time ago, when we were teenagers. She made us beneficiaries on each other's policies. I'm guessing a couple of hundred thousand dollars."

"This doesn't look good," Raven said.

"You don't think I know that?" he said.

"How's business, Diamond?"

He didn't say anything. In the silence Miss Molly walked out to them with new plates of food to replace the ones she dropped. She was breathing hard and limping. Raven got up to help her, but the woman waved her off. When she finally got to the table, she said, "Y'all ready to eat?"

She set Diamond's loaded plates down, and gave Raven a glass of ice water even though Raven hadn't asked for anything. When the woman left, Diamond started fussing over the food.

"Answer my question," Raven said. "You said you had enough money without Zeke's inheritance. But you also like things that glitter. Are you liquid?"

"Business is good," he said. "Could always be better. Most of the cash is tied up, but we have a promising investment opportunity coming up, and we're expanding. We're not hurting."

"You don't have to talk to me like I'm one of your investors," Raven said.

"And you don't have to talk to me like a cop, but here we are," Diamond said.

"How long you've been back in town?"

"A few weeks," he said. It wasn't lost on her that he hadn't called her.

"You staying?" she asked.

"No," he said. "Maybe."

"You didn't visit your mother or Zeke all that time?" she asked.

"Me and Zeke didn't always see eye to eye. Why don't you answer that other question for your damn self," Diamond said.

"Why are you in town?" she said.

"Business," he answered. "Confidential."

She leaned forward as he shoved a forkful of grits into his mouth. Too full, she thought, and here he was trying to shove more things into his body, and his pockets. When was enough money, enough jewelry and fancy cars sufficient to prove that you lived, that you mattered?

"Confidential, huh?" she said. "Let me tell you what's not confidential. You are now officially a suspect in this case. I'd tell you to get a lawyer, but I'm sure you're already going to do that if you don't have one already. If you did kill Zeke, Marcel and Lionel…" She ignored his groan. "If you did kill them, I'm going to find out and bury your lying behind right beside them. It'll be in a pauper's grave with no headstone, where no one will ever visit. No one in this town will ever know your name. They'll forget you ever existed."

"Come on, Raven. I'm still the same man, the one you dated, went on trips with, and was in love with. Was that all an act? I mean I'm the guy you wanted to spend the rest of your life with."

"I know," Raven said. "That's what scares me."

Chapter Thirty-One

After talking with Diamond, Raven spent the afternoon in the air-conditioned cool of BLPD, digging with the rest of the team. Raven told them why Diamond said he was at the scene. Marna reread witness statements. She called in favors to find out more about Diamond's business in Byrd's Landing. Cameron secured and then scoured the financials for Diamond's development company, which was called Bet on the Future. They specialized in transforming blighted strip malls into shops and eateries. One they owned in Bossier City had a quaint shop that sold crystals, another specialized in gargoyles, and still another sold rare hoodoo roots, books and spells. Cameron learned that Diamond didn't exactly lie about the business. They were doing all right, but if the promising investment opportunity Diamond mentioned didn't come through as Diamond had hoped, the business would cross the divide between all right into big trouble.

Stevenson and Marna argued for bringing both Lois and Diamond in, and were pushing both Raven and Cameron. Marna wanted to get a confession just like they did on the cop shows. Cameron and Raven advocated for building a case. It was well after eight at night when they settled back in their chairs in the murder room. Everyone was exhausted and looked it. Except Stevenson. He had a wide smile on his face.

"What you so happy about?" Cameron asked.

"If I tell you, will you kill my vibe?" Stevenson asked.

"Absolutely not," Cameron said. "I'd be just glad that somebody has a vibe, a happy one at that, even it is you. That's how hard up I am."

"Appreciate that. I think," Stevenson said. He had been eating a bag of chips and now wiped his greasy hands down the front of his shirt. Raven was bemused because usually he wasn't so laid back.

"Talked to my wife again for hours last night, even ran out of batteries. She's willing to take me back. We're going to try to make it work," he said.

Raven smiled, the first time she felt like smiling in days. Marna gave Stevenson a high-five, and Cameron congratulated him, told him to not screw up because he never wanted to see his ugly face again. Stevenson nodded, grinning through it all. He was happier than Raven had ever seen him.

"Does that mean you're leaving us?" Raven asked.

"As soon as the case is over," he said. "I don't want to leave you hanging."

"Motherfucker, we can handle it," Cameron said. "Why don't you leave tonight. I'll help you pack."

The chief stuck his head in the door and told them to go home, get refreshed and hit it hard tomorrow.

When Raven got home, she walked into a house that looked like someone lived in it. Gervais had helped her find furniture for the empty rooms by doing something she hated: shopping. He even agreed to visit furniture stores and send her pictures via text messages. She remembered when he gave her a handwritten list on yellow legal paper of potential stores one morning while they stood at the kitchen counter.

"What's this?" Raven asked.

"All the furniture stores we should hit," Gervais said.

"You mean *you* should hit. I can't understand any of this, though," she said. "I never heard of Lizard furniture."

"That don't say 'lizard'," Gervais said. "That says Levi's. You can find some cheap shit there. I thought we'd hit that for the bric-a-brac. You know, the pretties."

She turned toward him and gave him a long look. "Do I look like someone who scatters accessories or what you call pretties all over the place?"

"What you look like is fucking scary to me," he said. He looked closer at the note. "I get my words and letters mixed up sometimes. They say that's how my brain thinks. That's why I rode the short bus in school."

"So, dyslexia?" Raven asked. "Words inverted, backward letters. Looks a mess, Gervais."

He grabbed the paper and crumpled it up. "Thank you for making me feel like shit. I got hit in the head a lot when I was a kid. Could be anything."

She shrugged into her jacket. "Leave me a voicemail. Say it instead of trying to write it."

He flipped her off as she walked out the door. She smiled. They were getting along just fine. The man didn't have bad taste. She told him what to buy. He rented a truck, and the two of them carried the furniture in, her laughing at him for carrying a leather chair into the wide front door all by himself, his scared face like a crab peeking from under its shell.

Now all decked out with furniture, the place started to feel like home, her home. After she showered and got ready for bed, she sat on the porch and searched the velvet night for a long time. Instead of hearing the leaves whisper in the wind, she heard Diamond's voice. *He was trying to protect you*, he said. But from what? She asked the trees, the night, the yellow moon. She left the porch and went back into the house, locked the door. She opened a window to let the breeze in before climbing into bed.

Sleep claimed her in seconds, sleep and dreams of Floyd.

Chapter Thirty-Two

Floyd

Them two cops, that Early Sawyer and Victor Broussard, waited for Raven to explain why she disagreed with her old man about Mrs. Jefferson's name. Floyd got up and crossed the room. He sat down in the seat of that big chair that Raven perched on. He took hold of her hand and squeezed hard.

"My daughter and the dead woman were pretty close," he said.

"But not you and Miss Jefferson," Sawyer said.

"Me and her didn't get along too good," Floyd said. "She did things that I wasn't raised to do. She ate while walking around. Home training say you eat at a table. She never wore no shoes, her feet just as black and bare as a freshly tarred road. Still, up and down The Hill she went ordering everybody around like a fat queen of hearts. This woman was making my girl forget her manners."

Sawyer was all geared up for another question, but Broussard grabbed his empty Kool-Aid glass and shook it at Raven. "More," he grunted.

After she left, Broussard said, "Where were you the night she died?"

"You mean when she got stuck?" Floyd asked.

"What did you say?" Sawyer asked.

"Pardon me, gentlemen," Floyd said. "I grew up on a farm. Lots of killing. Of animals. You just get a different perspective."

Raven returned to the room with Broussard's Kool-Aid. He took it and drank it like he was dying of thirst.

"Mr. Baxter," Sawyer said. "Please answer the question."

"Let's see, that was Fourth of July? Right? Never was my favorite holiday. I was here with my girl. We watched a little television, I took a bath, a long one. I was working all day and wanted to wash the stench off me," Floyd said.

"You work on the Fourth of July?" Sawyer asked.

"I'm a handyman in these houses. Burst pipes don't wait for the holidays."

"So, you and your daughter?" Sawyer said. "Is that right, sweetheart?"

Raven kept her eyes on the scrubbed wood floor. Floyd sat there thinking the entire time. *Look at him, Birdie Girl. Just look at him*. But she wouldn't.

"Do you mind if I talk to your daughter alone?" Sawyer asked.

"I most certainly would," Floyd said. "God put me here on earth to take care of her, and that certainly don't include her talking to any nosy policemen."

"She wouldn't be in any danger," Broussard said.

"And how am I to trust that? You cops love putting answers to questions that haven't been asked into people's head. Visions that they think they own. I watch *Dateline* and *60 Minutes*. You screw up memories of grown men. I ain't about to let you get your hands on my little girl."

"Nobody's trying to screw up your gal," Broussard said.

Floyd went on as if he hadn't heard a word. "First you ask me where my mother birthed me, and now you want to defile my daughter," he said.

"No one is talking about defiling your daughter, Mr. Baxter. We just want to question her," Sawyer said.

"You want to question her to make me a liar. Lord knows why. I swear on my dead wife's grave that me and my daughter watched TV, she drew me a bath, a little too hot but it worked out okay, and then we went to bed. If you don't like that you can put the glasses back in the kitchen your own self and get on up out of my house."

"Did you see anything that night? Somebody in the neighborhood who wasn't supposed to be here?" Broussard asked.

"You mean like you?" Floyd said.

"Careful, now," Broussard said.

"We just want to find out who killed Miss Jefferson," Sawyer said.

"You looking at her family, ain't you? She took a lot of boys in, bad boys that come out of them Bottoms. Some of them they mama didn't even want them. She had one that was a young hellion. Chasing folks through the woods for no good reason, claiming he was going to kill them."

"Do you have anybody in mind you want to tell us about?" Sawyer said.

"Why, I say all of them," Floyd said. "They all killers."

"If I could hear, not a nod, but hear your daughter corroborate your alibi, we'll be on our way. You said you and Miss Ruth didn't get along. Let us do our job, Mr. Baxter," Sawyer said.

Floyd eyeballed Raven. He thought about the times when she would show that tough-as-nails grin, or turn her little face into stone. Sometimes her stone face scared him more than his own. He'd be shaving his whiskers with his prized Sheffield straight razor and catch her reflection in the mirror. At those times, her gaze pierced his flesh, froze his bones. He'd wonder how in the world he could be afraid of his own face, his own self. That's what she was to him, not a whole person, but a piece of him. But here she was ready to turn on him, to make him a victim like those he killed. And he'd find himself thinking all sorts of crazy things. Would he bore into his own belly like he did Mrs. Jefferson, knife out his own insides? Would he slit his own throat and claw at the wound? One day, would he turn on himself because Raven was in his mind and told him to?

Now with them two policemen sitting there ready to put him in handcuffs, she returned Floyd's gaze with a fierceness he could feel. He had no idea what would come out of her mouth when she finally started talking.

"Me and my daddy watched a *Gunsmoke* rerun like he said," Raven finally said. "The TV wasn't working good, so we had to slap it a few times, and then gave up. He asked me to run him a bath and I did it. He yelled at me because it was too hot."

Then she looked at him and said in a little girl's voice, "Sorry, Daddy."

That wilted Sawyer's bloom. Broussard's true self almost came out.

He shoved the fox tail key fob back in his pocket and started saying what he really felt. "I don't care if y'all kill each other. Have at it. Come on, Sawyer, we've done what we can here."

Sawyer stood, sent a right mournful look Raven's way. Watching what he thought of as two useless sacks of flesh walk down the porch steps, Floyd wondered about the real business Broussard got up to. And he wondered, too, what kind of grown man would fiddle with a baby fox's tail, something fitting for a twelve-year-old. Floyd knew the moment he saw it that he wouldn't be going to jail over the way Mrs. Jefferson exited this life. Broussard wasn't a serious man, and Floyd would bet his freedom that his lack of seriousness included how he upheld the law.

Chapter Thirty-Three

Raven had to battle the boo hag to free herself from sleep. That's what Miss Ruth called sleep paralysis. Floyd called it witches riding your back. Whatever the name, it plagued Raven. She kept her eyes shut, trying to remember the dream, but it was like trying to put smoke in her pocket. The images wouldn't come. When she finally opened her eyes, she noticed her Android dancing a jig on the nightstand table. She picked it up. Billy Ray. But when she answered, no audible human speech came from the other end of the wireless. Just a long, clicking breath.

She hung up.

The phone rang again. She dragged a pillow over her face, enjoyed the coolness in the warmth of the room. She pressed the pillow harder when the phone wouldn't stop ringing. She answered with a frustrated, "What?" What she got in return was a whooshing breath, which sounded to her like a tortured snore. She considered calling Billy Ray back, but that got her nowhere the last time. Since she was already awake, she got up, showered and dressed, and made a cup of coffee to take with her to the station. If she was awake, she might as well work. As she pulled into the parking lot, she got the call. Another murder, this time in a neighborhood where the cops came quickly.

★ ★ ★

The home of Fabian Long and his wife, Edmée, hadn't changed much since Raven and Billy Ray sat in the parlor with its mustard-colored pillows and white marble fireplace to question Edmée about the murder of Ronnie True several years ago. Same looming white walls, same garden of edible fruits and vegetables spilling on either side of the wide front lawn. Now police cruisers cluttered the street, a morgue van occupied the flagstone driveway. Patrol had isolated the house from its neighbors with crime scene tape.

Ain't never seen nobody grow vegetables in their front yard, Floyd said in Raven's head as she made her way to the front door. She was reminded of the time she and Ozy sat across the street from that lawn helping her search for a murderer. Then, Ozy had made that same remark. But Edmée had been bold enough to do so in her *Better Homes and Gardens* neighborhood. She had also been bold enough to kill her predator and walk dangerous neighborhoods in search of addicts to cure. Raven wondered what else she was bold enough to do.

Newell, Marna's cop husband, kept a crowd of curious neighbors at bay on the other side of the street. Some had dogs with them this early morning. Middle-aged men and women in jogging gear craned their necks, trying to glimpse what was happening behind the tall white walls.

"You ready?" Stevenson asked as she walked up the sidewalk.

"I was born ready," Raven said. She stopped so suddenly he bumped into her.

"Hey, use your brake lights, partner," he said.

She didn't want to say it, but she couldn't help herself. "Do you realize that you ask me if I'm ready at every crime scene?"

"I do," he said. "Do you realize that every time you respond that you are born ready?"

"Crap," she said and started making her way to the front door.

"See, partners," he said, laughing. "It's a partner thing. You're going to miss me when I go back to California."

"Shut up, Stevenson," she said without bothering to turn around.

The conversation between her and Stevenson, and their signing into the crime scene, were the only orderly things that happened that morning.

★ ★ ★

Raven walked past Gus who stood just inside the front door as if she were ready to bolt. Once inside Raven ran straight into the chief trying his best to pace a hole into the black-and-white marble floor. His hands were shoved into the pockets of his slacks, the edges of his white linen suit jacket flared out like angels' wings.

Edmée was there, too. Marna flanked one side of Edmée, holding an arm tight telling her not to move. Edmée's pink satin nightgown was covered in blood. Billy Ray flanked the other side. He ordered Marna to back off. Another man in a royal-blue tracksuit – lawyer, Raven surmised – yelled in Edmée's face to not say anything, to keep her mouth shut, and to remember what happened the last time she said too much during a murder investigation.

"We need her clothes," Marna was saying.

"And I need to get pictures," Tim, who Raven hadn't noticed, jumped in.

"You ain't taking pictures of her, man," Billy Ray said.

"I'll take them," Marna said.

"Stop touching her," Billy Ray told Marna. "You're making her more upset."

Stevenson walked into the fray. "Hey, you, back off," he told the lawyer. "You, Billy Ray, you're a civilian here. Carry your ass outside."

"Man, if you try to touch me, I swear I'll beat you like a rented mule," Billy Ray told Stevenson.

Edmée's sobs were like background music to everybody yelling to be heard over her grief. Or guilt. Raven hadn't decided which. She went to stand beside the chief, who was now still as he watched the entire thing as if he were at a play. She mimicked his pose, and then glanced over at him.

"What we got?" she asked, her voice low and even.

"You ain't going to help?" the chief said, jerking his head at the tugging and shouting bodies.

"Marna and Stevenson will get them calmed down," Raven answered. "I don't see you hotfooting it over there."

"Suit's new. I don't want to get blood on it," the chief said.

"Tell me," Raven said.

"Husband of Yours Beautifully covered in blood," he pointed at

Edmée, who was now hiccuping instead of sobbing. Stevenson was telling her to breathe. Marna insisted that she change her clothes. "He's upstairs in the master bedroom."

"Dead?"

"Most definitely. This time the perp may have used an axe. Or at least that's what Rita is thinking. She won't know for sure until the autopsy," the chief said.

Gus, bracing herself against the doorframe, dry-heaved.

"Don't be vomiting in here!" Stevenson yelled. "Get outside behind the yellow tape."

Edmée had quieted. Tim was nowhere in sight. Marna led her away while Billy Ray watched them with suspicion in his eyes.

"He's the first person she called," the chief said. "Even before she dialed 911. What you think of that?"

Raven thought a lot about that but kept her mouth shut.

"Body's in pieces?" Raven asked the chief.

"Yes," he said.

"I'm guessing she found him?" Raven asked.

"You guessed right."

"When?" Raven asked.

"Early morning, when she woke up," the chief said.

Raven stared at the chief.

"That's right," the chief said. "Your friend said they kissed each other good night, she read for about twenty minutes, answered some email, put her computer on the nightstand and went to sleep. In the morning, she woke up and rolled into bloody pieces of her husband."

"You serious?" Raven asked.

"As a heart attack. She said she slept through the entire thing."

* * *

There was less chaos in the upstairs master bedroom of the home of Edmée Crowley and Fabian Long, but chaos nonetheless.

Tim gave Raven a warning look as she poked her head in the doorway.

"This is where you ran off to," she said.

"Wasn't getting anything done down there," Tim said.

She glanced into the room. Rita was by the hacked body, which was surrounded by a heap of bedclothes stained with blood.

"Is Rita done with the body?" Raven asked.

"Just about. Where's Gus? Rita could use her," Tim said.

"Making Rorschach designs on the sidewalk. In color," Raven said as she moved into the room.

She stooped where Rita knelt beside the bed, "Hey, Rita," she said.

"Second person I know I'm staring at dead in these past few weeks, Raven. First Zeke, and now Dr. Long. He may have been an asshole, but he was a decent asshole."

"I heard that Edmée said she slept through it. Could that be possible?" Raven asked.

"I would say I doubt it, but it's not impossible. She sleep hard?" Rita asked.

Raven smiled, remembering the sleepovers from their high school days.

"She did back in the old days, but I don't know about now," Raven said.

"If the first blow was to the head, he may have not been able to make a sound."

Fabian Long's head was in two pieces.

"Could someone have drugged Edmée?" Raven said.

"I don't know. We'll need a tox screen. I couldn't find any sleeping pills around," Rita said. "And Tim's almost finished bagging the evidence."

"You mean if we can get a tox screen from Edmée," Raven said, thinking about the lawyer in the blue tracksuit. The lawyer may even be so bold as to object to photographs of Edmée to see if there were any cuts, scratches, or anything indicating that she'd been in a fight, and a blood-spatter examination of her nightgown.

"Could he have been killed somewhere else?" Raven asked.

Rita snorted when she tried to stifle a laugh. "You see all this blood, Raven?" And then, as if reminded, she said louder, "Tim, since we lost our intern, get my team up here so we can pack him up. I don't want to roll him here, and I'd like to keep as many sheets as possible together when we bag him. We'll have to pack the comforter separately. Maybe find some hair or fibers that don't belong to Edmée or Dr. Long."

"No sign of forced entry?" Raven asked as Stevenson walked into the room.

"No," Stevenson said. "Maybe somebody invited the killer in like he was a damned vampire. Or maybe he had a key and a soft step."

"Had a key and a marriage license," Rita said bitterly, wondering if Edmée had made her second kill.

Seeing already where this case was about to go, Raven straightened up. Tim came back into the room with the two morgue assistants. Rita directed them how to pack the body. Tim finished searching the room and bagging the evidence. He placed the bags in a plastic box.

Raven stayed until the morgue assistants placed pieces of Dr. Long into a body bag. They used the sheets to hold him together as much as possible, as if they were trying to carry a highly treasured, but broken, china doll.

Chapter Thirty-Four

Upon returning to the BLPD, Raven had to park in the back lot because the mayor's car was in her parking space. She would know his bright red Cadillac anywhere, fat rather than long, as they had been in the old days, its logo shining brightly in the hazy sun. On one side of the caddy was a Lexus that she knew belonged to a longtime City Council member. On the other side of the Lexus was the car of a prominent businessman. She imagined all three of the vehicles swinging into the parking spaces at the same time, three driver's side doors flying open and Byrd's Landing's elite stepping out. She could see them hitching up their pants and getting ready to give the chief the business.

Raven hoofed it toward the glass double doors, passing more vehicles that she didn't recognize. Protestors poked homemade signs in her face. *BLPD can't keep us safe. Impeach the chief. Fire the murderer. A killer can't catch a killer.*

I think them last two are about you, Birdie Girl, Floyd said in her head. *A poop storm is raining its stank all over Byrd's Landing. Why when that happens it always hits you first?*

Raven didn't have time to respond to Floyd's banter. She was too busy smacking signs out of her face and pushing protestors aside. A uniformed officer named Olson did what he could by creating a tunnel with a fellow officer that Raven could move through unimpeded.

She'd almost made it inside when Imogene Tucker stopped her.

"Not now, and not again, Imogene," Raven said, walking faster to the door.

As if she hadn't heard, Imogene hurried toward Raven anyway, her white stilettos clicking against the asphalt.

"You kidding me? Now, right now, Raven," Imogene said. "Fabian Long has been murdered. I need a statement."

"Don't wear so much red lipstick," Raven said. "It bleeds onto your teeth. You look like a well-dressed vampire."

"Do you think I give a fuck what I look like? Talk to me, smartass," Imogene said with her cameraman ready to start filming behind her.

"We still have our folks processing the scene," Raven said. "The blood's not even dry and here you are sticking a camera in my face."

"It's Fabian Long, Dr. Fabian Long. CEO of Memorial Hospital," Imogene said. "His name is on buildings in this town, for fuck's sake."

"I promise as soon as I find out anything you'll be the first person I call," Raven said.

"You're lying," Imogene said.

"I give you my word. Is that better?" Raven said.

Imogene crossed her arms over her chest. "Marginally," she said with a warning in her eyes.

"It'll have to do," Raven said. As she walked away, she heard Imogene ask the cameraman, "Do I really have lipstick on my teeth? I've been talking to people all morning, including the mayor. Why didn't you tell me? Get a mirror."

⋆ ⋆ ⋆

Raven could hear the mayor in the hallway just outside the chief's door. Stevenson and Marna were in the hallway. Marna looked like somebody had been beating her.

"How long have they been in there?" Raven asked.

"About a half an hour. The only voice I heard has been the mayor's," Stevenson said.

"Hope he doesn't bust a blood vessel," Marna said.

"We got other problems," Stevenson said. Sweat slid down his bald head even though the air conditioner was running full blast. Raven handed him her handkerchief.

"I find that impossible to believe," Raven said.

"Lois Wareham is in the box," Marna said. "Not saying much at all, but she's been in there a while. Says she wants to see you. Won't talk to anybody else."

"She's going to have to sit tight until we talk to Edmée," Raven said.

Marna opened her mouth to say something but closed it again. The chief and his companions had come out of the office in time to hear Raven's last comment.

"What, Marna?" Raven asked. "Don't play dumb now."

"Edmée lawyered up," the chief answered for Marna, his voice grim. "We've made an appointment for her to come in to speak with us."

"An appointment?" Stevenson said. "We aren't a caterer for one of her garden parties."

The chief looked pissed, but the mayor looked apoplectic. His fleshy cheeks wagged as he swiveled between the chief and Stevenson. His straightened hair fell into his face, leaving only one visible mean eye. It sparkled with rage. The businessman, who owned a string of Laundromats around town, didn't look any happier.

"Edmée Crowley just lost her husband. She was the wife of Fabian Long. We will show her some respect," Marcus said.

"She's also a convicted felon," Raven cut in.

"Manslaughter," the mayor retorted, spittle as big as BBs flying from his mouth. "Justified, if you asked me. If I had the power, I'd wake his ass up so she can kill him again."

"Preach," Marna said with a straight face.

The mayor gave her a scathing look. He turned back to the chief. "Get your team in order, Early. I want this handled quickly and quietly. This could be a disaster for more than Mrs. Crowley. I'm not talking about jobs or losing money, either. You get me?"

The chief leaned against the doorframe to his office, crossed his legs at the ankles. He looked like he didn't have a care in the world.

"I get you, Marcus," the chief said. "I always get you. Just make sure you get me. My detectives are going to do their jobs. The person they put in cuffs will be the person who did it. If it's fast, it's fast. If it's slow, it's slow. But it'll be righteous. You and your friends stomping around my office like two-year-olds ain't going to speed things up or keep Edmée Crowley out of prison."

The mayor blew up like a puffer fish. He brought a warning finger to accompany the next words he was about to speak. But whatever he was about to say died on his lips. The finger went down. He gathered what remaining dignity he had and marched down the long hallway with his two companions.

The chief turned his attention back to the three of them.

"I hope you don't think I meant any of that. I just don't like being pushed. Bring me someone fast so we can get back to normal around here. Marcus already talked to Edmée's lawyer to make an appointment for an interview."

"Marcus?" Raven said.

The chief put a hand up to stave off more protests. "It is what it is, Raven," he said.

"When is she coming down?" Raven said.

"We agreed to let her come down late tomorrow afternoon," the chief said.

Stevenson said, "You can't be serious."

"I am," the chief said. "And don't go making a nuisance of yourself trying to get her to talk without her lawyer. I'm talking to you, Raven. Ain't no way that woman hacked her husband to death."

"Why not?" Stevenson asked. "She bludgeoned Ronnie True to death with a golf club."

"He deserved that shit, though," Marna said.

"Billy Ray asked for a lawyer, too," Chief Sawyer said.

"What? Why would Billy Ray need to talk to a lawyer?" Raven asked.

Stevenson handed her his phone and told her to swipe. She did and stopped when she got to a picture of a gold watch. The Breitling that Billy Ray always wore was cradled in the blood and tissue of Dr. Fabian Long's body. It must have been tangled in the sheets at the crime scene, because Raven hadn't seen it when she was there.

"Lord have mercy," Marna said. "I cringe every time I see that."

"And his lawyer hasn't called in with an appointment yet," the chief said.

Chapter Thirty-Five

Lois Wareham lifted shaking fingers to adjust the purple headscarf covering her dreadlocks. She touched the rhinestone in her nose as if trying to tether herself to something real. Raven remembered what her stepmother always told her during panic attacks. She said to touch something, smell something, see something and hold on, it'll pass. Stevenson walked around the table. He made a racket on purpose as he pulled his chair out. Once he sat down, he leaned over the table and got into Lois's face.

"Tell me why you shouldn't be cuffed to this table right now," he asked her.

"Am I under arrest?" Lois asked. "I came here of my own free will. Diamond said you talked to him. That you know."

"You lied," Raven said. She took the other chair, albeit quietly.

Lois sat back. "I see," she said. "No good cop, bad cop act. Just two assholes."

"I thought you wanted to talk," Raven said.

"To you, not to him," Lois said.

"You get us both," Raven said. She didn't know what Lois wanted to tell her, but she'd bet her paycheck that it wasn't to confess. All Raven wanted to do was find out why Billy Ray's watch was at the crime scene, and why he lawyered up. She wasn't thrilled at Lois's self-serving detour.

"Why did you lie?" Stevenson asked.

"I had to," Lois answered.

"Because you killed them," Raven said.

Lois clasped her hands together on the table. Raven noticed that though the rag she had wrapped around it at her salon was gone, two thick Band-Aids covered her right palm.

"Show us your hand," Stevenson said.

Lois peeled back the bandages. Raven couldn't tell if it was the remains of a burn or a cut from a knife. She surmised from his silence that Stevenson couldn't tell, either.

"I hear you got another murder going. Maybe that person killed Zeke and them, too." Lois smoothed the bandages back in place as she waited for an answer.

"Unrelated," Stevenson said. "More like a lover's spat than two cold-blooded executions and a stabbing."

Raven kicked him under the table. She knew that Billy Ray didn't have anything to do with Long's murder. Stevenson didn't flinch.

"You didn't do this by yourself. Who helped you?" Stevenson said.

"Nobody helped me," Lois shot back.

"I respect that. Independent lady," he said.

"That's why you stabbed Zeke all those times after he was dead," Raven said. "What did you do? Hold the gun on Marcel and Lionel while they cuffed each other? Then chase down Zeke when he ran? You're bigger than he is, taller. You could've taken him."

"I told you that I didn't do it," Lois said.

"Come on, Lois," Stevenson said. "I know how it is. Zeke was going to cut you out, after you stayed with him when he was sorry and broke. When we talked to your friends, they said that made you mean mad."

"I don't have friends like that," Lois said.

"Acquaintances then," Raven said. "We heard Zeke had a relapse about a year ago, right? You stayed with him, held his head while he vomited, rocked him while he was shitting and sweating out the poison he willingly put into his own body, but you stuck it out. Now that he was about to come into more money, he dumps you."

"You're lying," Lois said. "Zeke never relapsed. You trying to trip me up."

Raven *was* lying and trying to trip her up. It was a desperate play to get a confession and get this conversation over.

Without missing a beat, Stevenson said, "That would have pissed me off. You needed money, right? We've seen where you work, grimy as fuck, hardly any customers."

"What happened, are you about to lose that place?" Raven slipped in.

"Stop it!" Lois was sobbing now. Stevenson shoved a tissue box at her. She threw it back at him. She wiped her eyes with the sleeve of her thin cotton shirt.

"Zeke never relapsed. He's been clean for years. If I did kill him and his friends, do you think I'd be stupid enough to ask to talk to Raven?"

"I have no idea as to the depth of your stupidity," Stevenson said.

"I didn't need Zeke's money or his help with anything. I have my own way of making things right. Papa, I mean Lucien…"

Raven sat back. "Go on."

"It's a business relationship," Lois said. "It has nothing to do with this."

"Funny," Raven said. "That's the same thing Diamond said."

Raven wasn't sure but she thought she saw fear flash over Lois's face. Lois touched the nose ring again and took a deep breath. She didn't speak, just sat there.

"Look, we don't have time for this. Just get on with the story you came here to tell us, the one you think will keep you out of jail," Stevenson said.

"I knew you'd find out I lied," Lois said. "Smartphones track everything these days. I was just so scared when I heard what had happened I said the first thing that came into my head. Lucien and I had a meeting and Zeke needed to meet someone out there. He said it was a friend of his."

"Who was this friend?" Raven asked.

"I don't know!" Lois said. "I told you we gave each other space."

"You didn't just say the first thing that came into your head. You double-downed on the lie. Why?" Stevenson asked.

"I just couldn't let it happen again," Lois said.

"What do you mean not again?" Raven asked.

"I know how the cops treat you when you're the last person to see someone alive," Lois said.

And here it comes, Raven thought. The self-serving story. She felt her leg start jittering impatiently, the way Cameron's did when he wanted whatever was happening to end, and end fast. But she knew she had to wait. And listen.

"I was the last person to see my sister alive. There are people in this town who still think I killed her. Even my parents didn't believe me."

Before she could continue, Stevenson stood up so fast that his chair fell over. He slammed the door hard when he left. Raven wished she was right behind him. She had things to do that involved a certain restaurant proprietor. But she stayed because she thought she'd learn something that would lead her to the person who killed Zeke.

"Tell it," Raven said without acknowledging Stevenson's departure.

Lois sniffed. "When I was in high school, I thought I'd be some great poet, you know. I dyed my hair black, wore these long scarfs, combat boots," she said. "I wanted to suffer because I thought that was the only way to do art."

Raven's fingers danced on the table. "Where did you go to high school?" Raven asked.

"Emerson, across town from where you and Zeke went," Lois said.

Raven nodded. Emerson was the rich school.

"You have to understand how boring my life was," Lois said. "My dad sold insurance and my mom owned a tech business. I had to make up things to be sad about. At night I'd lie in bed, read *Anna Karenina* and cry."

Raven stifled an urge to scream at Lois to get on with it. Instead, she asked, "What was your sister's name?"

"Fleur. She was six years old, had these bouncy curls and big brown eyes. She couldn't say my name when she was a toddler, so she called me Lolo. My parents loved that girl like air."

"They blamed you for her death?" Raven said.

Lois bowed her head. "Everybody blamed me. I was supposed to be watching her, but I snuck out. She followed me. I yelled at her, told her to go back home, to run. I stamped my feet and told her to scat like she was a stray cat. I didn't think she'd get lost. We were only a block or two from our house. When the police got involved, I lied."

"Why am I not surprised?" Raven said.

"You don't understand," Lois said. "When they found out I lied, they treated me like a criminal. Took pictures of me, my hands and face. Cleaned beneath my fingernails, questioned me for hours."

The family imploded after Fleur's abduction, Lois told Raven. Her father put a gun in his mouth a year later. Her mother let her business sink into a black hole. After several years of drinking like she was dying of thirst every day, she joined Lois's father in the graveyard. Lois went to live with her father's sister.

"She politely asked me to leave when she read the police reports," Lois said. "I became homeless while I was still a minor."

"That's a sad story," Raven said. "I still don't see what that has to do with Zeke's murder."

Lois rubbed the back of her fist beneath her nose.

"I snuck out of the house to see a boy," she said. "Strike that, a man. He had at least a decade on me. He was weird, you know. Into what I was into. Root work, hoodoo, poetry… I don't know how to explain it. But he knew the importance of…"

"Suffering?" Raven asked, unable to keep the mockery out of her voice.

"Yes," she said. "Middle-class angst, I guess you call it. I thought he was my soulmate."

A picture started to build in Raven's mind, but she let Lois go on.

"I promised myself after Fleur's disappearance that I would never put myself in a position to be the last person to see anybody alive. When Zeke died, not only did my world drop beneath me, but I thought I had seen the last of my freedom."

"Why is that?" Raven asked.

"Because the man I had gone to meet the day my sister disappeared was Lucien Toussaint."

Chapter Thirty-Six

Lucien Toussaint. After her conversation with Lois, Raven was more convinced than ever that the murders in the churchyard pivoted around this mysterious man. But he would have to wait. Besides, it would take a bomb to blast him out of the Old Bottoms. He was a king who would not willingly leave his kingdom. He wasn't going anywhere.

She wanted to tackle Billy Ray right away. But instead, she had no choice but to focus on the murder of Fabian Long. She spent that day picking through the evidence and preparing warrants for phone and financial records. By the time the sun went down, and the moon became a scythe of silver in the sky, Raven, Marna, Stevenson, Tim and Cameron were punch drunk and useless. The chief sent them home to get rest. The others may have followed his orders, but Raven drove straight to Billy Ray's.

Billy Ray's prized Chastain's Creole Heaven was deserted. Not a soul in sight in the now-dark double-barrel shotgun that was one of the most popular places in town. The lights didn't twinkle around the screen doors. No white headlights of new customers pulling in, or taillights of sated customers leaving the parking lot. The bottle tree Billy Ray made to ward off evil spirits tinkled in the soft wind. It was probably the first night the place sat empty since it opened.

Raven parked her Mustang close to the front door. She was not a fan of the dark, especially a Byrd's Landing dark, full of secrets, and eyes as old as time watching her from the shadows. She opened the door of the Mustang and climbed out to the sound of cicadas chittering. Using her pocket flashlight, she found the stone path that led to the shotgun behind the restaurant where Billy Ray lived. No light in the house, either, just a dark, hulking shadow against the darker night.

Where the hell was Billy Ray? She could understand closing the restaurant after Fabian's death, but his house, too? She was letting the beam of the flashlight guide her to the front door when a flicker like a bird's wing darted in and out of the light. Her feet froze her in place. She shifted the light. A patch of sidewalk, a tree, a window and a closed front door flashed in the yellow glow. She clicked the light off. She knew it was stupid, but she thought it'd help her hear better. And there. She heard someone breathing just ahead of her.

"Billy Ray," she tried.

She was answered by running footsteps and someone crashing through the trees into the woods near Billy Ray's shotgun house.

She switched on the light and ran after them. Her practiced feet flew just as they did when she was on a trail run in the state park. But she didn't know this trail, didn't know when to duck, dodge or pivot. Branches whipped her face and chest. Rotten wood snapped beneath her feet. She tripped, fell on her face, her arms flung out above her head like an offering. She heard Floyd's cackle inside her skull. *Why you chasing whatever fool that is, Birdie Girl?* All Raven could think to answer was, *Because they're running.* She needed to know why. She got to her feet and ran on.

When she realized that she could no longer hear, let alone see, the person she had been chasing, she skidded to a stop. She extinguished the flashlight and dropped it into her pocket. She drew her Glock. It had its own flashlight mounted beneath the barrel. With both light and protection, she felt better.

"Hello," she said, "anybody there?"

The silence of the woods answered back, a barn owl called out in the distance. She pivoted in a circle. Torn branches and crushed plants skated in and out of view. She had lost the advantage by barreling headlong into the trees while every living thing with sense scurried out of her way. The person she was chasing could have walked out of the woods, circled back and started chasing her. She could have kicked herself. Why didn't she check the house before running into the woods? There was an axe murderer terrorizing Byrd's Landing. What if Billy Ray were hurt? She flipped around and headed back the way she came when something hard slammed into the back of her shins. She crashed toward the ground, squeezing her eyes shut on the way down. When she opened them again, the barrel of a weapon along with a stream of bright light was aimed at her face. She shielded her eyes with her forearm. That's when fear gave way to curiosity and then annoyance. She recognized the shadow holding the gun on her.

She smacked the barrel out of her face and retrieved the Glock that had fallen a few feet away.

"Hey!" he shouted. "Careful."

"Get that freakin' gun out of my face," she said. "What the hell you doing?"

"Me?" Billy Ray said. "What are you doing, Raven? And stop hitting the gun. It might just go off."

"Only if you wanted it to," Raven said. "Or are you saying that since you whacked Fabian Long you've developed a taste for blood?"

"You know damn well I didn't kill that idiot," he said.

"How would I know that? Your watch was at the crime scene. And you covet his wife."

Billy Ray's laugh was soft. He grabbed her arm and helped her up. Unfortunately, it was the arm she fell on at the church. She was bleeding.

"Covet his wife," Billy Ray said. "You sound like your old man."

"What are you doing out here anyway?" she asked.

"Obviously chasing you," he said. "You can answer the same question back at the house. Come on, follow me. You wouldn't want to step on a snake."

Raven took several quick hops. She pointed the Glock toward the ground. Her heart beat so fast she thought it was going to jump out of her throat. She swore that she'd scream like a three-year-old if she stepped on a snake.

Billy Ray led the way through the woods back to his house behind Chastain's. Once inside, he turned on the light. The front room doubled as his office. A whiteboard covered with recipes, calendars and handwritten notes was pushed against a window next to his desk. A secondhand couch covered in orange and red flowers sat along the wall. Owls peered from every nook and crevice. Porcelain owls, ceramic owls, clay owls and even stuffed owls that friends and customers had given to Billy Ray after finding out he was a collector. Raven felt watched every time she stepped inside his house.

"Sit down," Billy Ray said. "Let me take a look at that arm. Take off your jacket."

Raven sat on the couch and took off her jacket. The bandage around her upper arm was bleeding.

"Goddammit, Raven," Billy Ray said. "It's infected."

He left the room and returned with antiseptic, a box of Band-Aids and white gauze. He sat down beside her.

"I didn't see your car," Raven said as he worked.

"It's there," he said. "I parked it on the side of the house."

He dabbed antiseptic on the cut. She winced. "Why?" she said.

"Got some phone calls I didn't like," he said. "Don't want people to know when I'm home. Thought I'd close the restaurant just for tonight. Give everybody a chance to cool down. What were you doing back there anyway, Raven?"

"You first," she said. "Why did you trip me, and stick a gun in my face?"

He peeled the back from a Band-Aid and placed it over the wound on her arm. He repeated the same move for the second Band-Aid.

"I told you, I've been getting threats. Didn't know it was you," he said.

"You sure kept that gun in my face a good long time after you found out it was me."

"That's the fear talking," he said. "It may have seemed like a long time. It wasn't. Why would I want to shoot you anyway?"

"Oh, I don't know," Raven said. "To keep your girlfriend out of jail? Maybe slow down the investigation?"

He ignored the question. "You want water? Beer or something?"

"I don't have time for beer or water or anything. People are dying, Billy Ray."

"People will continue to die whether you drink a beer or not. It's nature. You can't control everything."

"Fine," she said. "Sweet tea if you have it."

"With mint?" he asked.

"Yes, and muddled."

"As you wish," he said.

He went back into the kitchen. She heard cabinets opening and ice cracking. He returned and handed the cold glass of sweet tea to her. He sat on the edge of a green armchair with his own glass of tea.

"Good?" he asked as she drank.

"It is," she said, eyeing him.

"If I wanted you shot, you'd be shot," Billy Ray said.

"Maybe you changed your mind," Raven said.

"Why?" Billy Ray laughed. "Because of your sparkling personality?"

He was right. It was ridiculous to be suspicious of Billy Ray, but he had changed so much lately that it scared her.

He took a drink from his own glass and said, "I came home. Thought I heard someone rummaging around in the backyard. So went looking. Never thought it'd be you."

"I didn't hear your car," she said.

"I didn't take my car. I went out for a run," he said.

In blue running shorts and a clean, white t-shirt, he was surely dressed for a run. But something was off. Raven decided to let it go. For now. The tea was gone, the ice cubes melting in the glass. She held the cold glass with both of her filthy hands. She didn't take her eyes off Billy Ray.

"Why is your t-shirt dry?" she asked.

So much for letting it go, but she couldn't help herself. She was too much of a cop.

"I said I was going on a run but just couldn't do it. I changed my mind before I was half a mile out," he said, a small smile on his lips.

Raven didn't respond, just kept her eyes on him.

"Why you eye-fucking me, Raven?" he said.

"What was your watch doing in Edmée's bedroom?" she asked.

"Why do you *think* it was there?" he said. "Come on, you tell me, you're so smart."

"Don't be an ass," she said. "Why must you always be an ass when we need to discuss something serious?"

She set the glass on the coffee table, knocking down a porcelain owl. It didn't break, just lay on its side with its goofy eyes staring at her. She wanted to smash it. Billy Ray set it upright. She stood and hobbled toward the middle room, her body sore from running and falling in the woods.

"Where you going?" Billy Ray said. "You need a search warrant before you start throwing shit around looking for a bloody axe."

"Pound sand," she spat back.

"Is that your version of fuck you?" he asked, laughing.

She went into the bathroom and shut the door. She sat for a few moments on a claw-foot bathtub that Billy Ray was restoring. She tried to get her breath back. Her old friend and partner had changed in these last few years. More combative, closed off. Nowadays, most of their conversations centered on Raven. Her sins past and potential future redemptions. Before Billy Ray was burned, the conversation had been bidirectional. Raven told him about her life. He told her about his. She was aware of the father who took his own life, and Billy Ray's early dream to be a psychologist. He shared the reality of his mother's bills after his father passed, forcing him into police work. There was never a calling. He just needed the money. He spoke often of his twin sister, and his nieces who were also twins. How old were they now? Two? Three? Raven couldn't remember. The walls he had erected around himself after the fires? Raven left them intact, and then went a step further. Instead of helping him escape, she bricked up the windows.

She got up from the edge of the tub and went to the mirror above the sink. She twisted the faucet open, took the soap from the dish and washed her hands. Brown water and bits of twigs swirled down the drain. She took the soap from its dish and washed her face, looking into her own eyes, one green and the other blue just like Floyd's. All the while, she marveled at her own selfishness. She hoped Billy Ray hadn't gone so far that he would never be able to return.

She walked out of the bathroom to find him in the kitchen ripping the heads from crawfish.

"Knowing you, you haven't eaten," he said when he saw her.

She leaned against the doorjamb, folded her arms.

"Billy Ray," she said. "Talk to me."

He grabbed a cast-iron skillet from a hook on the wall. He wielded the heavy metal like it was made of cardboard.

"Didn't your partner tell you that I have a lawyer?" he said.

"Not as a cop, but as a friend," she said.

He didn't answer right away, just cut a pat of butter into the pan, and squirted olive oil from a plastic bottle over it. He turned on a burner. The Wolf stove clicked until a blue flame appeared. He didn't speak until the butter and olive oil sizzled. He shook the skillet against the burner.

"I've got some cut-up celery, onion and green pepper in the fridge. Get it for me," he said.

She did, and set the bowls on the counter next to the stove. She stood so close to him that he couldn't ignore her presence. He opened the containers and tossed handfuls of each into the pan.

"Do you think I killed Fabian Long?" he asked, sending her a testing glance.

"You hated him the moment you laid eyes on him, remember? When we were investigating the Lovelle murders? Even before you met Edmée," Raven answered.

"You know how I feel about rich, fake, snobby motherfuckers," he said.

"Him being married to Edmée didn't make you feel any better about him," Raven said.

Billy Ray added some garlic and shook the pan for a full minute. The smell filled the room.

"You think I snuck into his house and cleaved his skull in half?" he asked, shaking creole spices over the vegetables.

"No, I don't think that," she said.

"So why you going on about a watch?" he asked.

"Because it was there, Billy Ray. In Long's bedroom covered in Long's brains."

"Any of my blood on it? My DNA? Did y'all test it, yet?"

"They're looking into it," Raven said. "You know we wouldn't have the results by now, anyway."

He threw some white flour into the vegetables, stirred them around a bit with a wooden spoon.

"Listen to me good, Raven," he said. "I've always wanted to punch that motherfucker in the throat for the way he treats his wife. That's a long way from killing."

She watched as he poured some homemade stock into the vegetables and stirred.

"The Breitling, Billy Ray," Raven demanded. "The watch."

When the sauce was good and thick, Billy Ray said, "I don't know." He cut a lemon in half and drained it into the sauce before returning the pan to a simmer.

He swiveled to face her.

"Edmée ain't my girlfriend. I never wanted that with her, and I don't think she wants that. She just likes to jive, that's all. It's a game to her. I have no idea how that watch got there. Neither does she."

"Somebody's setting you up?" she said.

"Yes," he said. "Has to be." He turned and dumped the headless crawfish into the simmering liquid.

⋆ ⋆ ⋆

Billy Ray scooped the étouffée over piles of steamed white rice. It was like heaven on a fork. They ate in silence for a few minutes. And then Raven said, "I'm sorry, Billy Ray."

"Don't be sorry," he answered. "I didn't like Fabian Long well enough to grieve his passing."

"You know what I mean," she said, not looking at him.

"About your navel-gazing since we've been in this hell town? Well, I figure you just can't help it. You got a lot going on," Billy Ray said.

"But—"

"Raven," he said. "Shut the fuck up about it."

"I'm here now," she said.

"No, you ain't, but that's okay," he said.

The words felt like a slap in the face. She would just have to show him.

"When was the last time you saw the watch?" she asked.

"Night of my birthday party," he said. "I took it off because it had gotten loose. It was hanging on my wrist, bugging the shit out of me. I remember throwing it on the table. But when we were cleaning up, I couldn't find it. I thought someone who thought they were helping just put it somewhere."

"And that's it?" Raven asked. "That's an expensive watch."

"That I bought for twenty-five bucks at an estate sale. I really didn't think too much about it," Billy Ray said.

"Maybe Edmée picked it up? Meaning to give it to you later?" Raven offered.

Billy Ray shook his head. "She said she didn't."

They went over all the people who were there that night. Rita, Edmée, Cameron. Even the chief had swung by to pat Billy Ray on the shoulder. She couldn't remember him being there during cleanup. The zydeco band playing that night were in and out as well. Any one of them could have picked up the watch and planted it at Long's murder scene.

"Shit," Billy Ray said. "Maybe Fabian took it himself just to fuck with me. Or maybe play some game with Edmée. Use it for leverage to get Edmée to fess up to cheating on him."

Billy Ray may have a point. But with Long dead, it was a point that could never be proven.

Chapter Thirty-Seven

Late afternoon the next day, after Raven's conversation with Billy Ray, Raven decided that it was time to do what she had been wanting to do ever since she rolled Zeke's body in the barren churchyard. To the chief's infinite irritation, Fabian Long's murder case had been bumbling along all morning and past mid-afternoon. Edmée's lawyers negotiated a delay for her interview with homicide. Billy Ray's counsel threw roadblocks in the way of his client talking to detectives. Instead of signing search warrants that in any other case would have been routine, the judge sent back one inane question after another. Stevenson could deal with that fiasco while she paid Lucien Toussaint a visit.

She had called Lois to find out which house was his and drove the red Mustang to the Old Bottoms. She parked at the mouth of Toussaint's porch steps. An old, light blue Ford truck grumbled along the road, turned into Toussaint's yard, and nosed its front bumper right up to Raven's back end. *And that's when you know you're about to take a trip up poop creek without a paddle*, Floyd's ghost said in her head. Raven left the Mustang and stood in the July heat. The hot sun punched through the haze. Sweat beaded on Raven's forehead as she turned toward the Ford. Two men got out of the truck with assault rifles cradled in their arms. *Don't allow guns in here, my left foot*, Raven thought as they closed in on her. The screen door creaked, and Toussaint stepped through the slender opening. The white do-rag on his head was as bright as the ushers' dresses at Marcel Thibodeaux's funeral. It almost looked like it was part of a religious uniform. But the undershirt and gray sweatpants reminded Raven that this man was as far from a preacher as a demon, and this hellhole was not a church.

The two men from the Ford scrutinized her with gazes that felt like they were cutting into her flesh. Coming here might have been a mistake.

She left the office without telling anyone where she was going, even left her radio in the Mustang. If Toussaint thought she was worth the bullets, he could just tell his men to shoot her right there. He wouldn't even have to hide her body. He could just throw it in the swamp as a snack for the alligators. She waited with unease that didn't wane when Toussaint pushed the screen door wider to invite her in.

Inside the house was much darker than outside. Raven waited for her eyes to adjust. The smell of collard greens simmering on the stove drifted into the living room. She heard a woman in the kitchen singing to an old jazz tune. Her voice was good, reminded Raven of the Ella Fitzgerald records she used to listen to…and there her thoughts fled. Listen to with who? The smell of the collards and the gentle song tugged at a memory that should have been a pleasant one. But it wasn't. Not at all. Toussaint staring at her like a stain amplified her unease, not to mention the two men on either side of him holding weapons that could snuff out her life in seconds.

Toussaint twirled an old-timey straight-back chair from the table. It reminded Raven of the heavy wooden chairs they might use in an old schoolhouse.

"You here now," he said. "You might as well sit."

"I hope those cannons aren't stolen," she said, trying to sound unbothered, cop-like. This was one of the few times she was thankful that Floyd rode shotgun in her head. His face settled over hers like a glass mask. *I ain't going nowhere, Birdie Girl*, he said in a soft voice. *You just need to stay ready. This son-of-a-biscuit-eater Toussaint with the knife hanging out the pocket of his sweatpants is ready to cut your throat and save the blood for a cool drink later.*

"Whether they are or aren't ain't your business," Toussaint said. He took a matching chair opposite her.

Raven grinned. "Let me figure out what's my business."

"You trespassing," Toussaint said.

"How can that be when you don't own this land?" Raven said. "The city does, right? You're leasing it." She stared into his eyes, so he'd get her meaning. "For now."

"Why are you here, Detective?" Toussaint said. His voice was mild. Raven hoped it was because that's how he was feeling.

"I'm only here because of the bodies in your churchyard. I just have a few questions. I didn't come here to roust anybody," she said.

"We told those other cops everything we know. They wrote it all down. Go ask one of them," Toussaint said.

"They wrote down that nobody knew anything," Raven said.

"That's right," he said, shifting in his chair. "We ain't seen nothing. We ain't heard nothing."

"You heard gunshots," Raven said.

He answered her with a grunt.

"Or somebody did. They called it in, right? Can I talk to them?" Raven said.

He looked over his shoulder at the two men behind them. "Tell her, Moon," Toussaint said.

"I'm the one who called it in after the shots were fired and waited for your silly asses to get here," Moon said.

He still held the rifle, but pointed down to the floor. He reached up, gripped the silver moon and purple crystal charms dangling from a thick, silver chain around his neck. She tried to catch his eye, but he turned his head away.

"Did you hear anything odd at the church before that? A car, anything?" Raven asked

"Just the shots where there wasn't supposed to be any," Moon said.

The ceiling fan whirring over her head fought with the heat in the room and lost. Raven touched her fingers to her parched throat before she could stop herself. Toussaint told the other man, who he called Terry, to go and tell Mama Jo in the kitchen to bring out some ice water. Terry left. Toussaint turned back to Raven.

"He answered your question," Toussaint said. "What else?"

"What's your relationship with Lois Wareham and Zeke's brother, Diamond?"

"They say they got business with me?" Toussaint asked.

"Yes."

"Ask them," he countered.

"I'm asking you."

"If they keeping they mouth shut, maybe I better, too," Toussaint said. "Wouldn't want y'all to ruin it."

"You used to date Lois?" she asked.

He laughed quietly, shook his head. "I wouldn't call it date. She was a troubled child. I just tried to help her."

"By abducting her sister?" Raven asked.

His face went hard. "I ain't abduct nobody," he said.

"What do you think happened to Zeke and his friends? Why were they killed on your turf?"

"Ain't you heard the stories? People want to do bad, they come to the Old Bottoms," he said.

"You want to know what I think?" Raven asked.

"With a passion," he said, and smiled.

"I think you and Diamond struck a deal about the land. Lois came along for the ride. That shop of hers is hemorrhaging money. The only thing standing in your way is Zeke. For some reason, he doesn't agree to the deal. So, you and Lois get rid of Zeke. His friends were just in the wrong place at the wrong time."

"It's not lost on me that you left out the brother, Diamond." He grinned wider. He was enjoying himself.

"Diamond wouldn't kill his own brother," she said.

He placed an elbow on one knee, and laid his head against a palm. "You so want that to be true, don't you?"

When imagining the conversation that she would have with Toussiant, she never thought it would be like this. She thought she would have the upper hand. He would be on the defensive. She tried to dampen the anger rising in her gut, and in an even voice she asked, "Why are so many people afraid of you?"

He threw his head back and laughed, a long, powerful laugh that exploded from his gut. He flung both hands over his belly, his sneakers tap-danced against the wooden floor. He sat up straight, still laughing, flashing one gold tooth. And then he stood up, shot his fingers in the air like he was holding two pistols.

"Everybody scared of Papa Toussaint," he said. "Everybody scared to talk if you mention his name."

"That appears to be the case," Raven said. "I want to know why."

He went to the front window of the shotgun house and used two fingers to part the thick, black curtains. A sliver of sunlight fell into the dim room. He let the curtains fall back.

He sat down, sighed. A broad smile claimed his face.

"They make up too many stories about how powerful my spells are," he said. "Liberty High football player gets killed in a car accident, they say Papa Toussaint worked him. Preacher of First Baptist gambles away the church's money, they blame me. Everything bad happen in this town is because of me. Man, people just make up crazy stuff. I don't work roots that way, my roots heal. They help people."

The man Toussaint sent for the water returned with a stout woman by his side. Ice rattled in the tumblers as they set glasses on the table. Raven felt tempted, but didn't move to take a glass.

"Go on," Toussaint said. "It ain't poison."

He took a glass for himself, drank deeply. *You better drink it, Birdie Girl*, Floyd said. *Maybe the last good thing you taste before this mother-trucker slits your throat and shits down your windpipe*. Raven took a glass and drank, the cold water bringing instant relief to her throat. The old woman turned to leave, but Toussaint took hold of her wrist and told her to be still.

"Remind you of anybody?" Toussaint said, looking at Raven. "This here is Mama Jo. She takes care of folk around here, especially kids even though she ain't got none of her own. Been doing it for years."

The woman smiled at Raven, the only bright thing in the room the streaks of white in her short afro. Toussaint leaned toward Raven with his hands on his knees.

"I know you been asking about me," he said. "Trying to figure out what the chief and I got going. Trying to figure out why he lets me alone."

Raven put her glass on the table. "I want to find out who killed those three men. I want them to have some justice. They were good men."

"Who you to judge good men from bad? How many bodies your daddy got on him? What about you? The chief?"

"The chief may be a lot of things, but he's never killed anybody," Raven said.

His voice rose, bulldozing over her last words. He pointed a thumb at his chest.

"I ain't got no bodies up under me. When I close my eyes at night, no haints around my bed."

Raven snorted. "Come off your high horse. You drove your mother to a nervous breakdown. You probably had a hand in Lois Wareham's little sister's disappearance. Now, let's talk about murder. You may not have pulled the trigger, but you did time as a convicted murderer. That's how the world sees you. That'll be the first line in your obituary, not Papa Toussaint the root doctor and healer."

She touched a nerve. Strike that, she touched several nerves. Toussaint's face went so cold that his eyes froze. They looked dead. When he spoke, his voice was low, purposeful, but filled with outrage.

"You don't know anything about my mother, so keep her name out your mouth. Everybody say I come from good family, but my parents weren't so good when the doors were shut. One time I heard this brother poet say, 'My daddy beat my mama so bad she came down with a coma'. That was my house. And all the good citizens of suburbia did nothing about it. They just waited for my daddy to kill her so they could go on television to talk about how shocked they were. Now my daddy got milk in his eyes, cataracts he won't fix because they give him the excuse of not recognizing me when we see each other on the street."

"I'm not your therapist, Mr. Toussaint," Raven said.

"So you say, but that didn't keep you from bringing it up," he said. "What happened to Fleur was bad. Lois and I knew each other back then, but I'll swear on my own grave that I don't know where that little girl got off to."

"You can swear all you want. That won't change the fact that you're most likely responsible," Raven said.

Toussaint regarded her. "I don't think you believe that. For some reason you got it in your mind to hate me. I can't do nothing about that. You talk about me being a murderer. But my hands have never been directly involved in helping anybody from this world no matter what the cops accused me of. Can you say the same thing, Detective?"

"I'm not the one being investigated," she said. "I'm trying to bring a killer to justice."

Toussiant once again laid his eyes on her. He stared at her for so long that she shifted in her seat.

"Then I suggest you take a look in the fucking mirror," he said.

Without turning his gaze from her, he said, "Brothers, take our guest out to the swamps and show her how we do justice in the Old Bottoms."

Chapter Thirty-Eight

With assault rifles pointed at her back, Moon and Terry marched Raven onto the front porch. Terry ordered her to keep her hands up, mouth shut, and eyes forward. She turned her head to look at him, anyway. He laughed and muttered something about her not knowing how to listen. He emphasized his next order for her to stop by pressing the assault rifle's barrel into her back. She stopped but still looked at him over her shoulder. He smiled as he chewed on a toothpick. The barrel of Moon's rifle kept dropping toward the ground as if the earth were a magnet. She hoped it meant that he didn't approve of the turn of events. Raven cataloged the possible advantage.

The weapons themselves appeared to be well cared for, the barrels oily black. She wondered if Toussaint kept this place afloat with a little arms running. Once they were down the steps, Terry spoke.

"Put your hands up," he said.

Raven considered telling him to pound sand, but decided against it, not with a pointed assault rifle at her back.

"Pat her down," Terry told Moon. "Take her gun and her phone."

Moon took a few steps until he was in front of Raven. He was a couple of heads taller than her. She had to look up into his eyes. He avoided her gaze. He unclipped her shoulder holster and removed the Glock 19. Her jacket pocket shook as he reached in, pulled out her Android. He stared at it a few seconds before powering it off.

"You unhooked my holster like a pro. You used to be a cop?" Raven asked.

"Military police," Moon said. "Lifetime ago."

"Stop jawing, Moon," Terry said. "Give her gun to Mama Jo so she can clear it and wipe it down."

Raven twisted around to see Mama Jo glaring at her while humming a tune that Raven didn't recognize at first. And then she realized that it was 'Mack the Knife'. Mama Jo grasped the barrel of the weapon, careful to keep her fingers off the trigger. She released the magazine and caught it with a fleshy hand before it hit the ground. She dropped the magazine into the pocket of her flowered house dress. She then racked the slide, snatched the now-free spinning round like she was snatching a wasp out of mid-air. Instead of dropping the round into her pocket, she held it between her thumb and forefinger and showed it to Raven. Mama Jo's gaze was hotter than the heat of the day. It felt like a brand. Raven even felt her skin sizzle.

"Where your throwdown?" Terry asked.

"My what?" Raven answered.

"Your throwdown. Y'all always have a throwdown somewhere. Your second weapon."

"Come on, man," Moon said. "You watch too many movies."

"Look under her jacket in the back. This is Raven Burns. I hear this bitch be packing," Terry said.

Moon's eyes glided over hers at that point. He moved closer and leaned down. She could smell his sweat. He lifted the back of her jacket and unclipped the holster with the .22.

"Aww, Sookie, Sookie, now," Terry said, the toothpick working overtime in his mouth. "Didn't I tell you? Check for an ankle holster."

Moon squatted and said under his breath that he didn't sign up for this shit. He felt her right leg, grunted, and then checked the left. His hand froze for a moment. He glanced up at her face. Terry wasn't looking. Mama Jo was asking about what to do with the guns and phone, and Moon was telling her to put them in the Mustang.

Moon dropped his hands from her left leg. He stood up, slowly.

"Well?" Terry said, turning back to them.

"Nothing," Moon said.

"What you mean nothing?" Terry said. "Didn't you check?"

"Fuck yeah, I checked," Moon said. "You want to check, you check. But hurry up. It's hot in this motherfucker."

Terry looked around. Several people had emerged from the shacks to gawk. It did cross Raven's mind that these people weren't even supposed to be here. *Maybe they the ghosts who are going to kill you dead, Birdie Girl,* Floyd piped up in her head. *If I go, you go, ole man,* Raven thought back, and then sent him back to his grave. She regarded the faces around her. Most of them seemed to be enjoying what was happening, but doubt registered on a few faces. Terry must have seen it, too, because he nodded, poked Raven with the rifle and told her to move. *Which one you think we can take?* Floyd's voice. Raven almost laughed. *Shut up,* she whispered. *You're dead. You ain't taking nobody.*

"What?" Moon said.

"I didn't say anything," Raven said.

"I heard you whispering to somebody," Moon said.

"Maybe you just heard the clank of your cell door," Raven said.

"Big talk from somebody about to shit they pants," Terry said.

He was right. She was unmoored and set adrift by fear. She didn't walk over the wide dirt path that served as the main thoroughfare of the Old Bottoms. She floated. She was no longer in control. The body she had so trusted during her MMA training and on her trail runs threatened to tear itself into pieces at the slightest provocation. One strong wind would send limbs, head, heart, bones and flesh ripping into the scalding air. Floyd prattling inside her skull like he bought tickets didn't help. Her lizard brain whispering, *It's a dream, wake up, wake up* didn't help, either. In fact, it just assured her death. She knew she had to find her way back to reality if she was going to survive. She concentrated on what she passed while she stumbled to the woods edging the Old Bottoms, woods she knew from Marna ended in a swamp.

Shotgun houses lined either side of the wide path. She sought them out one by one, examined them in detail. Three young women sat on the steps of a newly painted pink shotgun. One of them had her hands buried in the others' half-done French braid. They glanced at her before going back to their business. A young boy in only neon green shorts harvested corn from a kitchen garden. He was all arms and legs, his blue-black body glazed by the sun. One shotgun had new wood haphazardly nailed to the rest of the rotting porch. If Miss May saw it, she'd have an aneurysm. Another's house doors and windows were boarded up with plywood. Someone had thrown a faded blue tarp over a derelict roof.

She looked to the left of her. Her eyes fell on a large greenhouse guarded by three men with assault rifles, and then a brown barn that looked to Raven like a drying shed. As she examined the things around her, she felt her feet touching the ground. She felt as if she had reclaimed her body.

"I said get your arms up," Terry said.

Raven raised her arms, but half-heartedly. She even used one arm to wipe the sweat from her forehead.

Terry laughed. "Papa Toussaint is right. You a real OG. Ain't scared of nothing."

"I'm as scared as the next person," she said, glad her voice didn't shake. "What are you going to do? Shoot me in the back? A cop? You think the chief will suck that up?"

"He'll suck up what the fuck Papa tells him to suck up," Terry said.

Even though the fear no longer crippled her, Raven was beginning to believe that they were going to kill her. Her brains, flesh, bones, her entire soul railed against what was happening. *This can't be it,* she thought. But the harder she railed against it, the surer she was that with each step she was entering the last few moments of her life. She could even feel the bullets from the weapons peppering into her skin like birds too impatient for her to become carrion. But she wouldn't let it end this way. Not as a sheep at the water's edge waiting for bullets and pink clouds on the water. She'd die fighting.

And her would-be executioners marching her to the swamps were so casual about it. Both of their voices had dropped, but she could still hear them. Terry was going on about some movie, and Moon complained about having to do Toussaint's dirty work.

"He hired me to be a digger. Not a goddamn prison guard or a kidnapper," Moon said. "Doing this kind of shit ain't gone bring anybody good blessings."

Terry told him that he didn't want to hear all that sad-sack shit.

"I'm a cop," Raven said, loud enough for the spectators to hear. "All of you watching right now will be an accessory to murder."

"Don't give us any ideas," Terry said, laughing.

No one said anything, they just stared at her as if to say if Papa Toussaint wanted her dead, she deserved it. If not for the crimes she committed today, then for those she committed in her yesterdays and yesteryears, and those she was ready to commit in the future.

Branches scraped the right side of her face and tangled in her hair as she entered the woods. She took her time removing them just to see what they would do. The muzzles of two weapons pressed against her back, first one, and then the other.

"Stop stalling," Terry said.

She walked into the coolness of the woods. It smelled of freshly dug soil and scat. Green water glinted through trees. The muzzle of one of the weapons pressed against her back again. She flipped around and caught the barrel of the rifle. She yanked it until it pointed skyward. Moon yelped in surprise. She kicked him in the chest as hard as she could. He fell with a splat into the muck. Terry was saying *wait, wait, wait.* She didn't wait. She swung the rifle around and caught him on the side of his face. He went down. When Moon started to regain his footing, she whacked him on the side of the head with the butt of the rifle. She heard Floyd's voice in her head. *Shoot him. What in the butthole are you waiting for?* She snapped the rifle around in her hand and pointed it at Moon.

"Put it down," Terry said.

Blood covered the right side of his face. His right eye was starting to swell. The assault rifle pointed at her chest. She stooped, let the weapon fall to the forest floor. Moon rose briefly, walked around in a circle a few times and then passed out.

"Oh, hell," Terry said.

With the rifle still trained on Raven, he went to his friend. He nudged him with his foot. Moon groaned and rolled over.

Satisfied, Terry said, "He ain't dead. You lucky. Now turn around and keep walking."

"Fuck you," Raven said, thinking that one round fuck was appropriate in life-and-death situations. "Just shoot me here."

He laughed then, a genuine laugh with lots of mirth in it, as if the thing he was pointing at her shot cotton candy.

"No one's talking about killing you. Now move," Terry said.

Raven turned and started once again walking toward the swamp. When she reached the water's edge, Terry told her to kneel.

"You're crazy if you think I'm going to die on my knees," she said.

The man sighed, as if he were tired of playing games even though he had been enjoying the fun.

"I ain't gone kill you, you dumbass bitch," he said. "You think we're stupid? Turn around and kneel. I don't want your dumb ass running after me, that's all."

Raven didn't know if she believed him, but the roller coaster of emotions had exhausted her. She started to kneel.

"Wait a minute, stay there and don't try nothing. Don't want an accident."

He moved behind her, stepping slow as if he were trying to sneak up on a rattler.

"Now, stay still," he said.

And that was fine with her. She was too tired to do anything. She looked up at the sky. White clouds scudded by. A crow or maybe a raven cawed. She closed her eyes, waited for the shots. Instead, Terry started talking again.

"To the south at the end of the swamp," he said, "there is a road in case you make it. Take that for about a mile or two down. You gone pass a junkyard with a bunch of rusted cars crushed all to hell. Don't stop because ain't nobody minding that place. Hasn't been for years. Just keep straight for five or six miles until you hit town. Papa Toussaint will have one of our boys drive your car to town, park it at your place."

Raven looked at him like he had lost his mind. He returned her look with a bright smile.

"I know what you thinking," he said.

A calm settled over Raven. "Tell me what I'm thinking," she said, her voice solemn.

"You thinking you gone go crying to the chief and tell him that we mistreated you. You can try that if you want, but there about fifty or sixty people who gone dispute that. Do yourself a favor and save your breath."

"That's not what I was thinking at all," she said.

"You one cold motherfucker," he said. "Anybody ever tell you that?"

He kicked her. She fell down into the mud, coughed and rolled over. He kicked her again until her nose touched green water, and again until she was face up.

"Good luck," he said. "Don't get ate."

He kicked her again and the world went dark.

Chapter Thirty-Nine

Raven woke on her side, lying in a patch of hot sun a few feet from the water. She coughed. The smell of rotten eggs and sulfur found her nose and trickled down her throat. She hurt from the top of her head to the tip of her boots. A cold finger traced a wet line on her cheek, retreated, then did it again. She felt the lightest pressure on the right side of her body, as if a thin blanket had been draped over her. Her stepmother, Jean, used to do that, drape a light blanket over her when she fell asleep on the couch.

But then the blanket rippled.

Raven slowly opened her eyes. Her head hurt too much to focus on anything. Only vague shapes and shadows were in her field of vision. Then it all came back with a rush. Lucien Toussaint. Moon and Terry with the assault rifles. Terry promising that he wasn't going to shoot her. *Well, they don't need to shoot you, Birdie Girl*, Floyd piped up in her head. *The swamp is a perfect killing instrument. Why, I'd use it myself if I could stay and watch.*

Raven's eyes fluttered at the sound of Floyd's imaginary cackle. He was right. Toussaint wanted the swamp to kill her, believed it would do his bidding. He thought the green water would drag her down, and spit her back up when it was done. He imagined that her corpse would decay with the dying plants on top of the water until she became one with the very thing that ended her.

And oh my, Floyd said. *What you feeling over you ain't no apple pie and spice blanket crocheted by the bony fingers of the sweet, dead Miss Jean.*

She opened her eyes wider and focused. A petite mouth treated her with a friendly, fanged smile. It was an alligator hatchling.

"Oh sugar," she whispered.

She moved her eyes but not her body. More alligator hatchlings had been using her to sunbathe. The one near her face cocked his head curiously at her. The distinctive black and yellow stripes made it look like it was wearing onesies. That may have been adorable, but it was definitely not safe. The mama alligator couldn't be far behind. Raven knew from spending time hiding with Floyd in the swamp that alligators found humans too big and too much bother for dinner. But if an alligator sensed threat, or if they were protecting a nest, all bets were off. Her thoughts stopped there. Mama alligator was in the water. Two dead eyes waited for Raven's next move.

"Jesus," Raven said, to which Floyd replied, *You rang?*

"Shut up," she whispered.

Raven tilted her head. The little passenger near her face slid off. The mama moved closer. In slow motion Raven tilted her body toward the water. Three more of the creatures slipped into the mud, their tiny feet scrambling for the water. But the mother's subzero gaze didn't leave Raven.

She stiffened. She waited until the hatchlings that had fallen off her body had reached the water. Then she lifted her body as if the mud beneath would explode if she moved too fast. The mother swam closer. Raven halted. A couple more hatchlings dropped to the ground and began making their way to the water. Once their feet touched the swamp, Raven sat all the way up. She checked her body. Nothing. They were all gone. The mama alligator dropped beneath the water. Raven breathed a sigh of relief. One swamp danger down, nine-hundred ninety-nine to go.

Chapter Forty

Cypress trees as wide as forever soared upward from the water. Spanish moss fell in drapes of elegiac lace from their branches. Most of the shotgun houses in Byrd's Landing used cypress siding, and people who lived in them, like Marcel, were buried in cypress coffins. It was as if the trees whispered, *I'll dress the house in which you are born, and make a cradle for the grave when you are dead.* The swamp was alive with birds cawing and insects chittering. A group of great white herons at least six feet tall glanced at her before turning away.

She sat on a fallen log away from the water and mentally scanned her body. Her ribs were sore from where Terry had kicked her. Her muscles ached as if she had just run a marathon without training. But they could be pressed into service. She drew a hand through her hair to feel her scalp. There was a lump, and sweat, but no blood. She thought about retracing her steps back through the woods and into the Old Bottoms. She decided against it. She couldn't find her way back to the Old Bottoms if she tried, not with all the running and doubling back she had done with Terry and Moon.

Her clothes were wet. But thank the Lord, it was summer and blazing hot. They would dry. Terry had said to go south until she reached the end of the swamp, and then follow the road past a junkyard until she reached town. She searched the trees looking for the side with the most branches and found it. That would be south. That's the way she would go. Dying sunlight fell between the branches and illuminated the vivid pink of the milk thistle. Not much light was left. She'd have to hurry.

Raven searched until she found wood sticking from the water. She fumbled with the hem of her wet jeans to free the Ghostrike from its ankle holster, the knife that Moon let her keep. She shaved the wood to a point, and heard Floyd again as she did so. *That's right, sharp enough to shave the whiskers off Santa Claus.*

When she was finished, she took measure of the trees again and headed south, making sure she avoided stepping on critters not as friendly as the alligator hatchlings. She jabbed the stick in the water to test its depths and used it as a brace to steady each step. The mud worked hard trying to suck the boots from her feet. For now, they were staying on. When the sun sank lower in the sky, mosquitoes as big as fly swatters came out to play. They dove for every bit of Raven's exposed skin. Other bugs she couldn't identify moved in for a taste as well. She needed to get all the way out of the swamp before the night ate her alive.

She walked for what felt like forever. At one point, she found herself nodding off, her cheek pressed against the sharpened stick sunk deep into the mud.

"You better get a move on, Birdie Girl," Floyd said.

He was no longer in her head. His voice floated from the water and twisted its way through the trees before reaching her ears. "You don't want no swamp monster to find you."

Raven opened her eyes, straightened and moved on, the thick branches on the cypress trees pointing south. She thought about what she would do to Lucien Toussiant when she got back to town. It didn't involve jail, but her hands around his throat. She would watch the light dim in his eyes. She'd smile.

The last thought stopped her in mid-step.

That was Floyd, not her. Floyd watched the light leave people's eyes as they died. She wanted to see Lucien Toussaint in jail for murdering Zeke. She wanted justice. She was so deep in thought that she forgot where she was. The lapse was no longer than a second, but a second was all it took. She jabbed the stick into the muck at a careless angle. It caught on something hard. The stick bent, splintered and then cracked. The momentum sent her body sprawling. Lying on her back she felt water beneath her. She was almost in the swamp. Raven stared up at the graying sky though the cypress branches. She didn't remember a time when she was so angry and in so much danger. She screamed, an enraged sound that accused the heavens. But it wasn't God who answered her call. She looked toward the swamp. An alligator, at least seven feet, weaved through the placid water, making silent but deadly progress. It came straight at her.

Still holding on to the stick as best she could she flipped onto all fours and scrambled toward dry ground. She was almost there when she fell once again into murky water. She flipped onto her back and scooted until she was on dryer ground. The alligator hurried out of the water. Raven's back was stopped by an old cypress with many branches. One part of her told her to be still, stay quiet. She was covered from head to toe in mud. Maybe the alligator wouldn't be able to see her in the branches' shadows.

The other part said to forget that noise. That part screamed. The alligator was on her in a flash. It lunged. She raised the stick. The sharp point was gone, but she raised it anyway and poked at the gator. He caught it in his mouth, whipped his big body around until the stick snapped in two.

Floyd cried from the swamp, *Find the knife. Kick him with those stupid boots you like to wear all summer long.* She reached for the knife which she had stuck in her jacket pocket. Her hand gripped the hilt. The gator lunged again. She dropped it.

Get your ass moving, Birdie Girl, Floyd yelled. *Jump on top of that son-of-a-biscuit-eater like they do in them survival shows.*

God, she thought. *Shut up!*

Not wanting Floyd to be the last thing she ever heard, she thought hard. She couldn't imagine trying to crawl away. Her legs would be the appetizer and her body the main course.

She groped in the mud for the knife. Instead of the hilt, she felt something wet slithering in the gunk. She screamed and snatched her hand up. Snakes. What seemed like a million of them slithering around and beneath her. She whimpered. The fear coursing through her veins didn't trouble her brain. It was too busy with the alligator who moved in again, pissed off and determined. She kicked him in the snout over and over as if she were trying to break down a steel door. She held on to the back of the tree for leverage. The alligator roared and spat. He started retreating, but Raven didn't let up. She kicked and kicked, her sole target the alligator's snout. On the final kick she connected with a dying branch. It snapped and bounced against her head. Before the lights went out, she could have sworn she heard Floyd's voice saying, *Nighty night, Birdie Girl.*

Chapter Forty-One

Floyd

There is a slim difference between stupid and mean. Stupid do because they don't know. Mean know but don't care. That was Victor Broussard. Sawyer, that young one, was just stupid. Oh, he got on to Floyd real quick, knew what he was. He just didn't know what to do about it. By that time Broussard and Floyd were buddies. He protected Floyd every time the wind blew in his direction for the hollering death of Mrs. Jefferson. That Sawyer boy despised Broussard. You could see it by the way he cut his eyes at him when he was with him around town.

Broussard didn't care for Floyd, but he needed him. Broussard had this habit of driving through the streets around The Hill just to be a bother to folk. You'd be walking along minding your business and he'd hit the squad car lights like you just spun up a row of cherries on the slot machine. He'd search you, sometimes hold you. He'd knock you around some. He didn't stop there. No sir. Sometimes he'd take a new bike right from under the birthday boy or girl. He'd bang on the door of someone who he thought done him wrong and demand a fifty for the trouble.

This one time an old man living on The Hill had a granddaughter who come home to get married. He was so proud of the fact that his grandbaby graduated from college that he put on his finest churchgoing suit and decided to walk to the wedding. He had this vision about saying 'howdy' and 'how you' to the folk he met on the way. He was going to make sure everybody he passed knew his grandbaby had a degree and now was about to get a husband. Nobody at the wedding even knew he was coming.

Broussard saw the old granddaddy walking along Moore Street all smiling and greeting everyone that he passed. Maybe he didn't like the set of the old man's shoulders, the pep in his step, or the smile on his lips. He hit the lights. Said he fit the description for some robbery that happened on the other side of town. Made that old man sit on the curb for two hours. By that time the preacher had said his piece. The groom had kissed the bride and everybody was eating cake.

Broussard terrorizing poor folk went on for some time. How can a man be so hated and not walk on all fours the Lord will never know. But Broussard? He thrived on the hate and walked on two legs like he was the only person who had a right to.

Folks soon got to know what would happen if you told on him. That's where Floyd came in. Broussard knew that Floyd helped Mrs. Jefferson from this world. And he wasn't shy about letting Floyd know that he knew. He promised to keep him out of jail if he would do him an occasional favor. Usually, those favors had to do with making folk who was about to make too much of a fuss disappear.

So, the folk on The Hill put up with Broussard like they put up with the weather. But then came the rumors that Broussard was starting to kill folk with his own hands. Some say he pushed a drunk onto the railroad tracks for sassing him. The oncoming train split him in two. And still others accused him of smothering the dandy granddaddy while the old man was sleeping because he wouldn't shut up about missing his granddaughter's wedding. Floyd can tell you, though, that Broussard had nothing to do with that one. Let's call it a favor between two like-minded individuals. By then people were squalling. They wrote letters to the *Byrd's Landing Review* even though the newspaper didn't print it.

It went on like that for a time. And then one day when the sun came up everything looked a little brighter. It was as if even the cosmos knew that Broussard wouldn't darken the doorstep of not one more law-abiding citizen in the good town of Byrd's Landing, Louisiana. Someone had disappeared him. They disappeared him forever and for good.

Chapter Forty-Two

The sound of birds singing woke her. The sun poured liquid gold through the trees. A great white heron flew over the water, its wings spread like a blanket of promise on the air. In a panic Raven lurched to a sitting position. There were snakes, but they didn't seem to be paying her any attention. It was as if she were just another part of the swamp's ecosystem.

"Now I wouldn't be thinking about that," Floyd said, again like he was outside of her body. "I'd be checking to see if I had all my parts."

"Oh, Lord," Raven said, remembering.

She shot to a standing position. She hurt all over, was scratched all to hell, but whole. She didn't know why the alligator left her alone. Maybe the branch that knocked her out got him, too. Maybe it was the rabbit kicks to his snout. She didn't care one way or the other, was only glad that she was alive.

She found south again, and started walking until she saw the dirt road at the edge of the swamp. A road not necessarily back to civilization, but at least to Byrd's Landing, to what she knew. After an hour or so of walking, she passed the junkyard Terry had told her about. She hadn't walked much past that when she heard the engine of a car. A white Ford Escort with one black door swerved toward her. For a minute Raven thought it was attempting to finish what the alligator started. It skidded to a stop at the last second before hitting her. Doors swung open. Gervais jumped out of the driver's side and Cameron the passenger's side.

"Oh, God," Cameron said, throwing a blanket over her. "What the fuck?"

"Get her in the backseat," Gervais said, pulling open the right passenger door.

She dove in, and fell sideways against the seat. Her head banged against the opposite window.

"Oh shit," Gervais said. "She smells like shit."

"How do you expect her to smell?" Cameron said. "She's just spent the night in the devil's asshole."

Gervais pulled the car back onto the road.

"How did you find me?" Raven asked.

"Turn here," Cameron said. "We're taking her to Memorial."

"No," Raven said.

"Yes," Cameron said. "Your stubborn, knuckleheaded ass is going to the hospital."

"Why?" she asked. "So they can hose the mud off me? At least take me home first so I can get cleaned up."

"And then hospital?" Cameron said, looking back at her.

Gervais rolled down the window. Cameron gave him a nasty look before doing the same.

"Cleaned up first and then hospital," he conceded.

★ ★ ★

They told her that Gervais got a call from a friend of his in the Old Bottoms about an hour ago. He knew Gervais was doing some work for Raven. He said that Raven had wandered off into the swamps after talking to Lucien Toussaint. Gervais called Cameron. They lit out to find her. *Lucky breaks*, Raven thought, closing her eyes. Lucky breaks and coincidences. Something she didn't really believe in, but if it meant being out of that swamp? She'd take it. She was about to ask the friend's name when Gervais said, "Did you run into any swamp monsters?"

"What?" Raven said.

"Swamp monsters. My cousin's friend got lost in the swamp, not for a night but for days. There was light in the water, monsters tricking him to go deeper into the swamp. I don't know how he found his way out. But he almost died. True story."

"Man, shut up and drive," Cameron said.

Gervais did and fast. Raven steadied a hand against the window to keep from rolling to the floor as he flew around corners and crested hills on the dirt road. He parked at a slant in her front yard, and was out of the car almost as fast as Cameron. When they helped her out, they clucked like a couple of hens.

"Maybe we should call Marna to help you out of your clothes," Gervais was saying and Cameron shooting back that he sure as fuck wasn't doing it and Gervais accusing him of not caring about his sister and no one asked his ass anyway and Cameron teasing him about having a crush on Raven like a twelve-year-old and Raven finally understanding why they got along so well.

Raven hobbled to the door, placed a hand on her aching back as Cameron and Gervais played the dozens, traded insult after insult, the next one more outrageous than the last.

"Jesus on the cross!" Raven said. "Shut it. My head aches like it's about to explode and you jackasses are making it worse."

She twisted the knob, thankful that Gervais and Cameron had left it open. She made her way to the bathroom.

"Imma have Cameron call Marna," Gervais shouted through the closed door.

"Do it and I'll cut your balls off," Raven answered back. "You'll have to go through the rest of your life ball-less."

"Deal," Cameron answered for him.

Raven shut out their patter. She peeled her mud-caked clothes from her sore body. They were right, the smell was almost too much to bear. It took her a minute but soon she was as naked as when she entered the world. No place on her body felt like it hadn't been scratched or bitten. She glanced in the mirror and saw that she looked every bit of the person who had wrestled an alligator on his own turf. Did she win? Maybe. Maybe not. She grinned in the mirror, her white teeth flashing in her filthy, swamp-creature face. *Let's face it*, she told her reflection, the green and blue eyes boring into her own. The alligator won. It just got bored with the fight. But she was about to bring down a real swamp monster. This one had a name and a reputation that everyone knew about. Lucien Toussaint would regret for the rest of his life giving the order to abandon her in the swamp.

Chapter Forty-Three

Toussaint had the nerve to leave her Mustang at her house. She hadn't noticed it when they first arrived, not with Cameron and Gervais yakking. Toussaint's men had left her cell phone on the driver's seat. She opened the door with a gloved hand, retrieved her cell phone. Raven insisted on driving to the hospital in Gervais's car so they could preserve any evidence that would take down Toussaint and his associates. Raven smiled through the pain. When they reached the hospital, they took her right away. An old nurse tutted as she helped Raven out of her clothes, ignoring Raven's protests and cries for privacy.

"You should've thought about privacy before you decided to spend the night in the swamp. Chile, you know monsters live out there. Things Jesus wouldn't even mess with."

Raven quieted, letting the nurse do what she thought she needed to do. She didn't want to admit it, but she liked the feel of her sure brown hands, the smell of her nicotine-stained fingers as she helped Raven into a hospital gown. Once Raven was lying down, she began hooking Raven up to an IV.

"What's that for?" Raven asked.

"Saline for the dehydration, and the doc might want to give you something for the pain. Sleep now."

Raven slept.

* * *

Raven opened her eyes to the nurse and doctor talking.

"Oh, there she is," a cheerful voice said. "Looks like you're back in the world, Detective. How you feeling?"

"Like crap, Dr. Nguyen," Raven responded.

"I bet," he said. "You had a rough night. I'm not used to speaking to you while you're in a hospital bed."

Raven knew Dr. Nguyen from the job. He was the emergency room doctor she dealt with when an assault patient was expected to die. When they'd inevitably pass on, he'd call Raven and say, "People think we're magicians. There was only so much we could do with this one. They're all yours, Raven."

He removed Raven's left hand from beneath the covers, examined it as he talked.

"You get bit by anything dangerous while you were out there?" he asked.

"I don't know. There were a lot of snakes." she said.

"What kinds?" he asked.

"The slimy, slithering, fork-tongued kind," she said.

"Not helping. Give me some colors," he said.

"Light brown and black near the water. Probably laid in an entire passel of black ones."

"Woo-hoo, water moccasins. Those things are vicious. They stay mad. The black ones were probably harmless water snakes. Anything else cause you trouble?" Dr. Nguyen said.

"A pissed-off alligator," Raven said.

He laughed. "Well, if he'd bitten you, we'd have probably removed you from the swamp in pieces. So here is what we're going to do."

And he told her.

★ ★ ★

Raven felt like she was awake for her own autopsy as they examined her. They scrutinized every inch of her body, in some cases using a penlight to search for ticks, spider or snake bites. They checked every orifice, beneath her breasts, between her toes, even up her nose. Dr. Nguyen then rolled her on her back like she was a sack of sawdust and repeated everything again, daubing her with antiseptic as he went. He whistled and told jokes the entire time. After he was done, he pronounced that nothing was wrong with her that would kill her. He studied his notes as the nurse helped Raven back into her hospital gown, got her under the covers and sitting up in bed. While the nurse slid back the privacy curtain used to shield the room from the front door, Dr. Nguyen said, "I'm going to keep you here for observation."

Raven, feeling like a pincushion, said, "No, you're not."

"Oh yes, he certainly is," said a voice from the doorway.

Raven looked up to see the chief and Stevenson standing there, scowling like she was an errant child. She turned her attention back to Dr. Nguyen.

"Give me something that'll knock me out," Raven said. "And be quick about it."

Chapter Forty-Four

The next time Raven opened her eyes she was in a hospital room still connected to an IV. Stevenson had slung himself across a chair that looked like it was made for a kindergarten classroom. The chief was leaning against the door. She wondered if he'd worn that scowl the entire night.

Raven tried to lift herself up. The alarm beeped as every muscle in her body asked if she was out of her ever-loving mind. The same nurse who had been in the emergency room entered. Raven read her name tag. Evelyn. She fussed and readjusted Raven's pillows before leaving. Stevenson and the chief remained silent, scowling and judging.

"Why are you two looking at me like…" Raven started.

"Like you just crawled out of the swamp?" the chief asked.

"Well, yeah," Raven said. "Like this is all my fault."

"Isn't it?" Stevenson said.

"No." She couldn't believe her ears. "Why would it be?"

The chief straightened and walked over to her bedside. Raven knew she was in trouble when he bypassed a perfectly good working chair just to stand over her.

"I told you to stay away from Toussaint," he said. "He didn't have anything to do with the murders in the churchyard."

"With Zeke's murder, Chief," Raven said. "With Lionel and Marcel's murders. They had lives. They didn't deserve what happened to them."

"You just don't listen, do you?" the chief said.

"I do listen," Raven countered. "To the evidence you choose to ignore. When was the last time you investigated a murder? Not since you ascended to the ivory tower and started yucking it up with the mayor."

"Watch your mouth," the chief said. "I've been investigating murders since you and your father…" He stopped, pursed his lips together. Raven drew back from the sting of his words.

"Go on," she said. "Since me and my father what?"

"I was going to say since your father was turning living bodies into victims," he said.

"You said me and my father," Raven said.

Evelyn, the nurse with the comforting hands, stuck her head in the door.

"Shush up in here," she said. "I can hear you all the way down at nurses' station."

After she retreated the chief looked momentarily ashamed. Raven pushed down her rage.

"You need to show the chief some respect," Stevenson said.

"Who are you to tell me what I need to do?" Raven snapped.

"I thought I was your partner. I was worried sick about you," Stevenson said. And he looked it. Bags under red eyes, rumpled clothes that he probably slept in.

She relaxed and fell back against the pillows. The room smelled of Lysol and flowers.

"Billy Ray sent the flowers on your night table, and Stevenson the ones next to them. The yellow roses," the chief said.

"Where is Billy Ray?" she asked.

"He's been a bit busy," the chief said.

"Dealing with another murder, or don't you remember?" Stevenson said.

"I bet it's more likely he's been dodging you trying to make him for murder," Raven said.

"It would be easier on him if he cooperates," Stevenson said.

"Would you cooperate?" she asked.

He said nothing. Raven let the resulting silence play. Not being able to stand it anymore, she asked, "Did you bring Toussaint in, yet?"

"For what?" the chief asked.

Raven stared at him. She then turned her gaze to Stevenson. He shrugged.

"What do you mean for what? For what he did to me. Kidnapping. Stealing my car, taking my phone, abandoning me in the swamp. To a cop on your team, Chief."

"He didn't do anything to you," the chief said. "We talked to him. He told us what happened. I told you to leave it alone, didn't I? And yet you went in there anyway."

"Please, Chief," Raven said.

He held up a finger to silence her. "He said he invited you in, answered your invasive questions, gave you some sweet tea. He said y'all had a good talk."

"You kidding me?" Raven said.

"Well, is it true? What I just said," the chief asked.

"Yes, it is," Raven said. "But did he tell you what happened after?"

Stevenson nodded, and heaved himself up from the chair. He leaned against the wall opposite her bed. "He did. He said you shook hands and left. It was quite late, so he went to bed. When everybody woke up, your car was still sitting there. Not wanting any more visits from the police, he had one of his men drive your car to your house."

"One of his men?" Raven said. "You mean two of his thugs. And that's a load of crap."

The chief spread his hands. The nurse poked her head in the door and shushed everyone again.

"He marched me through the Old Bottoms like a war criminal," Raven said. "His 'men' had assault rifles at my back the entire time. I thought they were going to kill me. And it wasn't night, but late afternoon. The entire neighborhood saw it."

"He told us you would say that," Stevenson said.

"Wait a minute, you believe him over me?" Raven asked.

"Are we talking about the same person who said she'd throw Willie Lee to the ground on purpose and say he tripped?" Stevenson said, his voice grim.

"Don't pull that crap on me. What about the part where you're supposed to have my back?" Raven said.

"What happened with going with the evidence," Stevenson said. "The conversation with Willie Lee is evidence."

Raven brought both hands up to the side of her head. It hurt. She ignored the pain.

"Everyone saw it!" she said. "You need to get a warrant, Chief, and look for those guns. And I saw a greenhouse and a drying shed. It could be drugs."

"It's not drugs. Owning an assault rifle in Louisiana isn't illegal," the chief said quietly. "Hell, you don't even need a permit."

"Using them to force someone into the swamp and leaving them to die is," Raven said.

The silence in the room this time left her cold, alone and afraid.

"Did you question anyone else, or did you just take Toussaint at his word?" Raven asked.

"You think I'm dumb, Raven?" the chief said. "Of course we did. Marna and her team talked to multiple people. To a person, every one of them backed Toussaint's statement."

"Why would I leave my car?" Raven said. "Why would I run off into the swamp?"

"That's easy, Raven," the chief said. "Toussaint didn't give you what you wanted, so you did some snooping on your own to try and make him for the churchyard murders. You took a wrong turn somewhere, hit your head, and ended up in the swamp."

"Hit my head?" Raven said.

"You have a lump on your head," the chief said. "Proof."

"Now, since you didn't get what you wanted, you're using this story to implicate Toussaint. To force the chief's hand," Stevenson said. "Maybe it was your plan all along. You told me once how you and your pops lived out in the swamp for a time. You know how to survive out there."

"You two think I staged this whole thing," she said.

"More than likely, Raven," Stevenson said. "Remember, I know how it feels to be obsessed."

Raven threw the glass vase with the yellow roses at Stevenson's head. He ducked. The vase smashed against the wall. Bent stems and bruised flowers crashed with the broken glass to the floor. The nurse burst into the door. Like an avenging angel, she kicked both Stevenson and the chief out of the room. She shook her head as they left as if she could understand how someone would want to bean them with a vase of yellow roses. Instead of scolding Raven, she called in an orderly to clean up the mess.

Chapter Forty-Five

They released her around dinnertime the next day. Raven thought about leaving the hospital against medical advice, but to what end? She wouldn't do anybody any good stumbling her way through the rest of the case because of an undetected snake bite. She needed to be at her best if she was going to put away Zeke's killer. She called Billy Ray to pick her up.

After she settled in the passenger seat of his Buick Skylark, he gave her the once-over.

"What?" she said as he pulled the car onto the street.

"Why didn't you call Stevenson to pick you up?" he asked.

"The man's an idiot," she said.

"You say that like it's a revelation. Where to?"

"Oral's place," she said, and then corrected herself. "My house."

"Better," he said. "You don't want to go to the station?"

"I need to get back to my own shower. I can still smell swamp gas on me," she said.

She told him what happened. Everything. Her march through the woods, her lunge for Moon's weapon, and Terry kicking her until she passed out in the swamp. She didn't leave out the part with the chief and Stevenson not believing a word of it.

"I ain't surprised," Billy Ray said. "The chief likes things easy."

"What about illegal things? They had guns, assault rifles."

"That ain't illegal," Billy Ray said.

"Should be," she muttered.

"You think the chief will take you off the case?" Billy Ray asked.

"And do what?" Raven said. "Give it to Breaker in major crimes? The man who'd run a mile in heavy shoes from a murder scene?"

"The chief might not have a choice if you keep on doing stupid shit," he said.

"What do you mean?" she said.

He parked the car in her yard but made no motion to get out. Instead, he looked at her.

"For starters, begging for rides from a murder suspect," he said.

"You mean you?" she said.

"I mean me," he said.

Raven rolled her eyes and got out of the car. She told him to come in for a few minutes. Once inside he sat on a big brown leather sofa with his arms spread along the back.

"Get me a beer, would you?" he said.

"Get your own beer," Raven said. "I'm injured."

"How are you going to have your way with me, then?" he asked.

"Hey, you're a funny man with a murder charge hanging over your head," Raven said.

"I didn't kill Fabian Long," he said. "My conscience is clear."

While he was grabbing the beer she dragged a whiteboard she had in a spare bedroom into the living room. He returned and set the two Abitas on her new coffee table. Without saying a word, Raven put two paper state park coasters beneath the bottles. After all, she was her father's child.

Billy Ray sighed when he saw the whiteboard but caught the red marker she threw to him with both hands.

"I don't know how I let you talk me into these things, Raven. Stevenson and the chief are going to shit RVs if they find out about this," Billy Ray said.

"We don't have to tell them," she said. "Besides, they think I made the whole thing up."

"You don't think the churchyard murders and Long's murder are connected?" Billy Ray asked.

"I don't know," Raven said.

"Why? How?" he said. "A churchyard, a bedroom, a shooting, and a stabbing compared to an axe murder? The only thing they have in common is the timeframe."

"You forgot about terrorizing this town. Toussaint has no love for Byrd's Landing," Raven said.

She wrote the churchyard and the Long murders on the board in two separate columns. Billy Ray lifted his beer from the table and drank.

"Even I didn't know you could stretch that far, Raven. Do you have any suspects in the churchyard murder case?" he asked.

Raven wrote Toussaint on the board. Billy Ray scoffed. She ignored him. She then wrote the names Lois, Diamond and Miss Maybelline on the board.

"You got motive?" he asked.

Raven drew a circle around Lois and Diamond's names.

"Didn't you date Diamond at one time?" he asked.

"A long time ago in high school," she said.

"I bet you're going to tell me he's a different person now," Billy Ray said.

"He's the same person. That's the problem. I know both Diamond and Lois are hurting for money. Zeke had a trust fund that would revert to Diamond if he died. There was also insurance money. And the land."

"Land?" Billy Ray asked.

She took a drink of her own beer. "Yes. The Old Bottoms reverts to Maybelline after Toussaint's lease is up."

"Lois?" Billy Ray asked.

"Maybe Zeke was going to dump her," Raven said.

"You need more," Billy Ray said. "Why is Toussaint's name up there?"

"It all comes down to him. Diamond and Lois were in the neighborhood the night Zeke and his friends were killed. Lois has some business with Toussaint she won't tell me about. She used to date him, Billy Ray. I saw what looked like a grow house and a drying shed in the Old Bottoms. Maybe it's drugs."

"What about Dr. Long?" Billy Ray asked. "How is he involved in all that?"

He had her there. "Well, they're both doctors," she said, and laughed.

"Not funny," Billy Ray said. "Root work has a long history going all the way back to Africa. It's how slaves took care of each other. That shit works sometimes, Raven. It ain't no joke. Some roots are hard as hell to get. You can get rich off that shit. It's a billion-dollar business in this country."

"How do you know so much about it?" Raven said.

Billy Ray drained his beer. As he walked to the kitchen, he flung back, "You got any food in here?"

The refrigerator door opened, closed and opened again. Then the sound of cabinets swinging open and knocking closed reached her ears.

"Ramen," he shouted back to her. "You got to be fucking kidding me."

She ignored him bumping around in the kitchen, slapping pots against the stove's burners. She heard water running, the microwave starting.

Raven sat on the new couch Gervais helped her carry into Oral's living room, now her living room. She thought for a long time.

What if Diamond was trying to get in on Toussaint's drugs and possible gun running? She remembered seeing men guarding whatever was in that greenhouse with assault rifles, obviously willing to kill for it. And then there was the drying shed. What if it was drugs and Zeke threatened to expose him? He would've done it too. Drugs had ruined Zeke's life. Miss May said that Zeke died trying to help somebody. Those phone calls and text messages Zeke made to Raven in the weeks leading up to his death? Was he trying to tell her what Diamond and Toussaint were up to?

But Raven didn't think the Diamond she knew would be willing to run drugs or guns. He would find that distasteful, thuggish.

Billy Ray returned to the living room with two bowls, steaming and fragrant with the smell of onion and chicken broth. He handed one to her. She took it.

"Found some peas, and some shrimp," he said. "You ain't got eggs. I found an onion that was about to go over. Added a bunch of spices just in case it tastes bad."

She looked up at him. "Is this going to kill me?"

"Hope not," he said. He sat beside her and put his big feet on the coffee table. She knocked them off.

"Might make you sick," he said, putting his feet back on the table.

He shoved long strands of noodles into his mouth. They ate in silence for a while. The ramen was hot, and the spices that Billy Ray added made it taste divine. She hadn't realized how hungry she was until she had a couple of bites.

"What makes you think that shed had something illegal in it?" Billy Ray asked.

"Because Toussaint is crooked as hell," Raven said. The bowl thudded and wobbled a bit on the coffee table when she set it down.

"You mean you want him to be as crooked as hell," Billy Ray said.

"What do you mean by that?"

"Sounding like it's personal."

Billy Ray set his bowl down next to hers. She thought about Billy Ray in his restaurant, delivering plates to tables when the wait staff couldn't, stopping by to ask his patrons if a meal was good or if they needed anything, and sitting at the old folk's table playing spades or dominoes when it was near closing. All the conversations he may have overheard, important information he may not have known he had.

"You staring at me like you're going to eat me," Billy Ray said. "Talk. You giving me the creeps."

"I think Mama Anna and the old folk are mixed up in this too. They won't give me anything on Toussaint." She said the words slowly, measuring them out. She didn't want to annoy him. If she annoyed him, he'd bolt.

"Could be a fairly innocent explanation," he said.

"Like what?" she asked.

"I don't know." He threw a pillow at her. "Don't make me do all the heavy lifting."

Raven stood and strolled back to the whiteboard with her hands in the pockets of her sweatpants. She picked up one of the markers from the tray, popped the lid on and off again. The chief had an enclave in his town with a leader who called himself Papa, an expert root doctor. He cured the sick, the addicted and elderly. Whoever needed shelter could find a place with him, some of them would gladly lay down their lives for him.

"Ever since this case started, I've noticed something that I hadn't before," she said.

Billy Ray raised an eyebrow, waited expectantly.

"Leather straps around people's necks, necklaces." She stopped and fingered the collar of her own sweatshirt.

"Diamond has one. Lois does, too. And I could have sworn I saw one on Rock, Marcel's cousin. Even the barista at the Perc Me Up coffeehouse. Come to think of it, so did one of the old folks. Miss Vera. You think it's a cult?"

Billy Ray laughed softly. "That's a bridge too far," he said. "You're one of the smartest people I know, but sometimes you are as blind as a snipe when you get something in your head."

"I love you, too, Billy Ray," Raven said.

"Those are mojo bags," he said. "Toussaint has been selling them and people be buying. They wear them for luck. The old folk probably don't want to talk about Toussaint, especially Miss Vera, because it ain't exactly Christian. They might've been embarrassed."

"What in the hell is a mojo bag?"

"For fuck's sake, Raven..." He stopped, considered. "Never mind, forgot how you grew up. It's like a bag of good-luck charms. What's in it depends on what you need it for. You know, things like love, luck, or money. They put roots in it, stones, pyrite, even animal parts. I think Miss Vera's has a chicken foot."

"She's embarrassed but tells you about it?" Raven said.

"Maybe she'd tell you if you acted right." He stopped, considered. "That grow house you talking about. Maybe it's for Toussaint's roots."

"Why the rifles? The guards?" she said.

Billy Ray looked at her for a long moment. She slapped her head with the palm of her hand. He had said earlier that some roots were hard to grow. If you could get them to thrive, and if people thought you were legitimate there was a lot of money to be had. What did Billy Ray say, hoodoo was a billion-dollar-a-year business? She remembered something Moon was complaining about before she slugged him with his own rifle.

"What's a digger?" Raven asked.

"A digger is a person who knows how to dig up the root the right way, say the right words over them. They say if you do it wrong, the root will lose its power before you take it out of the ground."

"So, that's what's so valuable in the Old Bottoms. The roots that Toussaint grows. Maybe that's the business Diamond is trying to get into," Raven speculated.

"Could be. If you can grow those roots yourself, some folk say they have more power," Billy Ray said.

"But that still doesn't explain what he has on the chief," Raven said.

"Think about it," Billy Ray said.

Raven did. As long as Toussaint was in charge of the Old Bottoms, the homeless population in Byrd's Landing was under control. It could have been as simple as that. They had a place to go. Maybe the chief had relatives over there. Maybe the mayor and Mama Anna had relatives who lived there, too. To top it off, Toussaint had weapons, powerful ones. She saw five assault rifles just on her march to the swamp. Who's to say there weren't more?

"The chief's sitting on a powder keg, has been for years," Raven said.

"That's what I think," Billy Ray said. He downed the rest of his third beer. Pointed the bottle at the circle around Lois and Diamond's name. "I'd concentrate on them two, first. Stop poking the bear."

"You mean Toussaint?" she said.

"I don't think you have any evidence linking him to Zeke's and them murders," he said. "But if you do…"

"If I do what?" she asked.

He looked at her. "If you do think that Toussaint has something to do with these killings, as a famous man once said, can't you walk and chew gum at the same time?"

Her Android rang. Too preoccupied with her thoughts to look at the caller ID, Raven pressed the answer button. What greeted her was a long, slow, rattling breath. Unsure of what she was hearing, she cocked her head and glanced at the floor as if that would make her ears better. Another long, wet rattling filled the air. It sounded like a whimpering moan. Raven brought the phone around to her face to look at the caller ID.

"What is it?" Billy Ray said.

She spun the Android so Billy Ray could see.

"It says the call is coming from you," she said. "It's a death rattle."

Chapter Forty-Six

The two-story house where Marna lived with her husband Newell was on fire with light. Yellow light burned in every single window. Uniforms walked aimlessly along, police tape trailing from their hands. They looked like ants who had lost their queen. Rita, in her customary jeans and a Grateful Dead t-shirt, sat in the middle of the sidewalk with her hands covering her eyes. Gus, the strong one now, pulled at her arm trying to get her to stand up. She was losing the battle. A small crowd gathered on the street, and Raven thought she saw a news van.

Four men in uniform surrounded Newell, who twirled on the lawn like a kid playing airplane. He didn't sob. He reeled around and around with his arms akimbo. His bellowing was the most mournful sound Raven had ever heard. He was half-dressed in a pair of sweatpants that hung below his big white belly and threatened to fall to the ground. At that moment, Newell was like a man out of place and out of time. It was as if his soul had fled his big body so it wouldn't have to deal with the animal pain coursing through its veins.

The uniforms talked to him, screamed his name, told him to be still. But Newell wasn't capable of hearing anything at that moment. What made it worse was Stevenson was just standing there ignoring the entire nightmare. His hands were raised palms up toward heaven. His lips moved a million miles an hour in a silent prayer. She surveyed the scene again looking for the chief. He was nowhere in sight. It was the most chaotic, unprofessional scene Raven had ever seen in her entire career. God help her, she wanted to join them.

Marna was dead. They knew that much. Marna, the unofficial mayor of Byrd's Landing. Raven had received the call shortly after Billy Ray left her place. Stevenson told her that Newell had called dispatch screaming. Raven believed the man hadn't stopped screaming since the call. She drove to Marna's house with the lights on, running every red light along the way. And now as she sat in her car surveying the scene, she heard Floyd's voice in her head. *Well, Birdie Girl, you can either start acting deranged like the rest of them, except that Gus gal. I'd keep my eye on her if I were you. Or you can get in there and teach the flea circus the proper way to dance.*

She remembered when Oral died, how she had lost it, how it had almost gotten her arrested for murder and let a killer escape. No matter how much she wanted to lay down and wail, she sat up straighter and put steel in her spine. She took a deep breath and got out of the car, adjusting the badge around her neck. The yellow light from the house bounced off the gold shield. She started with hey, hey, hey, but no one listened. They were all lost in their own worlds.

You gone have to do it, Birdie Girl, Floyd said. She didn't want to. Wasn't there enough violence and hate in the world without needlessly adding to it with filthy words? It was stupid, but it was her rule, one she had lived by. But now she felt she had no choice.

"Hey, what the fuck you doing?" she yelled at the uniform trailing the police tape along the sidewalk. Everyone turned to her, stunned.

"Get this tape around the perimeter," she said, glad that he appeared to wake up. He dragged a sleeve across his eyes. Another officer came over to help.

"You four," she said to the ones surrounding Newell. "You afraid you're going to break a nail? Tackle that motherfucker, get him in cuffs. Gus, go get him a blanket from one of the squad cars."

Three of them just stood looking at her. One of them, the smallest one, a uniform named Olson, tried to tackle Newell but just ended up riding the man's back. Still, it broke whatever spell the other uniforms were under. They moved in to help.

"Rita," Raven said. "Get your ass up. We have a job to do. Where's Tim?"

"I don't know," Rita said, crying. Her entire body shook as she rose to her feet. "I don't think anybody's called him, yet."

Raven grabbed Rita by the shoulder. She shook her hard. When the woman wouldn't stop crying, Raven took a handkerchief from her pocket and thrust it into Rita's hands. The linen cloth just lay limp in Rita's palms. Raven reclaimed the handkerchief and rubbed the tears from Rita's face.

"Did anybody call the chief?" Raven asked.

Rita hiccuped. "I think Stevenson did."

Raven directed Rita to the house. She looked toward Stevenson, who was still praying. She walked over to him, her steps fast and hard against the sidewalk. She didn't stop until they were toe to toe. His eyes had been closed. He opened them not on Jesus, but on Raven with a fury on her face that she hadn't let free since he had blown his cover.

"Are you done speaking in tongues?" she said.

"One day your blasphemy is going to catch up with you," he said.

"Did you even bother to clear the house? Was praying the first thing you did?"

"We cleared it," he said.

Raven took a deep, calming breath. "Yeah?" she said. "You did? I say we do it again since you didn't bother setting up a perimeter before you started talking to Jesus. Where's the body?"

"The bedroom," he said.

Newell had been restrained. He was now sitting on the grass sobbing with a navy-blue car blanket around him. The other two uniforms had just about finished the perimeter. Raven was glad to see that another officer had been assigned to crowd control. Looks like they were getting it together. She switched her attention back to Stevenson.

"Follow me," she said.

With guns drawn, they cleared every room. Two uniforms searched the backyard. After they were done Raven crossed the threshold into Marna's bedroom. She did it fast before she could change her mind.

* * *

Marna had gone to bed with pink curlers in her hair, and a short satin green nightgown covered in purple forget-me-nots. That's where normalcy ended. Because the person who used to sneak Raven lunch in grade school and raise hell in high school had a gaping wound in her throat. Stab wounds covered her torso. Her dark brown skin was ashen, and her usually sparkling brown eyes dead. Still, they had a message for Raven. *Find out who did this*, they said. *Find out who did this and make that motherfucker pay*.

Chapter Forty-Seven

Stevenson, Raven and the chief sat with Newell in an interview room. Stevenson wanted to give Newell coffee in a paper cup, even wanted to cuff him to the table. Both the chief and Raven balked. Newell was a witness, not a suspect. Raven told Stevenson to get that paper cup crap out of Newell's face. While they all waited, she went to the break room and got the *Star Wars* coffee cup Newell used every day. They may not have gotten along, but Newell was one of them. He had even helped her with the Sleeping Boy case last year. Without him Raven's nephew would be a victim of yet another Byrd's Landing serial killer. And this man loved his wife. She made the coffee fresh and brought it to him hot. That was ten minutes ago. Newell hadn't touched it. Instead, he sobbed.

"Is there anyone we can call?" Stevenson asked.

Newell didn't say anything for a few long moments, and then he said, "My mom, my sister. Their numbers are on my phone."

"We have his phone?" Raven asked.

"It's in evidence," Stevenson said.

"Well, take it out of evidence and call his people," Raven said.

"Raven," the chief warned.

"What's the passcode, Newell?" she asked.

He told them. Nobody moved until Raven glared at Stevenson to make it clear that he was the one to make the call. Once the door closed behind him, Raven turned back to Newell. He was still wrapped in that stupid navy-blue blanket Gus had retrieved from one of the squad cars.

"Cameron is going to bring you some clothes as soon as Tim finishes," Raven said. Newell, who had managed to stifle his tears, sniffed and nodded.

"Can you tell us what happened?" the chief said.

"I don't know what happened," Newell said. "I stayed up playing video games late, headphones on and everything. Then I fell asleep in the den, you know. I woke up, you know, thought it was about time for me to go to bed. It was pretty late."

"You're practically newlyweds, right? Why weren't you together?" Raven asked.

"We had a fight," he said. "I thought she needed her space, so I gave it to her."

"How did you leave the fight?" the chief asked. "Y'all go to bed still mad at each other?"

"She told me that she was going to read her book, and said 'Good night, Willie Lee, I'll see you in the morning' like she always does."

"Willie Lee?" the chief asked. "Who the fuck is Willie Lee?"

"It's a thing we do," Newell said. "It's from one of her favorite authors. Alice Walker. Marna's done that since we got serious, no matter how mad she was."

Raven knew the poem. It was about love and forgiveness and the hope that the end wasn't the end. Raven didn't want to think about it. It was too hurtful to think that the end wasn't the end until it was.

"What was the fight about?" Raven asked.

Newell didn't say anything for several long moments. And then he said, "I need to go to the bathroom."

"Did you know your wife asked me for a recommendation?" the chief said. "For a job that was not in Byrd's Landing?"

Raven looked at the chief, stunned.

"I have to go to the bathroom," Newell said.

"She said you wouldn't be coming with her," the chief continued gently. "Were you two having trouble?"

"I have to go to the bathroom," Newell repeated, more insistent.

"Newell," Raven tried.

"I have to go," he said, his wide blue eyes staring at both of them in turn. "I'm going to pee my pants. Is that what you want? Ain't I humiliated enough?"

The chief relented. Newell stood up, adjusted the blanket around him. She watched as his big, bare white feet slid across the floor, the pocket of his sweats slapping against his thigh. His head was down and his nose was running like a river. Raven stood up to escort him, but Newell put his hand up to stop her.

"I know where it is," he said.

Raven sat down again, slowly. She sat all the way down when the chief nodded to her that it was all right. Something warned her that it wasn't all right at all. But she ignored the feeling. Besides, she wanted to talk to the chief.

"You knew they were having trouble," Raven said.

"I did. Didn't you?" he said.

"Yes," Raven said. "Newell loved her so much, too much, I think. He hovered. A lot. Marna never could stand a hoverer."

The chief ran his hand over his head. "Let me tell her parents," he said.

"Chief," Raven said.

"You're not getting this case," the chief replied. "Breaker's going to have to take it whether he likes it or not. But I'll tell her parents."

Raven argued with him, but he wouldn't budge. She sat back in her chair, waited for Newell, something still niggling at her. Him clutching the blanket around his broad body, his feet shuffling against the floor, the pocket of his loose sweatpants heavy, knocking against his hip... Raven shot up as if someone fired a starter's pistol.

"Raven, what?" the chief said.

She sprinted down the hallway to the bathroom, the chief jogging behind her saying, "What, what?"

She had almost reached the door when she heard the shot. The sound stopped her mid-stride and then drove her to her knees. The uniforms did exactly what she said. They restrained him, cuffed him, and gave him a blanket. But they didn't bother to search him. They didn't find his personal weapon, a .22, buried deep in the pocket of his sweatpants. The chief was looking at Raven. His face was full of devastation and resolution. Breaker wouldn't have to take this case after all. Newell's suicide had given the chief an easy way out. He killed his wife, and then himself, the chief could say. The gunshot pronounced the case closed.

Chapter Forty-Eight

Marna's death wasn't the end of it. Two days later, Suzie Speck found her estranged husband, Willie Lee Speck, that perpetually agitated former trauma scene cleaner, in their backyard. Just like the other victims, he had been hacked to death with an axe. Worse, before his death, Raven had received another phone call from Billy Ray that wasn't from Billy Ray. As she listened to the dying breath on the other end of the wireless, she knew that there would be another body. She just never expected it to be Willie Lee's. After Willie Lee's death, panic infected the entire town.

Late in the afternoon on the day after Willie Lee's death, she, Stevenson and the chief were in his office. The chief tossed his baseball back and forth in his hands, so hard that Raven heard it smack against his palms. It must have stung. In the middle of a sentence, he jumped up and snapped the blinds shut on the large window behind his desk. Protestors had figured out where his office was in the building. They tortured him with signs, shouts and chants for hours on end. Back at his desk, he picked up the baseball and threw it in the air. He missed it on the way down for one of the first times Raven could remember. It rolled across the floor and stopped at Raven's feet. Stevenson bent to pick it up.

"Leave it," the chief snapped.

The chief was about to speak again when the phone rang. He snatched it up. "What? Marcus," he barked.

Raven groaned inside. It was the mayor. Raven could hear him yelling. The chief picked up the remote and pointed it at the flat-screen TV hanging on the wall opposite his desk. Raven and Stevenson turned to look. Imogene Tucker, perfectly coiffed and made-up, was talking in her newscaster voice straight into the camera.

"There has been one triple homicide, three murders and a suicide within recent weeks in Byrd's Landing. And though this town has known violence before, these murders are unprecedented as one of the victims is a well-respected doctor, and the other is one of BLPD's own. Yet, the police are no closer to solving these crimes. To give you an idea of how the investigation is going, I invite you to view the following footage. The first clip that I'm going to show you was taken at the churchyard homicides. The second was taken at the murder scene of Marna Taylor, a beloved and well-respected police officer in Byrd's Landing."

Footage rolled of Raven, Marna and Stevenson exploding from the church of the Old Bottoms. When that was over, a video of police officers walking aimlessly around Marna's yard trailing police tape while Newell bellowed unrestrained in his front yard played. Then the camera cut back to Imogene.

"We wanted to know how people felt about the murders, and the performance of the BLPD. Do they still feel safe? For that, let's cut to Sophie Renault to hear from the citizens of Byrd's Landing."

Another reporter on the screen stuck a microphone in the face of a blonde woman with dark roots, and a baby on her hip. She said something about people not knowing how to get divorced anymore and how it was a damned shame. They bleeped out 'damn' but Raven could read her lips. When the reporter asked her if she thought Byrd's Landing had another serial killer to contend with, the woman said, earning another bleep, "Serial killer my left tit. Love will make you do crazy things. Don't you listen to Al Green?"

Another Byrd's Landing resident in an LSU t-shirt firmly pushed the microphone away. The reporter quickly rebounded saying something about not everyone wanting to talk.

"Everett," she said. "What are people saying where you are?"

The camera cut to another location, this one outside of Chastain's. A camera followed a reporter with a high fade haircut and a skinny blue suit. He walked up to the zydeco band taking instruments out of their car while explaining where he was and why. The next thing Raven knew Gervais's scarred face filled the screen. The reporter asked him what he thought about all the murders, and if he thought they were the work of one killer.

"Ain't no serial killer out here, man. It's just crazy-spoiled love," Gervais said. He spread his arms and laughed. "Now if it is the work of a nutjob serial killer, I heard that this OG is sneaking up on motherfuckers," he said, the curse bleeped out like the others. "He likes houses that are all dark and quiet. I don't know about y'all, but I'm leaving the lights on. He's going to know I'm home because I'm going to be playing some Coltrane or some Tupac. I'm going to blast me some fucking Kendrick Lamar. Feel me? And me and my friends Smith and Wesson are going to be waiting on his ass. I got something for him."

"Blast some zydeco for that fool," one of his bandmates shouted.

"That's good, too," Gervais laughed. "Come on down to Chastain's Creole Heaven if you want to see what we talking about. It's open tonight so come get away from the madness."

"Holy hell," the chief said, rubbing his forehead while holding the phone to his ear. Raven could hear muffled shouting from the mayor. She heard the words 'fools' and 'incompetents' and 'fire'. The chief hung up on him. He clicked off the television.

"She promised not to show that video," Raven said, knowing that didn't matter.

"I know her boss," the chief said. "Angus hates this department. Once he got wind of those videos, he probably pissed himself trying to get them on the air. Makes us look like fucking clowns. Y'all need to make some arrests."

"We don't have enough evidence," Raven said. "We need more time."

"Time for what?" the chief said.

"To find out what connects these victims," she said. "I'm telling you it's a serial."

"It's not a serial, Raven," Stevenson said. "You're stalling. You just trying to find evidence to support your narrative about Toussaint."

"I've been getting these phone calls before every murder, strangled breathing. Rita says they sound to her like death rattles. Cameron checked the phone records. Each phone call comes just before a murder."

"Who's calling you, Raven?" the chief said.

"It's somebody spoofing Billy Ray's number. I tell you we have a serial killer, Chief. He's taunting us with these warnings," Raven said.

"You mean taunting *you*. Why?" the chief asked.

Raven looked at the closed blinds and for a moment wished she was home recovering from her injuries. She bowed her head. "I don't know."

"And you think these calls are what?" the chief asked.

"I think they are the victims' dying breaths," Raven said.

"That doesn't make an ounce of sense," Stevenson said.

"Then what are they?" Raven said.

The chief had leaned back in his chair, laced his hands together and placed the tips of his index fingers to his mouth. He looked like a schoolteacher who was listening to a not-so-bright student, one that he liked enough to indulge.

"Any other evidence, Raven?" he said.

"The phone records, especially the burner, I'm going to have Cameron check the records again," she said.

"Future tense," the chief said. "Which means you have nothing but a crazy hunch. Who do you believe is the serial killer?"

Raven said nothing because she knew how it would sound. Instead, she focused on the footsteps in the halls, the muffled voices from the protestors outside the window, while trying to come up with an answer that would satisfy the chief.

But she was too late. The chief sat up and scooted his chair closer to his desk.

"That's what I thought. You think Toussaint is involved," he said.

Stevenson flung up his hands. "Who else? She's obsessed with him."

"All right, genius," she said. "What do you think's happening?"

Stevenson counted on his fingers. "Diamond and Lois killed Zeke and his friends over the land in the Old Bottoms. Billy Ray killed Fabian because he wants his wife. Willie Lee's wife, Suzie, killed him for the insurance money, and, though I hate to say it, Newell killed Marna because she wanted to leave him."

"That's a bunch of crap," Raven said.

"Both you and I heard Marna complain about Newell," Stevenson said. "Plus, the chief said she was looking for a job out of town and Newell wouldn't be going with her."

"Newell didn't kill Marna. He loved her," Raven said.

"Then why did he kill himself?" the chief said.

"Because he couldn't live without her," Raven said.

"Never took you for a romantic," Stevenson shot at her.

"There's nothing romantic about it," Raven countered.

"Hold on, both of you," the chief said. "I'm not saying I agree with Raven, but why all in a row like this, Stevenson? It doesn't make sense. All these people deciding to kill their partners?"

"And why so messy?" Raven said. "There are easier ways to kill people."

"You would know it," Stevenson answered.

"Isn't your wife waiting for you?" Raven said.

"Y'all are driving me crazy," Chief Sawyer said.

"You've heard of suicide pockets? I think that's what's happening here. It's a contagion," Stevenson said.

"All these people caught the desire to kill? Where has that ever happened before? Come on, Stevenson," Raven said.

The chief stood up, limped around his desk. She could tell that an old knee injury was bothering him. He retrieved the baseball and went back behind his desk. He eased down into his office chair. With his chin on his hands curled around the baseball, he appeared deep in thought.

"This town," Stevenson said, "isn't like any place I've ever been in my life. Nothing that happens here would surprise me."

"You're saying that the town is sick?" Raven said.

"This town's not sick. Y'all just need Jesus," Stevenson said.

Raven laughed. The chief gave Stevenson a pensive look.

"Come on, Chief. You think Marcus has the Lord on speed dial? Are you going to call the pastor of First Baptist down here to preach a good ole fire-and-brimstone sermon?"

The chief shook a finger at Raven. "I'm not thinking that. But Stevenson could be right," he said thoughtfully. "A sickness spreading through this town like a virus is more plausible than a serial."

"I don't mean sickness, I mean evil," Stevenson said.

"I know what you mean, but I don't think it's Jesus this town needs. It's therapy. And a curfew, just until everything cools down."

"What?" Stevenson and Raven said together.

"Therapy," the chief said. "We need to get this town on therapy. We'll set up some hotlines, place therapists in the schools and in the drug stores and at the urgent care, you know, where people frequent so they can talk to somebody instead of killing each other."

"You've lost your mind," Raven said.

"Exactly, that's why I'm going to do what I'm going to do. We all have lost our minds. I'll work on my side of things, you work on yours."

"What exactly is ours?" Raven said.

"Arrest Diamond and Lois for the murder of Zeke and his friends. I'll get the warrant. I've already been keeping the DA updated," the chief said.

"Toussaint?" Raven said.

"What about him?" the chief answered.

"He has the same motive that Diamond and Lois have," Raven insisted. "He was losing the Old Bottoms to Miss May and Zeke."

"Can you place him at the scene?" the chief asked. "Got DNA, anything connecting him to the murders."

Raven said nothing. She couldn't and she didn't.

"Bring Suzie and Billy Ray in as persons of interest for the Speck and Long murders. Lean on them a little," the chief said.

"Billy Ray?" Raven asked.

"His watch was at the scene," the chief said.

"That's flimsy as hell, Chief. You want to bring Billy Ray in and not Toussaint?" Raven said.

"You want me to replay the news footage? Remind you both of how much you fucked up this case?"

"Hey!" Stevenson said.

"And Marna? Who should we bring in for that?" Raven said.

The chief threw the ball up in the air. It fell smoothly back into the palm of his hands in a hard slap.

"Nobody. The main suspect offed himself in the men's room down the hall."

Chapter Forty-Nine

The chief picked up the phone, punched a couple of numbers. "Freida, let me talk to Marcus."

Raven slammed the door so hard that the framed certificates on the walls of his office rattled. This included the commendation he received for apprehending Floyd Burns years ago and the mayor's thank you for apprehending the Sleeping Boy killer. Those, along with other certificates with their fancy lettering and gilded flourishes, quavered. The sound satisfied her. Maybe the chief would realize that he had become a mouthpiece for the mayor, a pacifier who spent most of his time slathering frosting over feces. The light spilling from the fluorescents in the hall dispelled any notion that she was dreaming. The chief wanted her to arrest Billy Ray while leaving Toussaint to terrorize the town.

Stevenson fell in beside her. He grabbed her arm. She jerked it away. She hoped he would give up but giving up wasn't in Stevenson's bag of tricks. Not giving up was why he was in Byrd's Landing in the first place, and why he had another shot at being a family man and a better husband to the wife he so obviously loved.

He grabbed both of her arms, and gently but firmly placed her against the hallway's vomit-yellow walls. He looked down into her face.

"You need to take a breath," he said. "Calm down."

She felt as calm as she could be while hunting for serial killers in a town God had forgotten.

"Get your hands off me," she said quietly. "Or I will kick you in your balls so hard you'll finally get a glimpse of that heaven you've craved for your entire pathetic, boring life."

He let her go, but he was still nowhere near giving up.

"We have a job to do. The chief gave us direct orders," he said.

"The chief's lost it. He just took himself out of the game," she responded, and jerked away.

★ ★ ★

Raven shouldered her way through the crowd outside of the BLPD. Her red Mustang shone like a beacon in a parking lot filled with cars, the Louisiana sun glazing the bright red paint until it appeared liquid.

As she peeled out of the BLPD parking lot with one destination in mind, Stevenson's Camry pulled out behind her. She made a right turn on Beaumont, a left on Cecily, and a sharp right on Morning Glory. She floored it on the straightaway weaving in and out of lanes. When she was several cars ahead, she slipped the Mustang between two big rigs and watched his gray Camry pass her. She had lost him. She didn't think once about him guessing where she would go. In the days, weeks, months, even years later, she'd think about this moment and the consequences of letting the white light of her own rage blind her.

★ ★ ★

She sat in the driver's seat of the Mustang parked near the church, the place where everything started. She sat in her car long enough for the setting sun to leave a red shit stain on the horizon. *This is how you going to start talking and thinking now you ain't got your way no more, Birdie Girl?* Floyd said in her head. She thought maybe she would. Because the chief, once again, had betrayed her, and was about to betray Billy Ray. She was living in a world where her carefully constructed rules for the universe no longer applied. In her mind's eye she could see the chief in full uniform at a news conference telling the town what he had in mind for them. Therapy. Using Marna and Newell's deaths as examples, he'd probably blame the insanity ripping through the town right now on domestic violence. She wouldn't be surprised if he manufactured a single, perfect tear to fall from his left eye. After the news conference, he'd probably order Cameron to set up hotlines in one of the station's empty conference rooms for volunteers to triage calls. Knowing the chief he'd probably even deputize them. He'd go a step further by badgering the mayor for a new domestic violence campaign. He'd used the recent deaths of Marna and Newell as bargaining chips. But Raven believed that the key to solving this crisis hid in the hastily refurbished shotguns in a place the townspeople called the Old Bottoms.

She checked all of her weapons, including the Glock in her shoulder holster, the .22 at the small of her back, and the new Ghostrike knife in her ankle holster. Toussaint hadn't answered her questions. Now he would. She would make him. And in the process, she would see the person who killed Zeke and Marna punished. The bonus would be keeping Billy Ray out of jail.

Chapter Fifty

Raven strolled down the center of the packed-dirt street of the Old Bottoms unaware that she swaggered like she owned the place, or was about to. A group of children played Red Light Green Light barefoot in the dusty street, their faces sweaty and shining with the joy of the game Raven remembered playing when she was a girl. Red Light meant stop. Green meant go. They all froze when they saw her. They stood in absolute stillness for a moment before scattering, as if she were a lion walking into a pack of gazelles. They flew up wooden steps and flung open screen doors shouting that the police were outside to whatever guardians they had in what Raven perceived as a lost and derelict place. The panic in their voices troubled Raven.

She surveyed the haphazardly refurbished shotguns, the solar panels, the grow house, and the brown wood of the drying shed. She noted that one house, painted a gaudy shade of purple, was further decorated by three large pots of red and yellow chrysanthemums. The people who lived here cared. They were trying to make a life. She remembered when Marna gave her a history lesson on the Old Bottoms. She said that Toussaint had revived it. There was no judgment in her voice when she said it, nothing to suggest that she thought that this neighborhood being here was out of place and time, that it was somehow wrong. *But was she willing to die for it?* Floyd asked Raven, to which Raven readily answered back – no, she would have never been willing.

The residents of the Old Bottoms spilled onto the porches of the shotgun houses. About a dozen or so men carried weapons. Two teenagers, one wearing a *Star Wars* t-shirt, and the other an old-school Scooby-Doo t-shirt, carried shotguns. At least they didn't point them at her. She returned their steely gazes with one of her own, and moved forward. She didn't stop until she was facing the screen door of Toussaint's house. She drew her weapon and pointed it at the front door. The metallic clatter of rifles and shotguns being raised behind her filled the purple dusk. She didn't bother to turn around. Neither did they shoot. She expected they were waiting for Toussaint to open the door and give his order. Raven had no plans to let Toussaint choose what that order would be. After a long moment, the screen door creaked open. Toussaint stepped out to face the barrel of the new Glock now pointed at his chest.

"You better be a good fucking shot," he said calmly.

"I am," she said. She moved her finger to the trigger, squeezed it just before the firing point. "I'm an excellent shot. Tell your men to stand down."

"You better be fast, too," he said. He moved to the porch railing, leaned against it before crossing his big arms over his muscled chest.

Raven grinned. "Deadly fast. Haven't you heard? I'm a runner."

"You know," he said, unfolding his arm to wave a finger to the army that was behind her, "they could shoot you before you can shoot me."

"Maybe, but I'll pull this trigger before I go down, and your chest exploding will be a beautiful, dying sight."

"What do you want?" he said.

"Tell your men to stand down," she reiterated.

He tried waiting her out and lost.

"Lower your weapons," he said, and then after a moment, "You satisfied?"

"Tell them to put them in a pile by your front porch," she said.

She heard grumbling behind her.

"Do it," Toussaint said. "The kind of trouble she's bringing we don't need."

And they did. One by one, they piled the weapons they had carried out of their houses by Toussaint's porch steps.

He lifted an eyebrow. "Well?" he said.

Raven didn't know if they had all deposited their weapons on the pile. They may have, but there was no way to be sure. She played her hunch.

"All of them," she said, her voice hard. "Even the ones who joined when I had my back turned."

Toussaint gave her a half-smile, and a salute. "Reckless, but smart as hell," he said. "Do it."

Three more assault weapons joined the pile. She placed her weapon back into her holster.

"That's one way to avoid a war," Toussaint said. "Now please tell me what you're doing here. You're alone, so I don't think you came here to arrest me."

"I'm here to finish our last talk," she said. "I want to know what you have on the chief, and if you hate this town enough to terrorize it by murdering its citizens."

She didn't like his smile. It was amused, tinged with an authority that said she could never touch him.

"Go home," Toussaint said to the men who had rushed to protect him. "The detective and I are just going to have a friendly but hard conversation."

He held out a hand, one she had no intention of taking. "Come on in," he said, and sighed. "I'll tell you everything you want to know. But understand this. You won't like it."

She placed her boot on the top step, but paused when someone called her name. She turned in surprise to see Stevenson jogging up the road. She couldn't believe it. She took her foot down and started toward Stevenson. He stopped outside the gaudy purple house.

"You big dummy," she said, when she reached him. "Go home."

"Go home?" he said. "What the fuck are you doing here? You heard the chief. This is the most asinine thing you ever did."

"Don't be stupid," she said in a harsh whisper. "He's willing to talk to me, you jackass!"

"The last time you talked to him you almost ended up dead," Stevenson said. "I'm here to protect you."

"I don't need your protection," she said.

She shoved him in the chest as hard as she could. He stumbled back several feet, tripped over a rock and fell. Just as Stevenson was getting to his feet, Terry, the man who had marched her into the swamps, exploded through the front door. He charged screaming with an assault rifle aimed and ready. The bullets smashed into Stevenson, who jerked like a rag doll. Raven drew her Glock so fast that she'd swear later that she'd rehearsed it. She pivoted and fired. Terry went down. He died with the assault rifle in a death grip.

On automatic pilot, Raven holstered her weapon. She unclipped her radio, yelled, "Shots fired, officer down, Old Bottoms!" while darting toward Stevenson. She dropped to her knees beside him and took off her jacket to staunch the bleeding. When she looked at him, she realized how useless that was. Blood spurted from his chest, even leaked from his mouth and ears. She watched him for what she thought was a long time but was only mere seconds. He didn't look afraid, just preoccupied with the business of dying. His body convulsed as the rest of his blood left him. His eyes dimmed, and he let out one long, last shuddering breath.

Raven didn't scream. She threw her head back and shrieked. She had no more control of the sound than she had of the setting sun. As the last of the sound faded, she sunk her face into Stevenson's bloody chest.

"Wow," Toussaint said from above. "I guess you are pretty fast."

Chapter Fifty-One

Moon and a few other men dragged a struggling Raven to an abandoned shotgun that had yet to be renovated. They stripped her of her radio, her handcuffs, her weapons – all of them this time – and flung her in. Before Moon shut the door, Raven was sure she saw regret on his face. His look of sorrow didn't bring comfort. She leaned against the wall and sank down to the floor. She cried until she couldn't cry anymore. Stevenson. She had taken him for granted. She knew that now, but it was much too late.

She sat against the wall of the old shack with her wrists on top of her knees for a long time. She didn't move even when the chief's voice sounded over a bullhorn.

"This is Chief Sawyer, Lucien," he said. "You need to stop all of this before more people get hurt!"

Raven laughed when Toussaint answered. Of course, the man would have his own bullhorn.

"You mean killed, don't you, Chief Sawyer?" Toussaint said. "We already put one dead man outside the neighborhood. I'm sure you got him by now. I want you to know that wasn't our doing."

Raven got to her feet as the chief and Toussaint argued. She studied the small house for a way out. Every single window was boarded up with wooden planks. She checked each one and found that the boards were nailed tight. Both the front and back doors were locked from the outside. She threw her aching shoulder against them with all her might. The only thing she got for her troubles was more pain. Raven surmised that this house was used as Toussiant's jail. There was a filthy mattress in the corner of the living room and a green plastic bucket. She kicked the bucket with the toe of her boot, glanced inside. At least it was clean.

She peered through the wooden slats boarding the windows. She saw people running in and out of their houses with boxes while armed men watched over them. Raven moved her head until she could see a sliver of the grow house. People were going in and out with buckets of plants. She was about to move to another window for a better look when she heard her name.

"Is Detective Burns injured?" she heard the chief ask from the bullhorn.

"For the time being, no," Toussaint said. "Just don't piss me off."

"How about you release her," the chief said. "That'll go a long way in creating some trust."

Toussaint laughed. "There ain't nothing on this earth or in your heaven that can create trust between you and me."

"Think about all the people you are hurting," the chief said.

"All the people I care about are in here," Toussaint said.

The bullhorns quieted for several beats while muffled voices flowed into Raven's prison. She wondered what they were doing out there.

"Then what can I get you?" the chief said.

"Nothing," Toussaint said. "I've got everything I need here."

★ ★ ★

It must've been after midnight when the locks on the front door of the shotgun clicked open. Moon came in armed with an assault rifle. He watched Raven like she was some rabid dog as he stood aside to let Mama Jo into the shack. Mama Jo tossed a dingy sheet and an old crochet blanket on the dirty mattress. She then upended a grocery bag. Four bottles of water fell atop the blanket and mattress.

"You can make it up yourself," she said, contempt in every word.

"Can I get some clothes?" Raven said. "These clothes are caked." She didn't say caked in Stevenson's blood.

"They good enough for you," Mama Jo said.

Moon reached into his pocket and chucked four cereal bars toward her. They fell at her feet.

"Looks like you gone be here for a while," he said.

Raven studied him, looking for the softness she had glimpsed earlier.

"You know this isn't right," she said. "You're going to end up in jail."

"Maybe," he responded. "But not today."

⋆ ⋆ ⋆

Raven ate three of the cereal bars and drank two bottles of water. Then she started walking the shotgun like a trapped ghost back and forth between the rooms. She tested the windows repeatedly, looking for a weakness. She ran her palms over the drywall in search of rot. When her hands met a cool or damp place, she kicked hard hoping to make a big enough hole to crawl through. This went on for what seemed like hours. It *was* hours later as she was raising a boot to kick another hole in the wall when the front door opened. It was Moon once again but this time he was with Toussaint. Behind him was a light so bright that she had to shield her eyes. Helicopter blades whirred overhead.

Toussaint carried a folding chair in one hand, and a portable lantern in the other. The lantern was a good one, the kind people took camping. He placed the chair in the center of the room and placed the light beside him before sitting in the chair. Moon closed the door. He stood with his back to it and a solid hold on the assault rifle. His face dared her to make a move.

"You redecorating?" Toussaint asked. "Trust me, there ain't no other way out of here. You could've asked Terry; that hothead spent a lot of time here, but you killed him."

Raven stared at him in wonder. The man appeared as calm as a monk. He laughed at her expression.

"What, you think I thought we could hold on to this place forever? That I don't plan?"

"You know you can't win," Raven said.

He laughed again, and sat back in his chair. "The chief's right, you don't listen. You see all the light they pumping in here? Oh, wait, maybe you can't. Your window's boarded up. Trust me, outside is as bright as the center of a roman candle. Man, they got a motherfucking crane out there with a spotlight on it. But it took them a while to set all that shit up. Gave us some time to take care of business. I know I can't win. Not this place, anyway."

"Did you come here to gloat, or kill me? Whichever one, get it over with. You're making me tired."

"I come to give you what you want. Go on, ask me anything. Might as well talk or all this," he lifted a hand and whirled his index finger around, "all this is for nothing."

She blinked at him, wondering if he was playing with her.

"What? All of a sudden you tongue-tied?" Toussaint said.

"You're playing games," she said.

"I could be," he said.

Moon shifted his weight against the door, adjusted his weapon. Raven studied Moon's face for answers because Toussaint's gave nothing away. Maybe this was his way of torturing her, but she had nothing to lose.

"Did you kill Zeke Riverton and his friends?" she asked.

"Now why in hell would I do that?" Toussaint said.

"Did you have them killed?" she asked.

"No. Why you think it was me?"

"Zeke was going to get control of the Old Bottoms after the lease was up. His mama was letting him make the decision on what to do with it. You knew he wouldn't let you stay here, so you killed him."

"After luring him to the churchyard?" Toussaint challenged. "Why you think he would've come if I called?"

"Zeke was pretty gullible," Raven said. "He may have believed that the stuff you do is real. Maybe you threatened to work his mama with that hoodoo mess. Or somebody that he cared about."

"Maybe somebody like you," Toussaint said. He laughed at the startled look on her face.

She knew he had something there. Zeke could have been trying to warn her, but Raven couldn't let herself believe that. That would make everything her fault.

"I don't care what people told you about me, I don't do the kind of root work that would hurt people. Next question," he said.

"You could make a lot of money here by growing your own roots. That's why you needed Diamond? Right? You two had a plan. Zeke was about to ruin that."

"Yelling ain't gone make it true," Toussaint said.

Raven sat back, touched her fingers to her throat. It was raspy. She hadn't realized she had been yelling. She took a deep breath to steady herself.

"Now," Toussaint said as if talking to a child. "Diamond, and Zeke's girlfriend Lois, did come to me about some business they wanted to get into. Talking about taking what I do national and how we three could make it rain money. Lois thought she could make Zeke let the land alone, not take it. She came begging to me the night Zeke died to work with her and Diamond. I threw them out just as I did you." He grinned. "But they went out the front, not the back through the swamps like you did."

"You're saying that you didn't want to go into business with Diamond and Lois?" she asked.

"I don't do what I do for money. I make what I need to keep my place, feed and protect my people," he said.

"You mean by running guns," Raven said.

"I don't run guns, I buy them," Toussaint said. He turned to look at Moon, standing against the door with the assault rifle.

"They do come in handy," Moon said.

"I don't believe you," Raven spat.

"You don't have to," Toussaint said and stood. "If I were you, I'd start looking closer to home. You feel me?"

"You mean for the churchyard murders?" Raven asked.

"I mean for everything," he said quietly. "All of it."

"If you're such a saint, why don't you let me go so I can investigate? Or better yet, if you know so much, why don't you tell me who's doing this?"

"Don't worry, I do plan to let you go. But in a few days. As long as you here, the FBI won't come in here blasting."

"While you're in a giving mood," Raven said, "tell me what's going on between you and the chief."

"You mean the chief, the mayor, Mama Anna from Chastain's, dirty ole Mr. Joe, Zeke's mama and my daddy, you mean between me and all them? Even your pious Miss Vera." He stopped. "Don't look so surprised. I need to know what's going on to survive in Byrd's Landing. I keep my ears open."

"Are you going to answer my question?" she said.

"Ask somebody else," he said. "Start with the chief."

Raven waited, hoping the silence would prompt him to say more. He did, but not what she wanted to hear.

"If you want the killing to stop," he said, "you need to look at your own house, and try to understand why so many people around you drop dead when you walk by. You need to dig deep, all the way back to when you lived on The Hill with your killer daddy. Until you do that, you ain't catching a dog, let alone a serial killer."

"Save me time and just tell me," she said.

"Ain't my responsibility. I got enough to worry about."

"Well then, fuck you," Raven said.

He studied her face for a few seconds. "I'll leave you the light."

That night, she peeled off her blood-caked t-shirt. She couldn't stand smelling Stevenson's blood on her any longer. She thought about doing the same with the jeans but just couldn't bring herself to do it. No telling what creepy crawlies were on the mattress. She spread the sheet over the mattress and used the crochet blanket as a pillow. The cheap yarn was rough against her cheek. She left the lantern on, stared into the light thinking she wouldn't be able to sleep. But she was wrong. Her own personal boo hag surfed her entire body into her nightmares. Floyd, as dependable as ever, was there to serve as a guide. This time he decided to tell the truth.

* * *

She shouldn't have opened the door.

It was almost ten at night and already dark. She had lived on this hillside of leaning houses all her life. Her mother and grandmother had lived in the same house before her. But it was the night that scared her especially since Floyd and that child moved in two doors down.

She had closed the front door long ago, which signaled the entire neighborhood of shacks strung along The Hill that she had stopped accepting visitors. On this night she was especially afraid because she was alone. It was the Fourth of July, when fireworks needed the dark. Those who were able had gone to the park for a cookout and to watch the sky on fire. No one should be knocking at her door. But there it was again, someone on the other side rattling the screen door steady as a woodpecker.

"Go on from here," Miss Ruth said. "Y'all know I'm done for the night. If you looking for the cookout, they at the park."

The rattling stopped. Her heart stopped, too, but she stuck to what she knew was right. And then there was a child's whimper. Miss Ruth touched an ear next to the slivered gap between the doorframe and the door.

Raven tried to scream in her sleep for Miss Ruth not to open the door. She tried to wake up by wresting her body right and left, tried to open her eyes. Sleep paralysis had glued them shut. A world sat on Raven's chest, the force of its gravity pinning her to the mattress.

Miss Ruth did move her head back as if she heard Raven's struggles. But then she said, fear in her voice, "Raven, is that you. Are you hurt?"

"Yes," a tiny voice said. "I'm bleeding, Miss Ruth."

"Go home to your daddy. He'll fix it," Miss Ruth said.

In the dream, Raven's mind clawed at the muscles of her own face, hoping the effort would wake her up. But she couldn't escape. She wanted to scream, "No, no!" but couldn't.

"He's the one who did it," Raven said.

Miss Ruth had no choice. There was a child bleeding outside her door. She steadied herself before lifting the two-by-four lying across the door. She set it aside and then twisted the deadbolt open. She took one more deep breath before turning the lock on the knob to the open position. Her final act was to be brave, to let in the dark so she could help a child. It was Raven, but only for a second. And then it was Floyd 'Fire' Burns who stood there grinning.

⋆ ⋆ ⋆

Miss Ruth's screams hurled Raven back to reality. She was once again in the front room of Toussaint's jail but she could still hear them. The screams drove everything from Raven's mind. She even forgot the right way to breathe. Each breath was like a punch to the throat. She pressed both hands against her ears to drown out the sounds.

She did this. Her.

Not just Floyd. She lured Miss Ruth to the front door so Floyd could unleash those screams on the world. Her mind flashed back to the woman at Marcel's funeral asking her about life on The Hill. *I don't remember much about those days*, Raven had told her. Now she knew why she'd repressed those memories. Two boys found Miss Ruth. Floyd told her later that one of them chased him through the woods. Floyd said that boy would be something else, and by that he meant a killer like him.

Who else knew Raven's role in the death of Miss Ruth? There was only one person who knew everything about her life with Floyd. That person was Zeke. She may not have told him that she was the reason Miss Ruth was dead, but he could have pieced it together and confided in Marcel. And like a dark game of telephone, Marcel may have passed the story to someone with vengeance on his mind.

Chapter Fifty-Two

No new revelations came that day. No food or water, either. Raven ate the last cereal bar that afternoon. She drank the remaining water. As night drew near, the FBI started pumping music into the Old Bottoms at an earsplitting level. First, it was Elton John's 'Philadelphia Freedom'. Raven peered through the slats to see people laughing and dancing. When the song changed to 'Pomp and Circumstance', Raven was on her hands and knees looking for a way out. She ran her hands over the uneven floorboards thinking that the floor would give her what the walls refused. She could kick a million holes in the wall but not one of them would lead to a way out. The floor was her best bet. The floorboards felt spongy near a rusted-out sink in the kitchen. She stood up and brought the heel of her boot down on it hard. The floorboards gave, but not enough. She threw open the few remaining cabinet doors and scoured the rest of the house looking for a tool that would help her break through the floor.

She found nothing.

Back at the weak space in the floor, she dropped to her knees and stared at the spot for a long time. For a brief moment she thought this was it. She was stuck while a killer roamed Byrd's Landing and the entire BLPD plus the FBI were focused on Toussaint's Old Bottoms. How much more blood will be laid at her feet? How much more pain would she be responsible for? She sobbed but only once. She dried her face and remembered the camp lantern and Toussaint saying, "I'll leave you with the light."

★ ★ ★

Raven returned to the living room where the camp lantern stood on its metal tripod. She was able to pull it apart without too much trouble. It was like cracking a crab leg. She returned to the kitchen and sank down at the spot where she felt the spongy wood. She pummeled, pulled and pried until she created a hole big enough to drop through. She lay face down and peered into the hole. The light the FBI pumped in didn't reach beneath the house. She jumped back up, ran to the living room and grabbed her jacket. She rummaged through the pockets for her mini flashlight. It was still there. Back in the kitchen, she sent the light into the hole and then yelled as loud as she could into it while 'Pomp and Circumstance' blared for a zillionth time. Nothing scurried. Not even a racoon or opossum. And thankfully, no snakes.

Raven shimmied through the hole, scraping her shoulders along the way down. Beneath the house wasn't tall enough for her to stand up. She headed to the back of the house hoping that she wouldn't meet a Toussaint guard or an FBI recon team. But her luck didn't hold. When she emerged from beneath the house, she came face to face with Moon.

★ ★ ★

They stared at each other as if they were trying to come to an agreement as to who was predator and who was prey. Raven didn't give him a chance to decide. She swept his legs from under him with a roundhouse kick. A bag he had been carrying hit the ground, the contents rolling out across the mud and dirt. She jumped on his chest, hit him twice with two strong elbows. She jammed her hand on his nose and mouth and pressed down with all her might. A guttural cry came from deep in his throat. His head whipped from side to side. He tried to bite her but she held on. His eyes bulged. He brought one of his hands out from under her and pointed to the spilled bag. She risked a quick look. There was her Glock ready to give her a big fat hello-mama kiss. She swung from Moon and grabbed the Glock. He sat up and gulped air that must have tasted like honey to him. Scattered around Raven's feet were her knife, her .22, and holsters for all. There was also a change of clothes. She recognized a rescue when she saw one.

She grabbed the clean t-shirt and pulled it over her head. "Where is my phone? My radio?"

"You're welcome," he said, his voice hoarse. "Toussaint smashed the phone and the radio."

"Sorry. How did you know I was back here?" she said.

He turned away while she took off her boots and peeled off her jeans. They were stiff and covered in blood.

He flipped his hand toward the house. "I came in through the front door, saw the hole in the kitchen, and went through the back. I figured you'd head out this way."

She pulled on a pair of black joggers he had brought for her, reached for the boots when he said, "I brought you socks, too."

She rummaged through the bag, found the socks and put them on, and then the boots.

"Why are you doing this?"

"Because Papa's gone too far this time," he said. "He's mad as hell and I don't think he's got control of it as much as he like to think he does. I ain't no killer."

When her shoulder holster was on, she said, "Let's go."

Moon shook his head. "I ain't coming with you."

"They'll kill you."

"He'll do a lot of yelling, I may get some punishment, but he won't kill one of his own. Just do me a favor?"

"Sure, anything," Raven said.

"Try not to let anybody see you for the next several hours," he said. "If they think you still in here, they won't storm the place."

"I'll do my best, but I'm not making any promises."

"That'll do," he said. "Go."

He didn't have to tell her twice. Raven went.

⋆ ⋆ ⋆

Raven walked away from the Old Bottoms. She crested a small hill onto a narrow, dark road. She stood and looked around. All the action was to the east of her. There were cranes, police vehicles, FBI vans, and satellite news vans. There were people, too, running around, as Floyd would say, like chickens with their heads cut off. She understood why no one was on this backroad. The only way to it was through the heart of the neighborhood. Toussaint wouldn't waste resources guarding an empty road, and the police couldn't get back here if they wanted to.

The bad news was that she too was stuck. She would have to walk into the lion's den by doubling back through the Bottoms and sneaking out into the fray of the FBI and BLPD. She needed to be cautious, but she didn't know how to do that. She asked herself what Stevenson would do. The answer came before the question was fully formed. Stevenson would wait.

She went back down the hill on all fours, glad this part of the Bottoms was not lit up like a birthday cake. Raven crouched under a shotgun near the entrance to the Old Bottoms. She crouched there on her haunches and waited for her chance. About an hour later the music stopped. She peered from beneath the house. Every house was buttoned up tight. She saw no one, but that didn't mean that it was safe to come out. Again, she stifled her impatience and waited for what felt like ten or fifteen minutes. When nothing moved, she crawled out keeping her body low to the ground. Toussaint in his white do-rag was talking to a white man in an FBI jacket at the entrance to the Old Bottoms. She heard words like 'good faith', and 'hurt' and 'go easy' from the FBI agent. Toussaint was shouting about children being there and police trespassing. While they argued, Raven slipped out of the Old Bottoms. She lay flat on her belly and crawled toward a group of patrol cars. The patrol officers were clustered near the entrance of the Old Bottoms waiting to see if the FBI agent sent in to negotiate would come out alive.

Raven tiptoed along until she was at the last cruiser at the very back of the line. She tested the door and found it open. She crawled inside and saw the keys in the ignition. She went to give Stevenson a fist bump and suddenly remembered. Stevenson was gone.

Lying across the driver's seat, and keeping the lights off, she backed the cruiser up and out of the Bottoms. When she was sure she was out of sight, she sat up, put the car in drive and let it coast for a long way. She didn't turn the lights or engine on until she was on the main road. It was then that she noticed the Remington shotgun. On the dash, she saw someone had left their badge. She picked it up, looked at it before placing it on the passenger seat. The badge belonged to Marna. She was driving Marna's cruiser. One of her officers must have left it in the car out of respect. The dead were everywhere.

★ ★ ★

The cruiser's clock said that it was almost three o'clock in the morning as Raven navigated the back streets of Byrd's Landing. She passed the four corners where Marna told her what happened to most of the houses and the people in the Old Bottoms. The headlights swam over the dirt road, the tall weeds. She could almost smell the slaughterhouse, and see the house lined with abandoned refrigerators as a defense against stray bullets. Marna's no-nonsense voice faded in and out of Raven's head, a message from a ghost.

When she reached the residential area of Byrd's Landing, almost every house she passed was ablaze with light. Front doors were thrown open to screen doors for people who had them, and to the open air for people who didn't. Music of all kinds raged in a chaotic cacophony. At a small house on Morning Glory near Cameron's apartment, a boy in a Tupac t-shirt paced his lawn back and forth with a rifle slung over his shoulder. Tupac's 'Hit 'Em Up' played so loud that it owned the street. Three doors down, an elderly woman in a long, purple nightdress hobbled up and down the sidewalk with her own axe while Ella Fitzgerald scatted from a portable speaker on her porch. At the next house a man sat on the porch with a sawed-off shotgun balanced on his knees. Garth Brooks' voice drifted from his windows.

Floating on a strident stream of dissonance, Raven drove to Cameron's place. His apartment building wasn't spared from the frenzy. Where there were windows, there was a light. Music blared from some of them, begging whoever was terrorizing Byrd's Landing to let the occupants within have their life. Raven had to bang on Cameron's door for a long moment before it flung open. He gaped at her before enveloping her into a bear hug so tight she couldn't breathe. He pulled her into the apartment. As always, his game console was the star of the show, but he had recently added an orange fuzzy armchair and matching couch. Evidence boxes from Zeke's murder were all over the couch and on his coffee table. His computer screen displayed phone records. Photos of the grisly crime scene lay over the back of the couch. Some of them were of Marcel's enigmatic writings.

He saw her looking.

"I thought if I could find out who's been killing everybody, things would calm down and it'd be easier for the FBI to negotiate letting you go."

Raven studied him. His skin had an undertone of gray, his eyes were red as if he had been crying. Any other time she would be ready to tease him. But not now.

"I'm sorry you were worried. They didn't let me go. I escaped, but I had help. No one can know that I'm out, Cameron. I made a promise."

"What? You crazy? The longer this case stays open, the longer people will stay ready to kill each other," he said.

"The FBI and BLPD will storm the place if they knew I was safe. I promised to give them an hour or two."

"Oh, fuck," Cameron said, falling heavily into the orange armchair. "You got Stockholm Syndrome."

"I don't have Stockholm Syndrome. Where's the chief?" she asked.

"The mayor sent him home," Cameron said.

Raven thought so. The town had come undone. A murderer was dispatching its citizens in a brutal and bloody way, not to mention a siege had caught the attention of the national news and the FBI. She was surprised that sending the chief home was the only thing the mayor had done. He was capable of benching the entire department and calling in help from another parish, or turning the entire mess over to the FBI.

She picked up one of the photos with Marcel's scribbling, remembered where she saw similar writing. It occurred to her that Marcel's note wasn't necessarily for him, but for someone else who was able to read it. She dropped the photo back on the couch and watched it slide to the ground.

"Why you here?" Cameron asked.

"Did you run the phone records again like we talked about?" she asked.

He nodded and handed her several printouts. She read them.

"You know what this means," she said.

"I sure as fuck do," Cameron said grimly. "What now?"

"Have you told anybody?" she asked him.

"I just found it," he said. "Before you knocked."

"Don't say anything, to anyone. Not yet," she said.

"What are you going to do in the meantime? Hide under my bed?" he said.

She smiled thinking about what under his bed probably looked like. "No, I need to run one more errand. I have to be sure this time," she said.

What she didn't say was that she had to make sure so she wouldn't go off half-cocked and put more people in harm's way.

"What am I supposed to do?" Cameron asked.

"Nothing. Just remember that you haven't seen me."

Chapter Fifty-Three

Front doors were closed in the chief's upper-class neighborhood. A few windows held small, yellow lights but the street was dark and quiet. Raven parked Marna's cruiser along the curb in front of the chief's sprawling one-story home made of pink and white brick. Raven grabbed the shotgun and got out of the cruiser. She walked past an old-fashioned cast-iron light pole at the edge of the wide lawn. Someone had knocked out all three lights as if they were begging the killer to punish the man who couldn't keep the town safe.

Raven banged on the door as if the chief were a criminal and she was there to arrest him. The door opened, and he stood there in a pair of striped pajamas and a black terry-cloth robe with a torn pocket. He didn't seem surprised that she was armed, just regarded the shotgun she carried for a brief moment. In turn, Raven noticed the Glock he carried. He waved her inside with his gun hand.

"You got out," he said as he walked into the living room without looking at her. "I know they didn't let you go, or I would have heard."

"I got out, yes," she said, following him.

He led her to a small wet bar in the living room. He traded the Glock for a round bottle of Pappy's he had beneath the bar. She laid the shotgun on the bar top.

"Who knows you're out?" he asked while he poured the whiskey into two crystal glasses.

"Just you and Cameron and I'd like to keep it that way. For the next couple of hours at least," Raven said.

He slid one of the glasses over to her across the bar. He brought his own up to his lips and tossed the whiskey into his mouth.

"Remember the mayor used to give me this for my bonus every year?" he asked while pouring more whiskey in his glass. "I told you that once you made chief after I retired, we'd celebrate with a drink."

Raven remembered but said nothing.

He regarded the second pour of the Pappy's and tilted the glass until the light from the bar refracted in the crystal. He drank slowly this time, as if he didn't want the taste of the four-thousand-dollar bottle of whiskey to die on his tongue too soon. After he finished, he poured himself another drink and told her to grab her glass and come outside with him.

His backyard was as wide as the front with an outdoor kitchen and a patio living room set. The sky was clear and thick with a thousand glittering stars. He flicked on the patio light on the way to a metal patio table.

"I don't know if I'm going to survive this shit, Raven," the chief said as they sat down.

"I don't care," Raven said.

"Don't blame me. I told you not to take your ass over there. Your partner's death is on you."

Raven knew it was her immediate fault. She'd have to live with that for the rest of her life. But if fault grew like a tree, she was just a branch. The buried secret the chief wouldn't give up was the root of all that had happened. Death would be the result as long as that secret lived. She wanted to tell him that, to shout it at him loud enough for his eardrums to burst.

Instead, she said, "You're the one keeping secrets getting people killed, Chief. This is your fault as much as it is mine. What are you hiding?"

"Are you sure you want to know?"

She waited. He sighed and took a drink of his whiskey.

"Back in the day," he started. "There was this crooked cop. He was my partner, a piece of shit by the name of Victor Broussard." He searched her face. "You remember him?"

"Should I?" Raven said.

"You should. You served the man grape Kool-Aid when you lived in that matchbox with your daddy on The Hill," he said.

She kept her face immobile. "Go on."

"Broussard terrorized Black people all over Byrd's Landing. For shit like jaywalking and loitering." He stopped and knocked the now-empty crystal glass against his knee. "It wasn't anything Black folk didn't have to deal with on the regular, but over the years he got bolder. By the time I was assigned to him back when I was a rookie, he was beating people up and rousting Black businesses for protection money." He studied her again for a long moment.

"Don't stop now. Tell it," she said.

"He and I were assigned to canvass The Hill after the Ruth Jefferson murder. That's when he met your daddy," the chief said, staring at her carefully.

Raven flinched, but she wasn't surprised. Every terrible thing that happened in her life led back to the man who gave her life. He committed evil beyond comprehension and then put the consequences on her tab. She would never be rid of him. She returned the chief's stare with a quiet one of her own.

"I met your father years before I arrested him for killing your stepmother," he went on. "Did you know that? I had met you, too, but I could see that your old man did something to your mind. You have holes where your memory should be. You acted like we never met when I saved you from your daddy."

"Why didn't you tell me this a long time ago?" she asked.

"I didn't see how it would do anybody any good," he said. "Anyway, I and a lot of other people on The Hill thought Floyd killed Ruth Jefferson. But every time we'd get close, Broussard defended Floyd. In return, we think that he did Broussard favors."

"What favors?" she asked.

"Everybody was too scared to say it out loud, but he would go after people who filed complaints against Broussard. Some say he even killed somebody," the chief said.

Raven leaned in close until she could smell the Pappy's on the chief's breath. "That's a damn lie. My father would never be somebody's lacky."

"Sounds like you were proud of your old man," he said. "In some ways."

"Get on with it," Raven snapped.

It was all some sort of sick cycle. People complained and got hurt, the chief said. But they wouldn't stop. They told their stories to the newspaper, but they wouldn't print anything. They ranted to the City Council, but it was all for naught. The more Broussard got away with terrorizing the Black people of Byrd's Landing, the more trouble he became. Then he just went too far.

"You said he had people killed. That wasn't too far?" Raven asked.

The chief shook his head. "Killing's a mercy when torture is on the horizon. This motherfucker, Raven, he started maiming people. He cut off body parts and shit. There was a rumor going around that he kept some parts in formaldehyde on his desk at the station."

"Come on, Chief," Raven said.

"They swore on it. I didn't believe it, either. Not at first," the chief said.

He rubbed his face hard. Raven wondered if he was trying to rub away the memory. There was blood on his hands when he brought them down. He had scratched himself. He went on. The detectives working on the case were closing in on Floyd. Broussard couldn't have that, the chief said. To take the focus off Floyd, he brought in one of the two boys who found Mrs. Jefferson. Raven heard a child's voice in her head correct him. *Miss Ruth*, it insisted.

"That young man was already messed up," the chief said. "He and his friend were bringing her plates from the Fourth of July potluck when they found her. Ribs, potato salad, macaroni and cheese. They dropped them when they saw what Floyd had done to her. You can imagine what that crime scene was like."

Raven could but didn't want to.

"The older boy kept talking about hearing her last breath, the death rattle," the chief said. "Everywhere he went, even in his sleep. Broussard said it was because of guilt. Even though it wasn't his right to do, he brought that kid in for questioning in the middle of the night. He locked me out of the interview room. I'm surprised I didn't pace a hole in the linoleum while he talked to that boy. I was just a rookie then. I didn't know what to do. Until the screaming started."

"The screaming?"

The chief continued as if Raven hadn't spoken. He seemed relieved that somebody had asked him about this horror.

"I pounded on that door for as long as my hands could stand it. Then I started kicking as hard as I could. Before I knew it the night sergeant was fumbling with a big set of keys. The screaming went on and on."

The chief brought his hands up to his ears but didn't touch them. He just let his hands hover there in mid-air for a while.

Finally, he said, "We got the door open, and we both fell into the room. Broussard was standing there with this fucked-up smile on his face. He said something about the kid falling and hitting his face on the corner of the table. Broussard's hands were bloody, so was his shirt. The floor was bloody, too, and the kid was there squirming in it."

"What did you do?" Raven asked.

"I couldn't do anything. The sergeant was cursing and pulling the kid's hands from his face." The chief looked down and swallowed. "Raven, he mutilated that boy. He cut him across the face from his right temple to his left ear. It was a deep cut."

Raven drew in a breath. "What was the boy's name?"

"You know him. Plays down at Chastain's. The same motherfucker on TV the other night talking about turning up the music and lighting up your home to ward off the killer. Gervais Armstrong."

Chapter Fifty-Four

They ignored the old church across the broad street from the Old Bottoms. The police. The FBI. The news trucks. All lights, weapons and cameras were focused on the clump of shotguns where Toussaint had created his brand of community. Now the neighborhood glowed from the lights as if it were on fire.

Raven parked Marna's cruiser on a side street. She grabbed the Remington and climbed out of the car, shutting the door softly behind her. Distant voices and the hum of running vehicles from the chaos of the siege drifted toward her.

But it was like they were in another universe.

On this side of the street, the woods behind the crumbing edifice feigned sleep. Like Gervais, they watched, waiting hungrily for what they believed would be inevitable violence.

She knew Gervais was here. Billy Ray said he was couch surfing, had no place to stay and needed money. That's one of the reasons he introduced him to the band. She couldn't imagine him staying in the Old Bottoms under Toussaint's thumb. And that flash she saw when she searched the church at Zeke's crime scene? She should have followed her hunch, and returned for a more thorough search instead of relying on someone else to do it for her.

She entered the church from a door at the back. She recognized the danger. The church had almost killed her once. It could do so again. She put the thought out of her mind. Above all she wanted Gervais. If the church was going to fall, she'd make sure it crushed them both. She owed it to Zeke who had called her in the weeks leading up to his death to warn her about Gervais's plan to avenge Miss Ruth's death. She owed it to Marna, who didn't have to die. And Marna's husband Newell. Both would be alive today if Raven hadn't run away from the memory of her time on The Hill. The investigation would have taken a logical turn. Gervais would have been in the crosshairs so much earlier. Most of all, she owed it to Stevenson who was cheated out of a life because he tried to protect her.

The side door opened onto an alcove. The cool gray before morning flowed through the open roof above. The floor was covered with rotted wood and moldy drywall. A strong, musty smell hung in the air. Raven stepped over the debris to another door. A sound like someone pounding the floor with a piece of wood penetrated the closed door. She jacked back the pump on the shotgun, mounted it on her right shoulder. She raised a booted foot and kicked down the door. It flew from its hinges and hit the floor with a loud boom. The next room was the altar with the pallid Jesus keeping company with graffiti from decades ago. What had Marna said? The graffiti wasn't even fresh.

And then applause. Gervais sat on the tipped Wurlitzer, a piece of old wood beside him, congratulating her with slow, mocking claps.

"She figured it out," he said. "What does she win, ladies and gentlemen?"

Raven side-stepped to the top of the altar steps with the Remington ready to fire.

"I'm not in the mood for conversation, Gervais," she said.

"So, why ain't I shot if you're not in a talking mood?" he asked. "You've had plenty of time."

He picked up a butcher knife next to the wood he had been pounding the floor with, and pretended to clean his fingernails with its long, fat blade.

"Do you know why they never found the murder weapon at Mama Ruth's place?" he said.

"I told you..." Raven started.

"Because I took it," he said, now waving the knife at her. "I didn't know why, but now I think I was saving it for you."

"So much for your crush," she said and fired.

He dove a millisecond before she pulled the trigger. His body skidded across the floor. He stumbled up, ran in a crawl toward her. She pumped the shotgun, mounted it again. Later Raven would say that he stood and flew but she knew that was impossible. The man was an athlete, nothing more. He jumped over splintered pews with arms spread like wings.

Before she could pull the trigger, he threw his arms around her waist and tackled her to the floor of the altar. It knocked the breath out of her. The shotgun sailed from her hands and clattered to the floor. With bulging eyes she watched the weapon skid out of reach and halt beneath the feet of Jesus. The only consolation prize was that Gervais had lost the knife.

But she couldn't think about losing hold of the shotgun right then. His arms were steel bands around her waist. They pushed her belly into her throat. She couldn't suck in the air she so desperately needed. She did the only thing she knew how to do. Using her elbow as a weapon she jammed him down on his head with all the force in her body. She tried it with her left, got tired, and tried it with her right. But he was too strong. His head was hard. She jabbed her right foot on his hip and pushed as hard as she could. Enough space to get back on her feet was the only thing that would save her. She hooked his arm and bridged up with her left elbow and left knee until she was able to finally push him away and stand up.

Gervais was laughing. He scrambled toward the knife, got to it before she did. He wasted no time before sinking it into her foot. Raven screamed. The sharp pain snatched away what little breath she was able to gain back. The burning felt like she had plunged her foot into scalding water. She pivoted. With her other foot Raven landed a soccer kick to the side of his head. He went down. She bent to pull the knife from her foot. But her hands were slippery from sweat and now blood. It was like trying to snatch a fish from a rushing river. Gervais was crawling toward her on all fours. He was much slower, but he was coming. She frantically rubbed her hands on her sweats and went for the knife again. She imagined her hands were Velcro. The next thing she knew, she had the knife and the advantage.

"Whoa!" he said with both hands up, turning his body toward the shotgun, but it was too far away and he was too late.

She limped toward him with the sole purpose of killing him with the same knife that had killed Miss Ruth. She wanted to watch the light leave his eyes. She wanted him to pay. He struggled to a sitting position and scooted backward until he was sitting beneath Jesus's crucified feet. He reached for the shotgun again, but she was close enough now to kick it away.

The sun had come up. A cool light fell in yellow streams through the open beams of the roof, laying gold stripes across Gervais's scarred face. Raven moved into striking range. This time she wouldn't hesitate. She raised the knife, but he spoke, and instead of his voice coming out of his mouth, she heard Miss Ruth's.

"Please," he said, bowing his head. "No."

His pleas brought her back to her senses. Gervais was crying. And the man who had hacked her friends to death, terrorized an entire town and then watched the aftermath with glee had pissed himself.

She realized something then.

She couldn't kill this man because he was already dead. Floyd had gotten to him first. Then Broussard finished him off. What lay before Raven was residue, a shadow. She lowered the knife by inches.

He would die in the execution chamber with a needle in his arm, not by her hands. Letting him live felt like allowing a fatally wounded animal a reprieve before death. And not using that knife put more distance between Raven's life now and her father's crimes in the past. For the first time in a long time, she felt free.

Epilogue

Raven's left foot was still in a boot a month after the church. She was standing in the field across from the abandoned shotguns on The Hill. The place was alive with activity. Cars whizzed by behind what was now a retaining wall separating the abandoned neighborhood from the highway. Now drivers would meet concrete instead of a chain-link if they couldn't keep all four wheels on the ground.

The mayor had just cut a bright red ribbon tied between two sawhorses in front of the third house. The photographer had trouble getting the picture, and the mayor and the City Council member helping him had to stand there grinning like idiots while holding a giant pair of scissors.

Diamond was over by a bulldozer talking to the supervisor. They held up a large piece of paper between them. Diamond's index finger skated over the surface as he talked fast. He wore a white hard hat atop his dreads and a white, long-sleeved dress shirt that was blinding in the sun. More of Diamond's plans, Raven thought.

He had called her a week earlier to tell her what was happening on The Hill. The shotguns would be demolished. In honor of Zeke's memory, he planned a low-income community with gardens, grocery stores and single-family homes, not apartments or projects, but houses with big front porches and wide front windows. Everything would be within walking distance, including a park and a school. No one would need a car. No one would need to leave. As she reflected on what he was trying to do, she wondered if this would be the idea that would finally fill him up. She wondered if it was a good one.

She leaned against the hood of her red Mustang. A black Lexus SUV pulled in beside her. The chief got out. It was the first time she had seen him in blue jeans and sneakers. She stayed silent as he walked over to her with his hands in his pockets.

"I was expecting Billy Ray," she said. He had promised earlier that he would meet her here, but he was nowhere in sight.

"Hello to you, too," the chief said as he settled in beside her.

Diamond rolled up the plans and clapped the supervisor on the shoulder. He gave her a small wave. Raven returned it with one of her own.

"Billy Ray told me you would be here," the chief said. "I know you wanted him for support today, but I told him that I needed to talk to you. If you had answered my calls, I wouldn't have hijacked all this." He nodded toward the houses that were about to be crushed under bulldozers.

"I can't imagine what we have to say to each other," Raven said.

He searched her face. "Can't you? You came to me last month, but didn't get what you wanted. You still don't know what Toussaint had on us."

"You want to tell me about Broussard," she said.

"I do."

Raven didn't want to hear it. She wanted his secret to stay buried. What he was about to tell her would turn her already tilting world upside down. She was too busy with her own guilt. It insisted on devouring her alive from the feet up. She hadn't been back to work. Every time she drove by the station she wanted to vomit. Therapy three times a week didn't help. She didn't know if she could bear dealing with anybody else's guilt.

But then she remembered Zeke calling those who bullied her 'bastids' when they were in high school. He wouldn't hesitate lending an ear to the troubled. Talking to the chief felt like doing Zeke a solid. The beep of a bulldozer backing up cut into her thoughts. She watched as it rumbled toward the first house.

"Go ahead, Chief," she said.

"I already told you that Broussard was terrorizing the neighborhood, that he had cut up Gervais's face." He stopped. The look he gave Raven was one of amazement. "You know the brass believed Broussard's story about that boy falling against a table? Everybody in the Black community was terrified. Not just poor folk, but people who had money."

"What did you do, Chief?" Raven asked. The asking felt like a ritual. She already knew it couldn't be anything good.

"We dragged Broussard out of his house in the dead of night. There were jars in there, Raven, awful things. We took him to the swamp, killed him, and cut up his body. We fed him to the alligators piece by piece. We did it slowly and patiently until every inch of him was properly chewed up and swallowed. It felt good doing it," Chief Sawyer said.

"We?" Raven said. Her voice was weak with the knowledge that he was about to hand her a present that she didn't want and couldn't use. And one that she had to take because he needed to tell this story to somebody.

"Me and Joseph Rochon, you know him as Mr. Joe, drug him from his house. Anna Lavigne, Mama Anna, brought the supplies needed to chop up his body. Buckets, hunting gloves, a couple of big carving knives, axes, paddles and shotguns to control the alligators. After, she let us wash up at her house. Marcus, the mayor, though he wasn't back then, shot him in the back of the head. That's all he wanted to do, didn't want to get his hands dirty. 'I want to be the one to shoot him,' he kept saying. But he watched us cutting Broussard up with this big weird-ass smile on his face. Vera Rivas…"

"Miss Vera?" Raven said, now surprised down to her bones. She couldn't believe a woman so steeped in the church could be involved in such a murder. But then she remembered what Toussaint had said: *your pious Miss Vera.*

"Yes, Miss Vera. It was her plan," the chief said.

Walls toppled and wood crunched as the bulldozer bounced over the fallen shotgun.

"How did Toussaint know?" she asked.

"Oh yeah, forgot somebody. Toussaint's mama and daddy? They let us use their swamp boat. Toussiant probably found out from them."

Raven waited for her world to shatter, but it didn't. The chief, the old folk. They had killed a man. People whom she had admired. She didn't think they had it in them. It shouldn't surprise her that they had lived entire lifetimes before claiming the live-edge mahogany table at Chastain's Creole Heaven as their own.

"What do you want me to do with all this, Chief?" she asked.

He wouldn't look at her, just watched the destruction happening in front of him as if he really cared about what happened to those old houses.

"I don't know," he said. "I just thought that after everything that happened, you deserved to know."

"If you had told me this in the beginning, it could have saved so many lives. We might have eliminated Toussaint as a suspect early on. Caught Gervais before Marna and Stevenson died."

"You could have trusted me," the chief said, his voice low. "I told you he had nothing to do with it."

The bulldozer was going for the second house. "Because you're just so trustworthy," Raven said.

"Gervais wouldn't have been easy to catch," the chief said. "He had an alibi for the churchyard murders."

"He said he was practicing with the band. That's true but we learned after the dust settled that he left early. And the Ruth Jefferson connection. We could have put it together. Zeke knew that Gervais was after me because he thought I was responsible for Miss Ruth's death. That's why Zeke met Gervais at the churchyard. To try and talk him out of it. Then the phone records. Gervais said Moon called him to tell him that I was lost in the swamp. Moon called the burner phone, Chief. Even the writing. Gervais and Marcel grew up together, made up that crazy writing to pass secret notes. I wish you'd talked to me."

"And you could have returned Zeke's calls and texts before the first body hit the ground. So, wish in one hand and shit in the other. See which one fills up faster," the chief said. "We can't undo what happened."

She wanted to say something but couldn't for the lump in her throat.

"Where do you think they went?" the chief asked.

He was talking about Toussaint's community. The FBI and BLPD stormed an empty compound. Moon had asked Raven for more time so they could pack everything they could carry and escape. The only things they left were Terry's dead body rotting in the street, and a few plants for Lois Wareham. BLPD scoured the swamps but they found nothing. Toussaint's people had walked out of Byrd's Landing into nowhere.

"I hope they went as far away from Byrd's Landing as they can get. I hope Toussaint found another place where he can do his root work in peace, where people like us can't get to him. And I hope…" She didn't finish her sentence. She was going to say that she hoped he would one day forgive her, but that was something she could never say to the chief.

When the bulldozers pushed over Miss Ruth's house, the conversation changed. She and the chief talked about the case, what it had done to his career, and if he would ever be allowed to resume his position as BLPD's chief. Raven was only half listening. She let the conversation wither away as she thought about Stevenson.

She had finally given him what he wanted. She confessed, but not to Lovelle's murder. She confessed to her part in Ruth Jefferson's murder. She gave a full-throated account in the case report. Stevenson always told her that the only way for her to move on was to lay her sins bare.

But it didn't work.

No one cared about the sins of a child. She wished that Stevenson was still here so she could tell him that he was wrong. Maybe one day she'd go a step further and confess to the Lovelle murder. But not today. She was just too damned tired. Before that secret could die, she needed some time to prepare for the consequences and to mourn its death.

About the Author

Faye Snowden writes noir mysteries, poems and short stories from her home in Northern California. Her poems have appeared in various literary journals and small presses, including *The African American Review*. Her short story 'One Bullet. One Vote' was selected as one of the best American mystery and suspense stories of 2021. Her novels include the *Killing* series, featuring homicide detective Raven Burns. The first book in the series, *A Killing Fire*, was released to fantastic reviews and was followed by *A Killing Rain*. Learn more about her work at fayesnowden.com.

FLAME TREE PRESS
FICTION WITHOUT FRONTIERS
Award-Winning Authors & Original Voices

Flame Tree Press is the trade fiction imprint of Flame Tree Publishing, focusing on excellent writing in horror and the supernatural, crime and mystery, science fiction and fantasy. Our aim is to explore beyond the boundaries of the everyday, with tales from both award-winning authors and original voices.

•

Other titles in the *Killing* series by Faye Snowden:
A Killing Fire
A Killing Rain

You may also enjoy:
The Sentient by Nadia Afifi
Junction by Daniel M. Bensen
Keeper of Sorrows by Rachel Fikes
Silent Key by Laurel Hightower
The Widening Gyre by Michael R. Johnston
The Heart of Winter by Shona Kinsella
The Sky Woman by J.D. Moyer
The Guardian by J.D. Moyer
Brittle by Beth Overmyer
Tempered Glass by Beth Overmyer
The Goblets Immortal by Beth Overmyer
One Eye Opened in That Other Place by Christi Nogle
The Last Feather by Shameez Patel Papathanasiou
Tinderbox by W.A. Simpson
Tarotmancer by W.A. Simpson
The Hatter's Daughter by W.A. Simpson
A Sword of Bronze and Ashes by Anna Smith Spark
A Sword of Gold and Ruin by Anna Smith Spark
Stars Like Us by Stephen K. Stanford
Idolatry by Aditya Sudarshan
The Roamers by Francesco Verso
The Night Ship by Alex Woodroe
Of Kings, Queens & Colonies by Johnny Worthen

•

Join our mailing list for free short stories, new release details, news about our authors and special promotions:

flametreepress.com